KERI HULME

Of Maori, Scots and English ancestry, the author was born in Christchurch and now makes her home on the West Coast of New Zealand – in a house she built herself.

In the past, she has worked at many jobs, ranging from tobacco picker to pharmacist's assistant, but now she is a full time writer, painter and whitebaiter. Her poems and short stories have been published in many magazines and broadcast on radio and television; THE SILENCES BETWEEN: MOERAKI CONVER-SATIONS – a book of poetry and prose – was published in 1982 by Auckland University Press and THE BONE PEOPLE, first published in 1984 by the Spiral Collective, has won both the Pegasus Prize for Maori Literature and the Booker Prize for Fiction.

sceptre

Keri Hulme

THE WINDEATER
TE KAIHAU

ACKNOWLEDGMENTS
Some of these stories have appeared previously in the periodicals
Islands, Landfall, Broadsheet, Untold, New Zealand Listener and
Manawatu Evening Standard. 'Pipi manu e', sung in 'A Nightsong for
the Shining Cuckoo' is by Hirini Melbourne

*The characters and situations in this
book are entirely imaginary and bear
no relation to any real person or
actual happening*

First published in Great Britain in
1987 by Hodder and Stoughton
Limited

Sceptre edition 1988

Sceptre is an imprint of Hodder and
Stoughton Paperbacks, a division of
Hodder and Stoughton Limited.

Printed and bound in Great Britain
for Hodder and Stoughton Paper-
backs, a division of Hodder and
Stoughton Limited, Mill Road, Dun-
ton Green, Sevenoaks, Kent TN13
2YA (Editorial Office: 47 Bedford
Square, London WC1B 3DP) by
Richard Clay Limited, Bungay,
Suffolk. Photoset by Rowland
Phototypesetting Limited, Bury St
Edmunds, Suffolk.

British Library C.I.P.

Hulme, Keri
  The Windeater = Te kaihau
  I. Title
  823[F]   PR9639.3.H75

ISBN 0-340-42374-9

For Pamela Tomlinson:

a strong and tactful editor,
a warm and vivid woman,
a friend, untimely dead.

ACKNOWLEDGMENTS

Many of the stories gathered here would not have been written without the assistance of the 1982 ICI Writing Bursary. Patronage of literature in New Zealand, outside of governmental funding, is rare, and it is deeply and sincerely appreciated by those writers who receive it – especially this one. Thank you, ICI, and the Literary Fund advisory committee of that year.

Bill Manhire – you're responsible for this lot, you realise, for making the suggestion I should make a collection.

Fergus Barrowman, your tolerance and patience as an editor is without parallel – I owe you a session at Whataroa one of these days.

CONTENTS

TARA DIPTYCH

The first wing

You are just lying there on the dry hillside, near the top, in the afternoon sun. Your hands are under your head, fingers inter-laced, your crooked arms making pointy wings either side of your head. Your body angles down towards the distant sea, and gulls are wheeling above you, silent and easy among the updraughts. There is not a thought in your head: you are gull-watching, hill-watching, sea-watching, nothing more.

You are just lying there on the hillside in the holy afternoon sun and the images are flowing through you, now a soap-opera – this character weeping tears of applied saline solution and this character stony-faced and stony-hearted and stony-voiced and *this* character, whilst tangling with a spinal ganglion, still en-deavouring to keep a brave fixed smile alight – and now a real-life blood drama [see the pistol jerk back and the head shove to an aside and the face just before dying grimace, similar grimaces from killer and killed], and right *now*, going through the atom-sieve of your left ankle, a barely boring barely interesting report on Ms Universal Torque Conservancy 1993.

This isn't any kind of fantasy: far from it. For instance, there is a skindiver off Cay Fear being penetrated by the gothic sonorific cathedral song of a solitary humpback cow a hundred leagues distant, and she is unaware of it, and her mother, nodding off in a fat armchair in Manchester, England, is being shot through and through with ten dozen heavy particles and straying microwaves and determined short waves not to mention next-door's telly dear, and *she* is unaware of it.

This isn't any kind of fantasy however: far from it. We are transit points and blubbery highways and temporarily fluid screens; indeed we are a finity of things to every light wave and every light particle and sonic particle and sonic wave, but mainly somewhere to pass through in a hurry without so much as a by-yr-lve or a pardon.

These are not the kind of thoughts that steal through your brain while you are gull-watching, hill-watching, sea-watching – these are afterthoughts. While watching, and watching yourself watching, and watching yourself watching yourself etcetera and so on in an infinite regression/procession, it is much more apposite to pick that bit of spiky grass-stalk dried to dunness like everything else on this hillside (except the thistles) and chew it, wondering when the sheep were here last and whether they'd been regularly drenched, and where, and – idly of course but exceedingly quickly because this particular wonder takes about an *nth* of one second – just what was the cycle of lungworm? scrapies? again?

You chew absently – geez nice spiral, gull – teeth leaving silvery indentations at first and then fraying the stem, and bring your other hand down to fiddle – haven't noticed that hollow before I don't think – with that rattler, tohu, cloak pin, a long dagger of pounamu you wear by the silver cross round your neck, and all the while the sun cooks you with practised ease and the gulls soar and the waves roll in and the hill just stays there as it has done for a while.

And there is a clink.

The tara, you think lazily, squinting as its green length, and the undertow of your thought goes

green: pounamu/plasma/prase
plasma/prase: Moeraki
Moeraki = Puketapu

hey funny! think of all the taras in there! Tara tara tara!

An errant grass-stalk tickles and teases your nose and a fibre from the stalk you're fraying tickles and teases the back of your throat and, just as you're building up to a sneeze, the word tara tickling and teasing round the interstices and fenestrations of your brain (it all happens in the gaps and windows) there is another clink! and the sneeze erupts.

[A long time later, in the afterthought period, you are pretty sure that not only is the second clink louder than the first, but also that it doesn't come from the tara round your neck singing against anything else solid.]

The sun has drawn sweatbeads out of your shoulder-blades and they are rivering down the spinal channel, the buttock cleft, no longer beads but rivulets, and abruptly the rivulets turn torrent. Your body is running sweat.

Because you have become a shadow in someone else's head and body, not a shadow passing through –

Silly to keep up the innocent pretence. I have become a shadow in someone else's body and head, while being a solid here on my holy hill. And it's not just a moment, there is a whole afternoon passing through me, a wine-tasting, a testing gossip-riddled party, a quarrel and a lover's meet, and such lovers! . . . and I *am*, *I* am, I am still in my skull as well, chewing grass and sweating very heavily under the afternoon sun . . . but here the sun has gone and the thunderheads are swelling and here the sun is making me swelter and here the cold rain is sluicing down and it is growing black night. And I am telling things the tonguing things and gasping over my grass-stalk with amazement and you're not me and *you*'re not me and I am myself alone.

Again.

Now I know about all the waves that barge through us because we're not really there – or here – and now I know that there are at least 21 meanings for *tara* grouped under everything from gossip to rays. Maybe it was because it all took place on hills similarly holy, identically named, or maybe it was because a sneeze and a sound sent the soiling dance of my synenergy swirling through another place and other people and even another time. Don't bother my head: set up the frame – one marvellous 21-jointed word, full of diversities – and because I am merely weaver, making senses for the sounds – I shall weave anew.

You'd be a brave human who would say where all the influences come from, but I think the word sets the whole thing up . . .

TARA

The other wing

(For
all the lonely seas of people
who don't know living till they die)

Here in the afternoon sun, the lesser shafts
stealing through a barrier of window/outside
thistlehead demons with bright devil faces
blowing on the silent wind/and inside

still, the stridulation of cicadas gossiping
clicking scandal from powerpole to tree
to holy hilltop rings in my head.

I clasp a peach in my hands/while he talks
– It's been bitter he says . . . the musk of the peach
sweet on my hands . . . bitter for who?
and deep inside, the cyanide pit.

– You disturb me he says . . . the peach juice drips
he grips a finger pointed to groin
until blood swells it stiff – I have this this
unthinking ache

I smile at the cream of the joke
my own addition
– the laughter
the great clouds bloom on the horizon/blister pearls

other guests eye us eye each other eye coming
cold & storm/a whining king still plaintive
he joins the carrion eaters.

– A fire? A fire.
The flames swoop unguided
send a surge of chancy energy through me
a dance intricate as tattoo lines
and linked/to the vast spirals heat-engraven on Earth's hide
linked to the looping whorls on my fingertips' skin
linked –

it twirls winks by her breast a long stabber
of cloaksinew, an eyed jade we call other names
dark green rich with apple-colour inclusions aware
translucent lens . . . I've seen similar spikes show choler
in a stingray's tail, warning in the dorsal fin
of a fish, colour all the viewing
of the horn of the crescent moon.

Cicada song stammers   falls suddenly   silent

my skin rises/goosebumps/papillae/rough hide
against of course the coming cold – see there! Puketapu!
he nods coolly/goes/flinging a goodbye over his shoulder
(nobody caught it nobody
was waiting for it)

obligatory last gulps and obligatory last cracks and then
a flock of goodbyes going giggling into the rain
and   silence

What can I say to you?
That is clean, new, untrammelled,
free of smears and fresh from mothertongue?

      and the rain is all around

    a pin to skewer a cloak of flesh.

'Solitary tall hills
sometimes walk, sometimes meet,'

    [sacred knob/holy top/Puketapu]

'and from ancient halls mounds vestibules
spinning out of the golden past
sometimes, the resonance of Words,
naming.'

    [O freebooter! A wing of seabirds aloft
    and hills shift and the clouds are in flight]

– the laughter of

this free gift
meant only entirely for pleasure for ever

– the laughter of

the quiet within:
hidden among the flowersoft pinksoft you think soft as skin
cleansed delicate newborn smiling thus soft/but it is excited
    lightning
toughened steel   a magnet ready gratuitous quick as
    sudden
sunlight/stronger than iron ever wrought/a brought gift/
a nexus between spirit and turquoise brain/centring soul/an
    impossible mixture

the ribald and the decorous/the woman and the other/the
    child
and the mother of worlds

– the laughter of

wild sparks running through the chimney pile
a blaze of starmaps made wholly night
a second after

a ruby glance, that gauge and alignment for a second
    bearing
Puketapu

– the laughter of

Hei! he atua pi –
koikoi! Hu!

– the laughter of

the joy we bear alone/sharing a canoe of great journey –
a groove of mellow fire/a feud in understanding
subtle
pulse of breathing
exhale

and death against the wall of my house
would suit me fine . . .

[I mean I'm old already and ready for it
the still the sour the afterthought
mirrored in the deep of eyes

even if I can smile (Look!
stainstarred silverstudded caries-scarred grinning
no ivories but a mosaic of enamel and filling clouded with
    rot.)]

'But aren't we more
than twoten bones and a dozen holes?'

'Ten my dear, all counted.'

– The laughter of

effigies of self
drawn by wishful thinking

– but, yeah
much more than skin and bone and cell
greymatter/eyejuice/energy curl
I am my by-the-wind sailor, the fisher of tomorrow
I have humours I think
what a nice skull I'd make
but a better head of hair

without
all that space

shifting now
replete with that free gift

the laughter . . .

        let the wind of the void
        take it all away.

Here beside
a dying fire
midnight/cicadas fret fully click and pause/the dandelions
are folded shut

the wind sighing
the last of the wine/only an hour to go?
There is always tomorrow and in leaving

it is so still:
the moon's in the near north
[at two in the morning
you're late in leaning
round the world, lady . . .]
and flitting over the hill
in happy stealth
an owl-child/songlight/raining
childsong/lightwing/rainshine
owl-light: rainchild: nothing else

KAIBUTSU-SAN

What I heard was this:

Lissen lissen hey man lissen

but I didn't hear it. A kind of mental sleeve-plucking.

Lissen we weren't doin' nothin' just plain Friday night in the Square lissen?

At first I thought it was the trees. Don't laugh. I was sitting quietly among the people swarm, sitting quietly on the bare tiles by one of the dying trees in tubs. If you listen carefully you can hear them waving their leaves feebly and gasping AIR AIR. If I were them, I'd up roots and head for the nearest bush. Leave the place freakily bare in the morning.

But it wasn't the trees. It wasn't real enough for that.

Lissen please lissen ahhh

I looked cautiously round. No-one near. I said, 'I'm listening.'

Ahhhhhhh at last at last at last . . . you can really hear? Wiggle your fingers by your nose?

O no. Not the sort of gesture I should make. But I wiggled.

Good. We started by scoring fivedollar hassling two thinfaced kids in a spacegame pit. They took one look at Mi all giant heavyjaw menace, another at our patches, and squeaked in terror. Handed over their money and scuttled away. Naturally we go outside to wait for more victims, take an innocent turn round the block meanwhile, but when we get back there's a demon lurking, swaying back and forth on his size twenties and caressing his long baton in an anticipatory sort of way. Smart little mothers, I think. I am verbally adroit but why waste words on rats?

I could – hear. I thought as I – heard, someone has spent a long time polishing this story. It does not sound verbatim. And as I thought that, I felt – someone. Hunkering down by me, ready to continue a long tale. Someones.

Yeah, there's both of us. Me and Mi. Mi doesn't say much. Not exactly a walking dictionary, old Mi. He only cares about food, drink, sex, and excitement. Excitement can be strife or perversions or anything, but excitement there has got to be. I think it's to keep his bulk moving. When you get to be seven feet tall (almost) at seventeen, you need more than just ordinary fuel and thrill to keep you going, eh?

'Yes.'

Me, I don't need much. All I got to do is keep finding things to hate, and the world's full of those. I even hate Der Gang, for keeping us honorary fringe members. Any decent tribe would've killed us stone-dead just for approaching them. I mean, who wants The Hulk, capable of eating you and your headquarters out at one snack? Or The Thing, scaled with an interesting greenish version of psoriasis and capable of remembering every word you say for ever? Like, gimme a chance to glance at your notes, earwig your talk, and zap! Total recollection, reproduce it anytime. Mutants, the both of us. But Der Gang gives us sort of patches and sort of tolerates us round unless they're all feeling bored. They were, Friday . . . you still there?

I nodded.

It's eerie man. You're there and you're not. Anyway, Friday and we got fivedollar. Not enough for anything much. Mi suggests Port? An evening blurred out of existence: it has appeal. But fivedollar will only get a half-g and a half-g'll only half-blur us. So I say Nope, and Mi, who thinks I'm God, just nods. He stands there hunched and huge in his patches and gear. He never takes his patches and gear off. You can't call them his second skin. They're his first. I am a little more uh healthy. I have underpants. And my chest boasts a delicate intricacy of greeny scales highly visible through the open denim jacket – you can't see?

'Not a thing.'

Ah shit. Nemmind. Anyway, there we are, strolling quietly through the Friday-night crowds, away from the spacepit. Mi lumps along, hands occupied with his cards. It's a twitch with him, a kind of tic, shuffling a pack in a flickering arc. Always has a pack on him, keeps them spruce clean inner secret pocket in his jacket. It's strange to see them come out virginal from among the carefully grown shit and grime. I've got the odd twitch too. Like reading signs, any signs, shop window neon store-top bus-side. I chant them out loud until I see there's another demon not a hundred miles away from us staring in a repulsively interested fashion. 'Centre,' I say, twitching Mi's jacket, and the cards vanish magically, back into their virginal hole. Centre is – you know the scarred remaining real tree? Not this scrawny thing in the pot trying to make it to bush-size?

> 'I know it.' The big one that has come to some unholy truce with good ol' CHCH pollution and now photo-synthesises soot instead of sunlight. The tree I'd come to see until I – heard.

Right. That's our centre. Our refuge. I squat by Mi on an outside root and the Friday-night crowd eddies round us. All those good straight people daren't get too close. Something might leap off us and sink its grimy little teeth deep into their skin ARRGGGHH! and suddenly they'll be like us, outlaws, streethappy. I sneer at the good people. I have 94 words for them, all extremely corrosive. I say them under my breath. Mi has his cards out again and is staring unfocused over their arc.

A crocodile of Japanese tourists is chivvied by, following a Leader and a Flag. They don't even blink at Mi and me. Don't even see us, I think. Not a registered tourist sight eh. Except there's one at the end of the crocodile, the wart on its tail. He trips along in little staggers, upright and sweating and obviously stewed out of his mind. He sees my stare, blinks, sees Mi, blinks again, and suddenly disengages from the crocodile. He is about four feet tall, flabby, and when he smiles at us, reveals appalling teeth. Great and yellow, like a horse's, and very wet-looking. He bows suddenly, like a pocket-knife folding, hisses through the teeth, and says

'Pray cards?'

Mi snorts. Stereotype, he is thinking, only he is not thinking 'stereotype', he is seeing comic-strip yellow men who can't say 'l'.

'Pray cards?' asks the gnome again, anxiously. He folds fluidly up beside us, and I hear tinkle tinkle and all of a sudden he has produced a briefcase.

And I gasp. It is made of some soft supple sueded leather, beige, brushed fine, achingly beautiful. I saw a dog with a hide like that and coveted it and plotted how to get it for months. But that is not all. The briefcase has ordinary dimensions and a curious handle. Little dials inset, lights like trapped glow-worms but enough to show electronic numbers and lines flickering away. An impossibly small television half an inch across but I swear to seeing tiny people cavorting on it. The briefcase looks rich, technical, elegant and somehow, heavy. I hunger for it.

The tinkle tinkle is from a fine steel chain running from the briefcase handle to the little man's wrist.

'Pray cards,' he states, in the brook-no-refusal tone of the very drunk.

And Mi giggles. He giggles so much he nearly loses control of his cascade of shuffled cards.

You take it from me, old Mi looks thick and clumsy as well as enormous. From the soles of his horny feet (I mean skin, he can't even steal a decent pair of steeltoes) to the top of his carefully felted hair, he looks like an oaf. Can't touch a thing without crushing it. Anything delicate or skilful is obviously beyond him. Except old Mi was born a card-shark. He was born knowing all card-combinations, the odds at poker, the possible hands in every game. He has razor-fine judgement in assessing other players. It is not a matter of memory for him to know what cards have been played, are to be played. It is a matter of instinct. Nobody who knows him plays with him of course. You get murdered, every game. That is why he shuffles. That is all he gets to do.

And here is this weird little victim offering himself to Mi.

I am getting a fierce electric sort of a buzz already. That briefcase is worth real dollars, hundreds of them . . . a furious rave of a Friday, not slow boring killtime at all! 'Gimme t'five' says

Mi and he giggles his high breathy giggle again. I heeheehee right along with him, and hand the money over. Mi spreads it on the root of the tree.

'Play cards for money,' he says slowly and emphatically, 'ah so' giggling again. Height of humour for him eh.

'Dorrors o-kay.'

He hugs his briefcase close to his chest, opening it so we can't see in. The amazing handle is flopped towards me and yeah: there really are little people on that impossibly small screen. My eyelids might be scaly and reptilian but the eyes inside are sharper than most. Then flip. Cards. Fresh cards in crisp Cellophane. And flip again. Fivedollars. About a hundred of them, neatly bent in bankers' tens, gathered together with a shiny fold of new white paper. He rips that, spreads them round in a fan; snaps off the Cellophane, pushes over the cards to Mi.

He sets his briefcase down carefully clinkle tink and beams at us.

'Ah so. Cards o-kay. Money. Prenty dorrors. Good.' He bows from the waist. 'Drink?' he enquires. 'Drink,' he decides. He picks up the case again. 'What genremen drink?' he asks us.

I'm goggling. I will have that bag if I have to personally saw it off the dwarf's wrist. But I say, 'The gentlemen love, truly relish, bourbon. We luxuriate in that delectable liquor,' malignly sticking in as many 'l's as I can think of in a second.

He blinks. He says something fast in Japanese and there is, I swear from inside the bag, a tiny mellow reply.

'Bourbon,' says the Teeth, and reaches in his briefcase and takes out three crystal shot-glasses. They are large glasses and they are full.

It *is* a travelling bar as well as an electronic marvel show! Mi doesn't think about the Amazing Bag, he just takes his glass and swallows the drink and goes Ahhhhh. So I try mine. Smooth and pure, holy best bourbon, god that's good.

The little Jap has already downed his. He holds his hand out, takes back our glasses, refills them (a long thin flask in there, vacuum operated? I think), and then licks his lips.

'Pray cards now,' he says definitely.

And so the slaughter begins. The purring power-machine that

is cardplaying Mi gears smoothly up. He toys a little with the Teeth, finding out his strengths (none apparently) and his weaknesses (everywhere). He loses our fivedollar, wins it and two of the banker's fold back, loses another . . . o you know as I do how to spin a sucker along. The fan of fivedollars shrinks. Mi giggles. The little man sweats. He opens the beautiful bag frequently. You hear his glissade of Japanese, a click, a tiny voice, then a swash noise. It honestly sounds like him saying I want three quadruple shots of best bourbon, and the bag saying Yes Teeth-san, and producing them . . . o the marvels of microchip technology!

We've had six seven neat sweet bourbons by now and the noise of the crowd eddying round our cardsharper and victim island has receded. The Teeth is talking in his fractured ell-less English,

'No mor dorrors, neary gone, sad horrorday now,'

but neither of us are really listening. I am staring fascinated at the game, at the bag, at the little man dealing his hopeless cards, wristchain ringing as he does. Mi is playing and sees nothing but the game in hand.

More bourbon from the bag-bar. Tinny voice, figures fluorescing on minute screen. No more Friday-night-in-the-Square crowd. Bourbon. The Teeth is sweating profusely, down his flabby cheeks, into the fissures of his neck. He giggles constantly. He still bows floppily from the waist each time he passes our drinks. He keeps dropping his cards. The chain from bag to wrist goes tinkle tinkle.

'What we pray for now genremen?'

That penetrates. The fan of fivedollars has folded entirely. I have it all in my back pocket, where it keeps our lucky first fivedollar warm. I nudge Mi. The bourbon vapours in my brain have produced a hell of an idea.

'No money, no game,' says Mi. He puts his giant hand on the pile of cards and discards, lovingly. His eyes shine. He foresees. And the future tonight is going to be Rampage. A rage of a night. We can really waste ourselves. Slit, booze, fists, you name it, we'll have it, thanks to the fan. But I want, I want

The Jap wrings his hands and the chain dingles.

'O but I *ruv* cards, prease pray more.'

I nudge Mi again.

'Money or nothing,' I say ruthlessly. Then bait my hook. 'Unless you got something worth dollars?'

He looks at his dandruff-spotted navy-blue suit, shiny black shoes, holds out the other wrist with a cheap chrome digital watch on it hopelessly. I shake my head. The sweat running down his face looks like tears. I snicker. He hugs the Amazing Bag to his chest desperately. The gleam in my eyes must be showing.

'Very precious, this case,' he says. 'Is everything to me. All my fun, all my life. What can you offer that is equal?'

Okay, normally that sudden improvement in a foreigner's English would have warned even Mi. It had 'demon' written all over it, their gambling squad or something. But the bourbon was roaring in our heads, and I saw only the gorgeous supple-skinned case with all its magic, and Mi saw only the greatest prize of his card-playing life lying supine and grovelling before him. As ready for the plucking as Mi was ready for the kill.

So I say, 'Well, we'll play you everything we've got against your bag. Fair exchange eh?' and Mi choruses, 'Everything, everything.'

'All the dollars? Everything?'

'Everything.'

'Clothes, jewels, skin, everything?'

'Yeah, yeah, *everything*,' damn the little bat I think, my fingers itching for The Bag.

'Everything you have and are?' whimpers the Teeth. 'Everything?'

'*Every*fuckingthing,' growls Mi. His cardshark fingers are riffling the pack.

'So. Everything?' he passes over filled bourbon glasses.

'Yeah yeah yeah,' we are melting with impatience and wouldn't see a warning if it sprang on us and throttled us We clutch our last glasses of booze.

'Ah so,' says the Teeth, and bows politely, and there is an infinite fat satisfaction about him now.

The cards are dealt, the hands are played, and Mi loses, of course.

The little Oriental gentleman stands fluidly, bows a last time, smiles.

'Keep the money,' he says. His face is becoming leaner. 'Keep your patches and gear.' He has stopped sweating. 'You can even keep the glasses.' He points the handle of the bag at us. We are sitting stunned, mouths O, Mi's hands limp as though the life has gone from them. 'I only want everything from you.' Somehow his teeth are more pointed than before. There is a flash and click like someone took a photograph. Immediately I feel something essential, vital, drain out of my belly, and Mi feels it too because he screams and the cards spray out of his hands.

Two more little figures suddenly appear on the tiny screen. I can see them, I disbelieve it. My ears hear a chorus of thin howls from the bag.

The Teeth smiles suavely, one last time.

'So sorry,' he says, and is back among the Friday-night crowd and lost. The Friday-night crowd is everywhere again, loud and rushing and rude and we're *here*. Man hey man, lissen, can you get us out?

> That's what I heard. I still couldn't see them but their agony was real. But somebody from the Friday-night crowd had seen me sitting by the trapped tree, seen me talking to seemingly thin air, and had called you. So here I am, back again, explaining. Do you comprehend what you hear,
> you,
> and your beautiful
> little black bag?

SWANSONG

I'm not concussed, I'm not.

Look, *listen.*

You're the one who wants to hear about her.

We had it all worked out, Cotton, McKinnon, and me. Go long to the next big stir, protest thing, get among those slimy commie liblips and do a leetle, a discreet stirring for ourselves. Right on the front line. Look like a powerhouse for good, their good, and be getting our own low jollies all the time. Poke 'em in the brisket. The groin. The brainpan yum yum. Got neat ballpoint pens that ain't ballpoint pens. Gotta scalpel instead of a pen. Does an easy slice like a razor. And sweet lils. Dunno what *you* call *them.* Bet you know them though – like soft batteryfed tubes? Long as your clenched fist? You touch any damn body and they get a kick. Electric kick. Punches a hole. Lay them flat. Sweet. Feels like holding your own meat and you stick it to someone and they lurch and scream and bend under at just the touch. Really gets to the gut and –

Well, I was waiting with the gear. March starts at noon. Way before, can hear all this action. Yatter and chatter through powerhorns. People tramping. Worries. Banners. The thocketty of chopper wings. Everybody gathering almost by my gate. Which was why we planned to meet at my place, why I had the gear. It all forms up just two blocks down. We plan to merge in as it goes past, filter out as it's driven back. The confrontation point is 'nother two corners up. The blue squaddies – you gotta hand it to them. They planned to squash this one *fast.* And we jus' wanna he'p.

Okay, talk proper, talk proper, I am just an innocent NZer and know no better though brighter than most. Personally I blame television *Okay* –

she was slender and tripped along, sort of small antique tripping steps slip slip one after the other a kind of cutey tiptoe almost-lurch (she said she was used to flying O my boring boring, she smothers a yawn, all that to-ing and fro-ing white feathers aflap midear you can get *tired* of swans)

and she had this hair, bobbing curls worse than Annie Fannie, brown but *bright* like each hair had an underside silver. Or gold. All flash flicker trip.

And the smile. She smiled most of the time and her teeth were small rounded pearly, each a little white glimmer. Stewardess I thought, with the flying and that. Smile.

– and SHARP, says Cotton.

– Where's McKinnon? You supposed to be here

(checking watch with withering look)

– an hour ago.

I said an hour earlier because Cotton and McKinnon never can get their shit together. Prefer to *im*bibe. Slurperers.

Cotton is going, Ah he, ahhh, and she's looking at Cotton and giggling. Shimmer laughter. A kind of musical tripping down up down a minor scale.

– He's ahh he's, goes Cotton.

– Busy, she glimmers.

Cotton hisses in my ear

– He was just drinking and chatting you know McKinnon he raves a bit but that's all just chatting her up and she says pretty quiet Y'talk *too* much and he kinda bows says O but the wit and sense of that comment m'dear and she smiles and says Eat it! and he looks puzzled then does the whole bloody glass!

I draw back, the inside of my small and pearly drizzled on, hissed in, wet.

– So where's McKinnon?

I'm truly puzzled.

– Hospital, hisses Cotton – seventy-six stitches so far.

All those sibilants. I shudder.

– O? So he's not comeen? Stiff. Are we ready?

Bugger McKinnon I think but I am cool for anything. Ready for anything.

She giggles her musical giggle and shakes her shiny curls. I'm dazzled. Cotton's gone blank.

– Ready! she says, crisp as a troopie.

– You? Girls don't

– Fight? she croons. You're telling me about battles? Fights? Mayhem? The golden fields of war?

I didn't think you got eyes that shiny black? Do you?

Well, yeah, getting on with it. One of us was out, we had three sets of gear, miaswell have her in. We dressed. McKinnon, whose daddy is something highup weird in the airforce travels to hell and gone, got us these t-shirts that weren't (I'd organised the pens and sweet lils but that's another matter, for the other lot, you just interested in the girl right? Okay.) These t-shirts – they had a lining that seemed soft until you poked it. The harder you poked, the harder it got. A fast whack jarred the hand of whoever gave it. They were prissy long, way over yer crotch. Came complete with a yank-type hat, those pokey things with beaks on 'em? The makers swore a bullet even would just bounce right back at whoever was numb enough to fire it. So there we are. T-shirted, hard-hatted, ballpoint pens in one hand, sweet lils in the other. I had stencilled peace signs on the t-shirts. A nice nice touch.

And we're feeling ready to break the world apart. A great urge. Shivery but fiery. Just from getting into battlegear. I wish we could've had some harness, any kind, but that would've given the game away. She looks strange enough as it is, dress sleeves poking beyond the t-shirt, pointy hat bouncing on the curls.

– Ready? Me, loud above the ill-disciplined tramping of protest wankers outside.

– Yeah o yeah, says Cotton, are we *ready*!

– Ready yet! Me, the marshal, crowing forward.

– Numbskulls, she says, no affection at all in her voice. Her smile glitters at us. Rather, her teeth glitter at us between tightly curving lips. You couldn't help but shiver. I mean, Cotton did. I just felt the war-fire ebb a little, the hard-on slide.

Then she trips past us out the door into the sunlit blaring

street out into the crowdmass chanting their palsied trendyleft
slogans and we had to follow. Push into the scummy bodies and I
can hear her voice in my ear though her face is turned the other
way.

– Don't you think you'll get tired of boarmeat and mead?

She sounds conversational.

– Though Heidrun does *try*. Gave us a damn good Scotch for a
while. She gets bored too, you know – and as for that poor bloody
pig! Words fail.

And then she's walking forward as though she's walking
through people and I've got to really worm and slither to keep
up.

Oho I think, jostling and being jostled, shaping my lips into
their slogans while my eyes are busy looking for unprotected
genitalia and vulnerable throats (but the rough stuff would be at
the police barrier ahead) O she is tripped out of her tiny mind, that
is why McKinnon chatted her up he can spot them a mile off
glitter-dollies with mushbrains good for *any*thing, that'd explain
him talking to strange ladies on the day of our Great Stir, good old
McKinnon organise the lay afterwards a good bloody prod maybe
even a loonnng snuff? lick my lips, I'll bet she's got no-one looking
out for her, but even when that thought hit me even as I licked my
salivation away my finelyhoned mind came up with NO look at
those clothes expensive whitefeathery dressthing cost the earth
ah hah better yet! A wild rich and weirdo one great one McKinnon
ol'boy! and the undertow puzzling me, What *was* that bit? About
stitches and glass?

The crowd's cooking now, slogan battles going on between
justfolks on the footpaths and yech us and now some treacly faded
folkies coming up with WE SHALL OVERCOME and there's a
really nasty group we're among now, bikehelmets with the visors
down and dyke written all over them, it's close *close* CLOSE to
the front. We'll get this lot I think, cool and marshalling still and
spin my head to look for Cotton and there he is right by, eyes
glittering and mouth open and goddammit a drool spinning from
his mouth. I lip to him, THESE ONES SLAY meaning these ones
stab dig punch rip and he nods, still dribbling the wanker and
high.

One of the dykes peers from their huddle, could call it a packed disciplined group but they wouldn't know goosestep from frogmarch – you should try it on *them* stead of us righteous okay *okay*. I get on with it. One of the dykes peers anyway and I see her do genuine double-take and what's she watching? Our curly girl tripping demurely along seeming closed in her own space pieces of white gown shining out from the t-armour-shirt her eyes bright as bright as bright. The dyke says something couth and cool like Shit! and edges out from her witchy sisters.

– Hey! she yells.
– Yes? demure smile, little white fangs hidden.
– What're one of you things doing here?
– Things? dangerously sweet and low.
– The butch bitch grins. Pushes back her black helmet visor, still keeping step alongside her sister-pack.
– Hardly born of woman!
Ours sniffed, miffed.
What do you mean, hearing?
Like before. Like she was talking in my ear. I could hear everything including all the raucous bellowing crowd. I do assure you I am not lying. As if it matters now.
Anyway, ours starts ranting We were the first, the battle-women deciders of the fates of men
– a few thousand years of that must've bored you to tears
– yawns dear actually, screaming yawns
– so what gives now?
Dozens of rabid lefties screaming things like FREEDOM and puerile suchlike tripe and there's this weeirrd conversation echoing in my ears. In Cotton's too: he's shaking his head like he wants those little insect words out.
O shit I know it all sounds wild
I know I took a beating on my head
No I am not concussed. I know who I am. I know where I am. And I want *out*. Would you seeeriously think doctor lootenant captain sir, I want to prolong this misery? With more misery waiting for illegal possession et cetera et cetera? I do have a high shall we say

I *am* telling.

It ends quickly after that previous snippet. The blue squaddies started going MOOOVE MOOOVE like berserk beefs
and stepping into us pistol batons out and the dykes lowering
shoulders pounding forward and the stupid chanting getting
louder LIBERTY STOPTHERTOR STOP and howls and
shrieks and scrunches all round and if you think I had much
time to shockpunch anyone slit anyone spike anyone, you
dead wrong – snicker ha ha I tell you that because I know them
out there are listening, course I tried give a poke there skid
a blade there but some of those freaks are big bastards and
they're all banded together and the dykes are a solid fisty wall
and I watch Cotton get a baton through his teeth spit spit and
a sticky bloodful gout and go under the feet and I'm screaming
and trying to find a friendly hand or shoulder someone to
cling on to stay upright and I get this warm almost frail feathery
hold.

She gives me one wild blackhole stare, and turns back to the
heavy lady.

– but what else is there? We search you know, we roam the
world entire for even the smallest pitched battle body to body
hand to hand. Our love and our duty but they're not even grateful
now, soon as we mention the daily slaughter and the pork and
mead forever and the eternal nightly carousing they scream hell
hell what else is there?

– Could try and show you a new world, offers the patu dyke
and her voice is I kid you not kind, even, calm.

And that's when it happened.

There was this piercing screech HUHUHU and wild booming
howling, words I think, and everyone round ducks.

Yes, me too.

And then she screams and I can hear it still

– anything*anything* ANYTHING BUT THE VALHALL AND
THE GOLDEN FIELDS OF WAR

and the black helmet grabs her, hugs her, face contorted, and
people are falling in a bloody swathe as though her words and
scream are knives cutting them in two.

And some cunt woodens me.

And that's all.
Except just before the blackness came I thought
– and McKinnon always drinks a handle the fool

KING BAIT

I think this season'll be the last, you know. Well, I mean, Coasters have their channels for spreading news, mainly ex-Coasters. From such people, news filters through to friends of ex-Coasters, not to mention relations, and eventually travels the length and breadth of the country. So maybe everybody knows why, and maybe everybody doesn't, yet.

Here I am, wound round in a welter of words, with a mystery on my hands, and very uncertain what to say about it. But this is the core of the matter, the heart of the nut: King Bait.

One thing everybody does know about the Coast is bait. Whitebait. That succulent little fish, quick and lucent, likened in an old haiku to the 'spirit of the waters' –

> The whitebait:
> as though the spirit of waters
> were moving.

And every beginning spring, Coasters in their hundreds flock to the rivers and streams to swoop and scoop and blind-drag as many as possible out of sanctuary. When it's a good season, tons are lovingly packed into freezers against the lean, non-bait portion of the year; tons more are railed and flown over the hill, weekly. The Coast becomes a joyous place, the Coaster a contented being.

Of course, quite a few hundred-weight get converted meantime into patties and omelettes and – well, whatevers. How did your mother cook them when she got them from the shop? I'm from Christchurch, we eke out the bait with flour and other foreign bodies. But here! Prodigality . . .

Take half a pound of bait per person, add an egg (two eggs, if you really like them), stir vigorously until fish and egg is a viscous froth full of strange little eyes. Add half a teaspoon of baking powder; a little salt, a smidgen of pepper, and fry the mix quickly, but with care. There you have a Coast feed, two right-sized whitebait patties, a subtly flavoured delight for anyone with a tongue in their head.

Last year, I missed the whitebait season. I was newly arrived from Christchurch and, unaware of Coast ways, I bought my bait from a local fish-shop, and was well-content to get it 40 cents cheaper the pound than the family over the Hill. Last year, I couldn't have told you the difference between a net for the Tere, and one used in the Grey. Nor what the advantages of supplejack over duraluminum. Set-nets were strangers, and the joys of very early morning tea in a tin shack on a river-side also unknown. The haiku was just a pleasant poetic fancy, blind-dragging was peculiar terminology and the great runs – well, myths of the past, a nice concept to beguile the tourists.

This year, I'm all enthusiasm. Buy myself the regulation round Grey net, and a bloody great pole to go with it. Equip myself with gumboots, get out old fishing clothes, and head down to the river at odd hours, waiting on changing tides. Drag that net, eyes strained, shoulders filled with a dead ache, hopeful of a nice little pudding in the bottom of the nylon bag. Or a very large one, for the season's started out a boomer. Tons of bait about. Happy faces all around, reflecting my smug grin. Full stomachs abounding, appetite satisfied, bankbook replete, and yet expecting much, much, more.

Things are just beginning. All over the Coast the hiss of hot fat and the crunching of little eyes . . .

And you know what? I think it's the end.

A very strange thing happened yesterday, twenty to nine under Cobden bridge; a strange, a horrible, a holy thing.

Friday night was a good night. I'd been to the local juicery, talked a lot, sung a bit, drank to capacity, happy among happy people. Came home with the white moon high over the sea. A windless peace-filled night, the only sound that liquid continuous chirruping of tree-frogs. I cooked a couple of patties, ate them with a last cold beer from the fridge, and went to bed. Relaxed, full, content, perfectly at ease . . . ah, sweet.

And then, the morning. I woke suddenly, dropped abruptly out of sleep. For a moment I couldn't place the awakening factor, and then, there it was. A most peculiar hysterical liveness, filling the quiet street, streaking up my quiet hill, a shrill cacophony of voices.

'Berloody kids,' I think, and go to turn over, back to sleep.

It penetrates then:

'Whitebait running WHITEBAIT RUNNING WHITE-BAIT . . .'

The words and the strangeness were enough. I shot out of bed, into my denims and t-shirt faster than it's said, grabbed my boots and the net, and screamed out of the door and down the hill far more quickly than I've ever done. In fact, I'd reached the bottom before I realised that I've left the pole back in the house. Or asked myself why somebody should tell everybody about a good thing.

But the street is alive as never before. The old lady recluse, who's probably never seen the light of day outside for years, is standing there, mouth open, staring-eyed, looking shrunken and untidy on the footpath. The new family at the corner is running in a graduated straggle round the corner, all eleven of them. As they vanish, the bloke next door and his wife with the new kid rush out. He's got the net and pole, and she has one arm full of kerosene tins and plastic bags, and one arm full of baby, and I swear it's not the former she's going to drop. I don't wait round looking anymore. Bugger the pole, I hive off through a short-cut down into Bright Street. And believe me, all ambulant Cobden seems to be there, I'm a heavy sleeper, late waker, and the street is now crowded with everyone before me, running, walking, staggering, hell for leather for the river.

Well, it's normally a ten-minute walk from my place to the bridge, but even with the crowd I make it in a three-minute run. After getting through the lame oldies and slow small fry, it's much easier of course. There was the risk of being skewered by poles, or having the breath thumped from one by a carelessly swung kero tin. Christchurch Friday-night-in-the-Square experience came to the fore here, though, and I'm in the van of the rush as we reach the river, that stretch just before the north end of the bridge.

Down the bank, trampling bush, slipping, kicking someone, grazing my hand on a tree I use to break my headlong eagerness a moment. All pulsing wild excitement to get a spot.

And stop aghast. Because, before God, the Grey is solid whitebait, bank to bank.

A fabulous mass of life, so thick in the river that water isn't seen. Just a seething froth of bait, frantic yet purposeful, a live river flowing in from the sea. And the hiss of disturbed water from their passing is louder than rain, louder than rapids, as spirited and loud as great falls.

I scoop, holding the rim of the net. It's FULL, absolutely chokka, and I drag it, elated, to the shore. The nylon is strained to its limits. Damn, nowhere to put the catch! But the bait, contrary to the normal lively whipping efforts to get out of the net and into the river, lie there like a sacrifice, and peacefully begin to die.

Strange. All my feverish desire to catch whitebait is gone. I lay the net with gentleness on the riversand at my feet, and all along the bank, as the people come slithering excitedly down, and then stop, stunned, they are now doing the same. Over on the Greymouth side, the weird thing happens, as the crowds gather and swell and burst to the riverside. Horrified reverence for this impossible dream-run.

Except one man.

I don't know who he is, a thigh-booted dungareed individual, made distant and inhuman by his action. For he is swinging his net like an automaton, scooping the bait, flinging it silver and any-where onto the shore. There is saliva hanging in a shining string from the corner of his mouth, and I am not so far away that I can't see the money-glaze on his eyes. It's inevitable, a feeling of disaster growing. Stop it you bastard, from voices in the crowd, leave them alone. But he continues shovelling up the unresisting harvest.

. . . an eddy in the river of bait, or an eddy of the crowd, pushing harder out? I don't know, but he is suddenly off his feet, falling with grotesque flailing slowness into the froth of eyes. The bait-river moves on, and how to swim when the water is gone, how to swim in a viscous moving jelly? His dark head is above the river once, shining all over with lucid bodies, mouth gaping open, nostrils flaring wide, but full of writhing fish . . .

If ever a man died in dream turned nightmare, that was him. And yet, not a movement or sound is heard from any of us. Just a shared feeling of wonderment, of rightness, and inevitability, as the whitebait we caught die on the shore. Things move to a conclusion.

And then there is an unforgettable sound, a vast wind of indrawn breath coming from the seaward end of the river. People astonished, bereft of all movement except the gasp of awe. Slowly it swells, welling along the banks of the river, both sides of the river, while we who have no knowledge, wait and there, midstream, lambent, borne on the living tide, the spirit of the waters, moving.

We disagreed how big today. Ten or maybe twelve feet of lighted perfection. Clear as the most clear water, except for the fine line of black speckling on his sides, and the slender dark-drawn rays of his four fins and tail . . . and the goldened brain in the top of his head . . . and the eyes, the great silver eyes, intensely circled black centres, burnished globes on the inward side of his head. They reflect neither intelligence nor love, nor malignity, but show forth pure being. Summation. A complete benign magnificence.

For as the multitude of whitebait had gathered to protect this one by sheer pacific numbers, so was there nothing to fear from him. Watch with calm incredulity as he passes.

King Bait.

And as much bait flowed behind in that protective solid wall, now unharried by fish or bird or man, as came to be preyed on before. I thought of the millions upon millions of ridiculous harmless little fish, who had been sacrificed to provide a safe passage for that majesty, and did not wonder much therefore at feeling echoes of their massed consuming joy.

There is nothing in the river, except the white slimefroth of their passing, and the water. And somebody says, loud is the quiet that follows after,

'Hell, I hope they make it to wherever that is going. I hope they get there.'

And somebody near me, voicing all the other thought of the people,

'God love us all, but are they ever coming back?'

A TALLY OF THE SOULS OF SHEEP

(NB: *Script*, *Notes, [Disinformation])

Location(s)

Kaitangata Bay is on the southern West Coast.
There, mussel-bearing rocks are swept by
the boisterous Tasman, which is casual about
snatching people with a swift white fist and
bearing them off to the deeps. There, suitable
low sandhills are covered with marramgrass and
pingao and sand convolvulus. There, high cliffs
and bluffs, and fascinatingly treacherous
swamps, abound. And the bush can be impenetr-
able.
There, the Southern Alps rear in the near
background. They are jagged fangs.

*Kaitangata is actually in
Central Otago. This is a
dislocation.
[Kaitangata means a
dispute over eeling
rights.]

*Ah, pretty nihinihi –
perhaps a lingering CU
on the shy pink flowers
before shifting on to the
winter-bronzed pingao.
[He nui pohue toro ra
raro.]

The car, to begin with – everything begins in the
car – is travelling any scenic road. Choose your
favourite route from any part of our thousand-
mile stretch. Sooner or later, it will run into some
sheep, grazing the long acre or moving from that
paddock to this paddock.

*battered 4-door family
saloon, year and model
immaterial.

The bach – we will come to the bach at Kaitangata
Bay shortly.

Characters

The man is a freezing worker on holiday. He is

*None of the characters
refer to each other by
name

middle-sized, solid, dark, and stolid (except for a nervous habit of chewing the nail of his left forefinger). His movements and actions are fluent, but aside from his eyelids (which flicker inappropriately) and his jaw muscles (which clench without, it seems, due reason) his face is frozen.

The woman is a housewife and mother, overtly devoted to kinder, kirche, kuche, and knitting. She is relatively tall, an ectomorph with a gaunt highly-mobile face. Her body is stiff and she believes it to be a rather messy casing for her soul. When she once unguardedly mentioned this to the man, he had a rare fit of hysterical laughter and was nearly sick into his sausages.

OED def. of soul: 'the essential fundamental or animating part, element, or feature, of something.'

The daughter is just pre-pubertal, noisy, bossy, aggressive, and outgoing. She collects and pokes and explores.

The son is two years younger, a plump rather passive boy whose one passion is drawing. Anything on anywhere.

The main characters are accompanied by a cast of thousands.

Two passing shepherds and their pack of eye dogs and heading bitches.

An enigmatic pirate figure, one eye covered with a black patch, who seems to fish the beach at Kaitangata Bay.

Plenty of gulls and oyster catchers, tree-frogs, a morepork or two, and a cynical korimako.

And all these sheep.

*Any member of the ruminant genus Ovus. Or, person displaying characteristics of the animal.

Action

A bunch of keys swinging, one of them in the ignition.

The car interior, the four people.

The car radio –

'and in Wellington, Nelson and Marl-borough, fine sunny weather. Overcast and mild in Buller, with showers expected later in the day. Rain on the West Coast and Fiordland increasing tonight, and in Southland, heavy rain and gale-force south-westerlies with mumble mumble mumble'

Woman (speaking over the weather forecast): What's this place like anyway?

Man: Quiet.

Pan to passing fences, back to his face –

Man: O shit.

– long shot of the road ahead. There's a solid wall of sheep coming on. Two drovers behind the flock, one on a horse, the other on a farmbike, are pushing them hard. Several dogs weave round the sheep, which engulf the car, swirl and muddle round it. The dogs get noisier. The woman and kids stare in a bored fashion. The engine-sound pulses, competing with the bark-ing and the bleating – the man is obviously revving the motor impatiently. A closeup of his face reveals his jaw muscles tightening. His eyes close quickly.

The long shot of moving sheep continues, but superimposed in the upper lefthand corner is a very swift montage of stills:

*sheep being flogged up the ramp to the sticking pens

*a shiny steel hook hanging from a shiny steel band

*a stuck sheep and a smiling butcher by its side

*a shiny steel knife and a shiny sharpening steel across each other

*a sheep, eyes tightly shut, hanging head down

*a CU of a steel hook driven through a heel behind the tendon

*A word about the sound track: it runs ahead of the action, sometimes. This happens in real life, too.

*Another word about the sound track: there is a phantom voice, which probably comes from the man's head because it is a masculine bass, but, gainsaying the character, it is rotund and flowery, an actor-poet practising his pieces.

[This montage will be used many times. It will even become slightly scratched with use. There is no accounting for the realistic FX of the playful mind.]

*a knot of freezing workers in their surgical whites clustered together: no-one is looking at the camera

The man's eyes open and his eyelids flutter. His jaw muscles unclench. The camera follows his gaze out the car window.

Some balky animals are close into the side of the vehicle.

Focus on one – on its loose lips and strange, empty, silvergold stare.

Sheep: Baaaaa.

Man (softly): Yeah.

Woman: Pardon?

Man: Nothing.

The sheep is shifted by a nipping dog. The last of the mob rattles past. A grinning dog runs after them. The drover on the bike is last away. He sticks one finger in the air in acknowledgement of their waiting, and roars off. He's grinning too.

*As he does, the phantom voice intones – *Phantom Voice:* When the heels hang from twelve o' clock, the fingers just touch six.

Action 2

The girl is tormenting her brother and he is whining for parental intervention. Outside, it is unremittingly scenic. The woman is knitting viciously.

Woman: Now what is this place like, *really*?

Man: Well Dave said. . . .

Woman: I don't know Dave. (She is frowning.)

Man: He's a nice enough bloke. Plays pool with the team sometimes. One of the admin lot though.

Woman: He's never been home.

Man: He's not that much of a mate.

Woman: Yet he lends you his bach for nothing and

Man: I mentioned at the end of the season I needed a damned good break – for christ's sake *shut up* –

(He doesn't yell, but says those five words very definitely. The children stop their squabbling immediately, though the girl pokes out her tongue, looking towards the backview mirror as she does. The woman compresses her lips hard, and inhales noisily.)

Man: a damned good break, so he offered it. Nice beach and good fishing he said. Sounded alright to me, particularly for nothing.

Woman: It wouldn't have cost *that* much to have gone to the camp as usual. The last five times have been so. . . .

Man: Exactly.

Woman: *I* like the camp. (She is stabbing the needles through the wool.)
The man grunts.

Woman: It's got everything just like home. It's a change though. You know where you are.
The man grunts.

Woman: How much longer?

Man: I don't know.

Woman: You don't *know?*

Man: Dave said when you get to the turnoff, drive to the end of the unsealed road. He didn't say how long the metal was going to go on for. So we just keep going down this road until the road runs out.

Woman: You do *know* which bach it is I suppose?

Man: Dave says there's not too many of them and his is the last one, right by the beach. We've got the keys. And we can ask someone.

Woman: *Dave* says . . . Dave *says*.
Silence. She stabs another stitch.

$\frac{M}{W}$ or W?
      [M]
WWWWWWWWW
MMMMMMMMM

The fanged equation

[Tally: to compare, for the purpose of verifying an account, etcetera.]

Location

The bach at the beginning of the beach, Kaitangata Bay

It has four rooms – a small bedroom full of doublebed that the adults will sleep in; a tiny bunkroom the children will share; a bathroom-washroom-cum-loo, somewhere in the background (it never figures as a location but for the sake of verisimilitude . . .) and a kitchen-living room, quite large, complete with fireplace and two doors. The furniture is dull, scarred, third-hand, dump-rescued. There is a collection of paua shells on the mantelpiece over the fireplace, ready to be ashtrays.

*You will have noticed many cliches already. These small worn truths are necessary.

Action 3

The man is fussing with a kerosene lamp. The woman comes in, flings back the hood of her parka scattering raindrops. She dumps an overflowing bag of groceries down.

Woman: O my g . . . goodness.

Man: Neat isn't it? You wait until we get a fire going!

Girl: Mum, there's no electricity. There's no fridge or TV or phone or anything.

Boy: Mum, it's cold.

She pushes her hair away from her wet face with a tired gesture. Her face is full of lines.

Woman: O . . . goodness.

Man: Just as good as the camp eh?

He turns away so she cannot see his secret smile. The lamp is suddenly away in a flare of light and his face is full of odd shadows, odd highlights.

Action 4

A scene of peaceful domesticity. The man has built a fire and feeds it carefully, humming to himself as he does. The woman is arranging slices of kiwifruit on top of a large steak. She places another steak on top of the kiwifruit layer, making a macabre sandwich.

Woman (frowning slightly): We can probably use it all up before any goes off.

Man: What?

Woman: The meat.

Girl: What does that do? (She is watching her mother closely.)

Woman: Makes it tender. Makes it more tender. (She smiles slightly.)

The man frowns suddenly into the fire.

Man: Don't leave it too long. The last lot went like bloody jelly. No chew in it at all.

Woman (as though she hasn't heard): I wonder if we could use someone's freezer here. They surely wouldn't mind? (To her daughter.) Would you like to go and see who's home and maybe ask them that? There must be someone with the power on.

Girl: Can I have first pick of the steaks?

Woman: Go on with you. (She's smiling again.)

The girl takes this for 'Yes', and pulls on her parka, and stamps outside. The boy is drawing on the grocery bag. He takes no notice of anyone, and shields whatever he is drawing with his arm. Whenever the camera, handheld, edges closer to see what he is drawing, he swivels slightly, but not obviously, so the drawing is never quite seen. The man continues to hum and build up the fire, the woman to build her stack of green fruit and redly bleeding meat; the boy, to draw.

*The wood he uses is rata, freshly cut, obviously made ready for the incoming inhabitants of the bach. The resin runs out profusely, hissing and sparking in the flames. Tree blood.

The door bursts open suddenly.

The girl has been running and her face is red as well as rainwet.

Girl: There's a dog up there and he's *starving!*

Man (standing abruptly): Where?

Girl: The last house on the hill. He's under the watertank and he's chained and he's *starving.*

Man: Did you try knocking on the door, see if anybody's home?

Girl: There's nobody home.

Woman: But where'd you look?

Girl: Every place.

Woman: Nobody home? But that's silly. There's always somebody, people, somebody home. . . .

Swift cut to fawning dog, jaws grinning, tail in a flurry, ribs very visible.

His chain is fastened round his neck with a padlock.

His water dish is under the tankstand and thus, dry, despite the continuing rain.

He is slavishly grateful for the chops the girl feeds him, gulps them, pukes eventually, and, being a dog, eats everything again.

The man watches his daughter feeding the animal.

Man (to himself): Dave never said anything about a dog. . . .

Action 5

The rain clatters against the windows.

The man and the woman are having a cup of Milo before going to bed. The fire has died down to a shimmer of coals and embers.

Woman: Are you *sure* there's no-one else here?

Man: Doesn't seem to be, just us. Good eh?

To her silence,

*Future generations will think the hardware we use on animals vicious, much as we view slave shackles and chastity belts now. 'Cattle prods? Snaffle bits? Dog whips and chains?' They'll shudder, stare horrified at electric fences and docking instruments, and denounce us as inhuman.

Man: Well, maybe they've all gone to a stocksale
   or a gala or something? Small country places
   are like this, everybody heads off together,
   right?
   The woman hunches her shoulders and
looks out the seagrimed windows into the
night.
   The rain keeps clattering at the windows.

Action 6

   We are focused into the man's eyes. They
stare. The eyelids flutter nervously. We draw
out a little. He is listening intently.
   The rain is still beating down, but the sound
seems too heavy for rain. It is as though a
thousand sheep are being driven at a fast trot
outside the bedroom window, their sharp little
hooves staccato.
Man: Rain. . . .
   The wind gusts, and the rain flock seems to
move faster. There is a distant howling, a very
distant clamour as though of miserable dogs.
Man: Wind. . . .

Phantom Voice:
Do not draw your breath
too deeply.
Blood bubbles through
the air.

[*Seems/As though:*
prevarications.]

Action 7

   Slow camera movement, pulling focus:
   first, a tideline (quietly pan left)
   then undulating sanddunes, topped by pingao
and marramgrass; darkgreen and bronze bush;
   the blackly-ragged treetop line;
   blue hazy hills, and finally,
   the sharp cruel white peaks of the mountains.
Woman: Isn't it pretty!
Man: Yeah . . . bit toothy for comfort though.
   The girl is yelling from further up the
beach.

Girl: Look! Hey look what we found! Guts!

An excised liver, neatly tied up in a plastic bag.

The boy is dawdling behind his sister, doodling with a stick on the fresh sand page.

Man: Fishguts.

It's a pronouncement.

Man: Somebody's been catching a lot of something.

There are more innards, unbagged, along the shore.

In the distance, by the misty edge of a bluff, a thin wavering line of smoke arises.

Woman (heartily): Well, not *every*one's gone to town.

Action 8

They stand in an uneasy cluster round the fire. Most of the logs have burned to ashes, but the butts remain.

Man: Must've been burning for hours.

Woman (laughing uneasily): Those bits of sticks look like bones.

Girl: They *are* bones. They've got knobs each end.

Man: Some fisherman having a snack on the beach.

*Brief focus on the opaque gold eyes: tighten into the vertical slit pupils.

On the other side of the fire, away from the family, towards the bluff, a dozen severed dogfish heads lie in a neat row.

*Brief focus on the coiled wet lengths.

There are also a lot more guts, shining pinkly in the unexpected sun.

But the bones, calcined and grey and ashy, the bones are long.

Man: Pig bones.

He is frowning.

Man: Pig or something.

Action 9

It might be later that day. The woman and the children are walking back along the beach to the bach. The man is nowhere to be seen.

With all the wide freedom of the beach round them, the three still walk on one another's heels.

As they round the point into Kaitangata Bay, a person walks towards them.

Woman: Hello! Hey!

The figure turns suddenly, as though a human cry affronted it.

[Tally: (rare) short for tally-ho.]

Woman: Just a minute! Please!

It walks rapidly sideways, to the surf, but close enough for the three of them to see that it has one eye covered by a black eyepatch.

Woman: I beg your pardon, hello?

The figure turns deliberately on its heel, striding with haste into Kaitangata Bay. Into the roadway, presumably into one of the baches.

Woman (uneasily, to the children): He can't like company.

She smiles fixedly. The girl is unaccustomedly quiet. The boy is scratching some kind of ideogram upon a piece of seaweed.

Woman: Well at least we know there's really people back again.

Her eyebrows are puckered. She cannot understand how the figure disappeared so fast. A wave breaks close by.

Action 10

The woman is cooking, cooking chops. They are middle loin chops, and some of them have clearly once been ribs. The woman is cooking rib-bones and breast muscles.

A thin blue haze clouds the kitchen-living room.

A quick shot of a corner of the ceiling reveals many fly spots and a busy spider cocooning a victim and the odd swirl of cooked smoke.

The children trail in, strangely subdued.

Man: All this fresh air too much for you?

Girl: Don't like the flies . . . and there's shadows round there.

Man: Round where?

Boy: By those cliffs.

Woman (sharply): What do you mean, *shadows*?

Boy (hesitant and whining the words): Shadows . . . just shadows.

The man snorts.

Man: You'll be seeing bloody ghosts next – wash your hands for dinner.

Action 11

The camera will track the girl as she takes the gnawed chop bones up the hill to the dog under the water-tank stand.

She will call it cheerfully.

Girl: Nice food, dog! More nice food!

There will be silence.

The chain will be shown lying at full stretch, the padlock clipped onto the last link. There will be a line of dark pawprints leading away from the chain as though the dog had been worked hard and had gone on bleeding pads. The padprints will be visible because the dog has worn away all the grass. It is bare and dusty ground under the tank stand.

Action 12

A door opens into the dark bunkroom.

The man stands black against the lamplight behind him. The sound track is full of night sounds from the bush. The liquid trilling of tree-frogs. A morepork calling, and its distant mate answering. The querulous gutturals of a possum.

A camera peeps over the man's shoulder as he stares at his sleeping children.

[Tally: to count, or reckon up.]

They sprawl peacefully.

Because the room is full of bush-sound we can't hear them breathing.

Action 13

Very similar to Action 5 – focus on the man's staring eyes, pull out a little until we have him MCU: his arms are folded behind his head.

The bush sounds are very loud in this room too, but underneath them, on top of them, is the odd pattering rustle as of a large mob of sheep driven down a tarsealed road.

*Fade down bush/fade up sheep.

There are no noisy dogs, no miserable howling.

The sound of the sheep rushing past, just outside the room it seems, has overwhelmed all other sounds.

We widen the shot until we have the woman in view, and then tighten upon her.

She is lying on her side, back to the man, resting her head upon clasped hands.

We tighten the shot further to CU on her face. Her eyes are widely open. She is clearly listening to something too.

Phantom voice (quite softly, just audible above the sheep-rustle): When the hooter goes the killing stops. The quiet is eerie: no bleating just my mate caressing/the steel to his knife 'See it shine?' crooning through the teabreak crooning to that blade 'See it shine?'

Action 14

Very brief. The man is hunkered down, head to one side, looking along the road that ends by their bach.

There is not a sheep dropping in sight.

Action 15

The man is pulling mussels off sea-guarded rocks. The surf smashes down and spray flies over him. He yells. His face for once is relaxed and triumphant and thoroughly happy.

He throws the mussels back to shore, and the children scramble to get them before the waves of the incoming tide do.

The woman is sitting on a high flat-topped rock. Her feet are tucked under her. She looks supple and at ease. She is knitting, her ball of wool tucked away in a shoulder bag. She shouts at the children, 'Be careful!' from time to time.

Action 16

[How's your mind's eye?]

What happens next demands fluency in camera action.

The family is coming back from the mussel rocks, the children skittering ahead, the woman striding with the man, the man carrying the mussel-sack.

The camera is now airborne, sweeps out over the sea in a wide circle, still centred on the moving family group, to touch back on the beach behind them.

It moves up to the parents, swivelling round to the seaward side to contain them in profile LS, as they laugh and shout at each other, the man roused by the sea wildness and the woman aroused by the man in his wet shorts.

The camera then crabs round behind them again, as they stop for a swift hug. In the distance, we can see the girl race up to the bluff, the boy bend down and scribble something in the sand.

The camera pulls back. The children have raced round the bluff, the arm-in-arm couple are approaching it. They look very small, now, almost unable to be seen as people.

Action 17

Two lines of children's footprints, stark on the wet sand. They come to an abrupt stop, as though a straight-edged wave had erased them 3 seconds ago.

*Possible ending
Number One.

If we decide to go on:
the two adult faces, seen in CU, are blank, uncomprehending.

[Action 18]

The parents will check the sea, the cliffs, the beach, frantically. They will then assume the children are playing some macabre kind of hide & seek, and they will become angry.

They will then become tearful, hurl recriminations at each other, at each self.

They will race back to the bach, arrive panting and dishevelled and exhausted.

[Tally: to haul taut (specifically sails, fore or main lee).]

They will look at each other in misery.

[Action 19]

While the woman marches determinedly up the hill to the baches there, the man leaps into the car. The engine keeps turning over, but won't catch. He checks the petrol – OK. The battery – OK. Everything seems to be

connected properly. He is sweating and muttering to himself.

When the woman returns, slumpshouldered
because there really is nobody anywhere here,
except for themselves, the man points silently at
the distributor cap.

Man: Somebody's taken out the rotor arm.

They look at one another, and then huddle
together.

They press their faces into each other's
shoulders and won't look up as the noise grows
ever louder.

*A discontinuous
soundtrack here, partly
the man and woman's
rushed breathing, partly
the distant clamour of a
pack of dogs
intermingled with
frenzied bleating.

*Possible ending
Number Two.

[*Action 20*]

The man shakes himself, shakes free of the
woman's desperate clutch.

Man: This isn't getting us anywhere. You check
the beach again. I'll walk out.

He walks rapidly away. The woman calls
after him.

Woman: But the nearest town might be miles
and miles away!

He continues striding away into the distance.

Woman (quite softly): But what'll I do if I find
them?

She turns wearily round to face the beach
again.

A glint of light catches her eye. There is a
camera on a tripod down towards the bluff and
somebody hunched behind it.

She races towards it, yelling incoherently.

She is about 500 yards away, when the figure
behind the tripod straightens – it is the enigmatic
pirate person, and as the figure bends down
again, it is apparent that it is looking through the
viewer with the patch-covered eye. To its left,
the landward side, stand two smaller people.

They look almost the right size to be the children.

The woman stops dead. She peers ahead, her mouth dropping open. There is quite a seafog from the heavily-breaking incoming surf, but she can definitely see 3 figures. She sinks to her knees in the sand, covering her face with her hands.

Woman: Dear God, I don't understand any of this, but thank you. Thank you.

She raises her head and opens her eyes.

*Seasound growing very loud as she does.

There is no-one ahead of her, no-one by the bluff.

*Possible ending *Number Three.*

[*Action 21*]

The man comes striding round a bend in the metal road and stops abruptly.

The way ahead is blocked by a massive slip.

Man: Christ, no wonder there's nobody home.

That must've come down in the rain just after we arrived.

He steps cautiously onto the side of the slip. It is alright for his first hesitant dozen steps, and then his foot slips on loose rock. He grabs at an uprooted manuka by his head. It pulls nearly free. The slope above and below him is starting to move.

*An impertinent korimako with excellent sense of timing begins to chuckle and chonk at this precise moment. Its call sounds over the ominous and increasing rumble of moving rock.

A CU of his face shows a beading of sweat but his expression is curiously stolid. Unmoved.

*Possible ending *Number Four.*

[*Action 22*]

The man and the woman are sitting either side of the kitchen-livingroom table. They hold steaming cups. They are hunched over them.

There is a grazed bruise down one side of the

*There is the sound of vast flocks of sheep going by, the patter of hooves like heavy rain, the bleating frantic and hoarse. Hundreds of dogs yelp and bay. Both

rackets are quickly
drowned by a heavy
shuddering beat, as
though an enormous
helicopter hovers
directly overhead.

[The man and the
woman don't look out the
roadward windows.
They already have
looked out, and the
moonlit road is empty.]

*Possible ending
Number Five.

man's face, and one of his hands is bandaged. His
lips are slack and his eyes are downcast.

The woman is trembling. She occasionally
raises one shaking hand to her eyes, touching
her lids.

The camera pans to reveal that both of the
doors are blocked shut with chairs.

The camera pans once more, settles on the
beachward window, focuses to where the bluff
must loom in the darkness.

Two bonfires burn brightly there.

Finale

Kaitangata Bay in bright broad daylight is a
pleasant busy sort of place. Outside one bach, a
man is polishing his car. Next door to the bach at
the end of the road (which is clearly unoccupied,
with long grass surrounding it, and a general air
of neglect) a sweetfaced white-haired lady is
hanging out washing. By the bach on the hillside,
a young couple frolic with their excited dog.

[Tally: a stick or rod of
wood, usually squared,
marked on one side with
traverse notches
representing the number
of sheep passed by the
counter.]

Down on the beach, a solitary fisherman
stands by a surf-rod. There is nothing tugging at
the end of the cast-out line, and although the
fisherman has but one eye, it gazes brightly,
benevolently, on the wide spread of the Tasman
sea, and he licks his lips.

ONE WHALE, SINGING

The ship drifted on the summer night sea.

'It is a pity,' she thought, 'that one must come on deck to see the stars. Perhaps a boat of glass, to see the sea streaming past, to watch the nightly splendour of stars . . .' Something small jumped from the water, away to the left. A flash of phosphorescence after the sound, and then all was quiet and starlit again.

They had passed through krillswarms all day. Large areas of the sea were reddish-brown, as though an enormous creature had wallowed ahead of the boat, streaming blood.

'Whale-feed,' she had said, laughing and hugging herself at the thought of seeing whales again. 'Lobster-krill,' he had corrected, pedantically.

The crustaceans had swum in their frightened jerking shoals, mile upon mile of them, harried by fish that were in turn pursued and torn by larger fish.

She thought, it was probably a fish after krill that had leaped then. She sighed, stroking her belly. It was the lesser of the two evils to go below now, so he didn't have an opportunity to come on deck and suggest it was better for the coming baby's health, and hers, of course, that she came down. The cramped cabin held no attraction: all that was there was boneless talk, and one couldn't see stars, or really hear the waters moving.

Far below, deep under the keel of the ship, a humpback whale sported and fed. Occasionally, she yodelled to herself, a long undulating call of content. When she found a series of sounds that pleased, she repeated them, wove them into a band of harmonious pulses.

Periodically she reared to the surface, blew, and slid smoothly back under the sea in a wheel-like motion. Because she was pregnant, and at the tailend of the southward migration, she had no reason now to leap and display on the surface.

She was not feeding seriously; the krill was there, and she swam amongst them, forcing water through her lips with her large tongue, stranding food amongst the baleen. When her mouth was full, she swallowed. It was leisurely, lazy eating. Time enough for recovering her full weight when she reached the cold seas, and she could gorge on a ton and a half of plankton daily.

Along this coast, there was life and noise in plenty. Shallow grunting from a herd of fish, gingerly feeding on the fringes of the krill shoal. The krill themselves, a thin hiss and crackle through the water. The interminable background clicking of shrimps. At times, a wayward band of sound like bass organ-notes sang through the chatter, and to this the whale listened attentively, and sometimes replied.

The krill thinned: she tested, tasted the water. Dolphins had passed recently. She heard their brief commenting chatter, but did not spend time on it. The school swept round ahead of her, and vanished into the vibrant dark.

He had the annoying habit of reading what he'd written out loud. 'We can conclusively demonstrate that to man alone belong true intelligence and self-knowledge.'

He coughs.

Taps his pen against his lips. He has soft, wet lips, and the sound is a fleshy slop! slop!

She thinks:

> Man indeed! How arrogant! How ignorant! Woman would be as correct, but I'll settle for humanity. And it strikes me that the quality humanity stands in need of most is true intelligence and self-knowledge.

'For instance, Man alone as a species, makes significant artefacts, and transmits knowledge in permanent and durable form.'

He grunts happily.

'In this lecture, I propose to . . .'

But how do they know? she asks herself. About the passing on of knowledge among other species? They may do it in ways beyond our capacity to understand . . . that we are the only ones to make artefacts I'll grant you, but that's because us needy little adapts have such pathetic bodies, and no especial ecological niche. So hooks and hoes, and steel things that gouge and slay, we produce in plenty. And build a wasteland of drear ungainly hovels to shelter our vulnerable hides.

She remembers her glass boat, and sighs. The things one could create if one made technology servant to a humble and creative imagination . . . He's booming on, getting into full lectureroom style and stride.

'. . . thus we will show that no other species, lacking as they do artefacts, an organised society, or even semblances of culture . . .'

What would a whale do with an artefact, who is so perfectly adapted to the sea? Their conception of culture, of civilisation, must be so alien that we'd never recognise it, even if we were to stumble on its traces daily.

She snorts.

He looks at her, eyes unglazing, and smiles.

'Criticism, my dear? Or you like that bit?'

'I was just thinking . . .'

Thinking, as for us passing on our knowledge, hah! We rarely learn from the past or the present, and what we pass on for future humanity is a mere jumble of momentarily true facts, and odd snippets of surprised self-discoveries. That's not knowledge . . .

She folds her hands over her belly. You in there, you won't learn much. What I can teach you is limited by what we are. Splotch goes the pen against his lips.

'You had better heat up that fortified drink, dear. We can't have either of you wasting from lack of proper nourishment.'

Unspoken haw haw haw.

Don't refer to it as a person! It is a canker in me, a

> parasite. It is nothing to me. I feel it squirm and kick, and
> sicken at the movement.

He says he's worried by her pale face. 'You shouldn't have
gone up on deck so late. You could have slipped, or something,
and climbing tires you now, you know.'

She doesn't argue any longer. The arguments follow well-
worn tracks and go in circles.

'Yes,' she answers.

> but I should wither without that release, that solitude,
> that keep away from you.

She stirs the powder into the milk and begins to mix it
rhythmically.

> I wonder what a whale thinks of its calf? So large a
> creature, so proven peaceful a beast, must be motherly,
> protective, a shielding benevolence against all wildness.
> It would be a sweet and milky love, magnified and
> sustained by the encompassing purity of water . . .

A swarm of insectlike creatures, sparkling like a galaxy, each
a pulsing lightform in blue and silver and gold. The whale sang for
them, a ripple of delicate notes, spaced in a timeless curve. It
stole through the lightswarm, and the luminescence increased
brilliantly.

Deep within her, the other spark of light also grew. It was the
third calf she had borne; it delighted her still, that the swift airy
copulation should spring so opportunely to this new life. She
feeds it love and music, and her body's bounty. Already it
responds to her crooning tenderness, and the dark pictures she
sends it. It absorbs both, as part of the life to come, as it nests
securely in the waters within.

She remembers the nautilids in the warm oceans to the north,
snapping at one another in a cannibalistic frenzy.

She remembers the oil-bedraggled albatross, resting with
patient finality on the water-top, waiting for death.

She remembers her flight, not long past, from killer whales,
and the terrible end of the other female who had accompanied her
south, tongue eaten from her mouth, flukes and genitals ripped,
bleeding to a slow fought-against end.

And all the memories are part of the growing calf.

More krill appeared. She opened her mouth, and glided through the shoal. Sudden darkness for the krill. The whale hummed meanwhile.

He folded his papers contentedly.

'Sam was going on about his blasted dolphins the other night, dear.'

'Yes?'

He laughed deprecatingly. 'But it wouldn't interest you. All dull scientific chatter, eh?'

'What was he saying about, umm, his dolphins?'

'O, insisted that his latest series of tests demonstrated their high intelligence. No, that's misquoting him, potentially high intelligence. Of course, I brought him down to earth smartly. Results are as you make them, I said. Nobody has proved that the animals have intelligence to a degree above that of a dog. But it made me think of the rot that's setting in lately. Inspiration for this lecture indeed.'

'Lilley?' she asked, still thinking of the dolphins, 'Lilley demonstrated evidence of dolphinese.'

'Lilley? That mystical crackpot? Can you imagine anyone ever duplicating his work? Hah! Nobody has, of course. It was all in the man's mind.'

'Dolphins and whales are still largely unknown entities,' she murmured, more to herself than to him.

'Nonsense, my sweet. They've been thoroughly studied and dissected for the last century and more.' She shuddered. 'Rather dumb animals, all told, and probably of bovine origin. Look at the incredibly stupid way they persist in migrating straight into the hands of whalers, year after year. If they were smart, they'd have organised an attacking force and protected themselves!'

He chuckled at the thought, and lit his pipe.

'It would be nice to communicate with another species,' she said, more softly still.

'That's the trouble with you poets,' he said fondly. 'Dream marvels are to be found from every half-baked piece of

pseudo-science that drifts around. That's not seeing the world as it
is. We scientists rely on reliably ascertained facts for a true
picture of the world.'

She sat silently by the pot on the galley stove.

An echo from the world around, a deep throbbing from miles
away. It was both message and invitation to contribute. She
mused on it for minutes, absorbing, storing, correlating, winding
her song meanwhile experimentally through its interstices – then
dropped her voice to the lowest frequencies. She sent the
message along first, and then added another strength to the cold
wave that travelled after the message. An oceanaway, someone
would collect the cold wave, and store it, while it coiled and built
to uncontrollable strength. Then, just enough would be released
to generate a superwave, a gigantic wall of water on the surface
of the sea. It was a new thing the sea-people were experimenting
with. A protection. In case.

She began to swim further out from the coast. The water
flowed like warm silk over her flanks, an occasional interjectory
current swept her, cold and bracing, a touch from the sea to
the south. It became quieter, a calm freed from the fights of
crabs and the bickerings of small fish. There was less noise
too, from the strange turgid craft that buzzed and clattered
across the ocean-ceiling, dropping down wastes that stank and
sickened.

A great ocean-going shark prudently shifted course and
flicked away to the side of her. It measured twenty feet from
shovel-nose to crescentic tailfin, but she was twice as long and
would grow a little yet. Her broad deep body was still wellfleshed
and strong, in spite of the vicissitudes of the northward breeding
trek: there were barnacles encrusting her fins and lips and head,
but she was unhampered by other parasites. She blew a rasp-
berry at the fleeing shark and beat her flukes against the ocean's
pull in an ecstasy of strength.

'This lecture,' he says, sipping his drink, 'this lecture should
cause quite a stir. They'll probably label it conservative, or even
reactionary, but of course it isn't. It merely urges us to keep our

feet on the ground, not go hunting off down worthless blind sidetrails. To consolidate data we already have, not, for example, to speculate about so-called ESP phenomena. There is far too much mysticism and airy-fairy folderol in science these days. I don't wholly agree with the Victorians' attitude, that science could explain all, and very shortly would, but it's high time we got things back to a solid factual basis.'

'The Russians,' she says, after a long moment of non-committal silence, 'the Russians have discovered a form of photography that shows all living things to be sources of a strange and beautiful energy. Lights flare from finger tips. Leaves coruscate. All is living effulgence.'

He chuckles again.

'I can always tell when you're waxing poetic.' Then he taps out the bowl of his pipe against the side of the bunk, and leans forward in a fatherly way.

'My dear, if they have, and that's a big if, what difference could that possibly make. Another form of energy? So what?'

'Not just another form of energy,' she says sombrely. 'It makes for a whole new view of the world. If all things are repositories of related energy, then humanity is not alone . . .'

'Why this of solitariness, of being alone. Communication with other species, man is not alone, for God's sake! One would think you're becoming tired of us all!'

He's joking.

She is getting very tired. She speaks tiredly.

'It would mean that the things you think you are demonstrating in your paper . . .'

'Lecture.'

'Work . . . those things are totally irrelevant. That we may be on the bottom of the pile, not the top. It may be that other creatures are aware of their place and purpose in the world, have no need to delve and paw a meaning out. Justify themselves. That they accept all that happens, the beautiful, the terrible, the sickening, as part of the dance, as the joy or pain of the joke. Other species may somehow be equipped to know fully and consciously what truth is, whereas we humans must struggle, must struggle blindly to the end.'

He frowns, a concerned benevolent frown.

'Listen dear, has this trip been too much. Are you feeling at the end of your tether, tell us truly? I know the boat is old, and not much of a sailer, but it's the best I could do for the weekend. And I thought it would be a nice break for us, to get away from the university and home. Has there been too much work involved? The boat's got an engine after all . . . would you like me to start it and head back for the coast?'

She is shaking her head numbly.

He stands up and swallows what is left of his drink in one gulp.

'It won't take a minute to start the engine, and then I'll set that pilot thing, and we'll be back in sight of land before the morning. You'll feel happier then.'

She grips the small table.

Don't scream, she tells herself, don't scream.

Diatoms of phantom light, stray single brilliances. A high burst of dolphin sonics. The school was returning. A muted rasp from shoalfish hurrying past. A thing that curled and coiled in a drifting aureole of green light.

She slows, buoyant in the water.

Green light: it brings up the memories that are bone deep in her, written in her very cells. Green light of land.

She had once gone within yards of shore, without stranding. Curiosity had impelled her up a long narrow bay. She had edged carefully along, until her long flippers touched the rocky bottom. Sculling with her tail, she had slid forward a little further, and then lifted her head out of the water. The light was bent, the sounds that came to her were thin and distorted, but she could see colours known only from dreams and hear a music that was both alien and familiar.

(Christlookitthat!)

(Fuckinghellgetoutahereitscomingin)

The sound waves pooped and spattered through the air, and things scrambled away, as she moved herself back smoothly into deeper water.

A strange visit, but it enabled her to put images of her own to the calling dream.

Follow the line to the hard and aching airswept land, lie upon solidity never before known until strained ribs collapse from weight of body never before felt. And then, the second beginning of joy . . .

She dreams a moment, recalling other ends, other beginnings. And because of the web that streamed between all members of her kind, she was ready for the softly insistent pulsation that wound itself into her dreaming. Mourning for a male of the species, up in the cold southern seas where the greenbellied krill swarm in unending abundance. Where the killing ships of the harpooners lurk. A barb sliced through the air in an arc and embedded itself in the lungs, so the whale blew red in his threshing agony. Another that sunk into his flesh by the heart. Long minutes later, his slow exhalation of death. Then the gathering of light from all parts of the drifting corpse. It condensed, vanished . . . streamers of sound from the dolphins who shoot past her, somersaulting in their strange joy.

The long siren call urges her south. She begins to surge upward to the sweet night air.

She says, 'I must go on deck for a minute.'

They had finished the quarrel, but still had not come together. He grunts, fondles his notes a last time, and rolls over in his sleeping bag, drawing the neck of it tightly close.

She says wistfully,

'Goodnight then,'

and climbs the stairs heavily up to the hatchway.

'You're slightly offskew,' she says to the Southern Cross, and feels the repressed tears begin to flow down her cheeks. The stars blur.

Have I changed so much?

Or is it this interminable deadening pregnancy?

But his stolid, sullen, stupidity!

He won't see, he won't see, he won't see anything.

She walks to the bow, and settles herself down, uncomfortably aware of her protuberant belly, and begins to croon a song of comfort to herself.

And at that moment the humpback hit the ship, smashing through her old and weakened hull, collapsing the cabin, rending timbers. A mighty chaos . . .

Somehow she found herself in the water, crying for him, swimming in a circle as though among the small debris she might find a floating sleeping bag. The stern of the ship is sinking, poised a moment dark against the stars, and then it slides silently under.

She strikes out for a shape in the water, the liferaft? the dinghy?

And the shape moves.

The humpback, full of her dreams and her song, had beat blindly upward, and was shocked by the unexpected fouling. She lies, waiting on the water-top.

The woman stays where she is, motionless except for her paddling hands. She has no fear of the whale, but thinks, 'It may not know I am here, may hit me accidentally as it goes down.'

She can see the whale more clearly now, an immense zeppelin shape, bigger by far than their flimsy craft had been, but it lies there, very still . . .

She hopes it hasn't been hurt by the impact, and chokes on the hope.

There is a long moaning call then, that reverberates through her. She is physically swept, shaken by an intensity of feeling, as though the whale has sensed her being and predicament, and has offered it all it can, a sorrowing compassion.

Again the whale makes the moaning noise, and the woman calls, as loudly as she can, 'Thank you, thank you' knowing that it is meaningless, and probably unheard. Tears stream down her face once more.

The whale sounded so gently she didn't realise it was going at all.

'I am now alone in the dark,' she thinks, and the salt water laps round her mouth. 'How strange, if this is to be the summation of my life.'

In her womb the child kicked. Buoyed by the sea, she feels the movement as something gentle and familiar, dear to her for the first time.

But she begins to laugh.

The sea is warm and confiding, and it is a long long way to shore.

PLANETESIMAL

I once knew a girl who –

sat apart at the party, down on the floor. A small almost-woman in a large blue overcoat, the kind sailors wear. She cringed within its folds. I sat beside her on a sudden kindly impulse. I offered my roach in its glittery skull holder. I was drowsed and calmhearted, gladly aware of all the patterns of laughter and the brittle flowering colour of the carpet. I wasn't upset when she refused the smoke.

'Don't like it?'

'Don't smoke or drink,' she said dully. Her head bowed. 'Because . . .'

'Because?'

'I think I'm going mad. If I fuddle things more, if I.'

Retreating into the midnight coat.

O dear. Another mixed-up strung-out febrile brain. I smiled, gently, buddhalike. I said, charity of the smoke

'They say if you can think it,' carefully between tiny exhalations, 'you are not going mad.' Perfect curve of smile, perfect curve of smoke. I once knew this girl who –

She looked back at me and winced.

'I can think what I like. The evidence . . . the evidence.'

'What evidence?'

She peeled back the heavy coat sleeve. 'Look.'

I bent forward politely.

It was an ordinary female arm, pallid, slightly hairy, a little too thick at the wrist.

The roach smoke drifted between us.

She pulled the coat sleeve higher.

Needle tracks, I thought dreamily. There will be the

footprints of needles and she will bore me with her tale of dirt and discouragement. Needle tracks.

'There,' she said.

The inner cup of her elbow.

Except it wasn't there.

It was the most exciting tattoo I had ever seen in my life, and I exclaimed with delight. The connoisseur taken aback. I said so, exalted. With bitterness she said,

'It is not a picture. Touch, but only the very edge. Where there is still bone.'

I leant my finger carefully over the outside rim of skin to touch that extraordinary black oval. The cancellation of her flesh. However with mere ink had an artist gotten –

I snatched the finger back.

'You see?'

Her smile was as crooked and hurt as her previous wince.

The lovely fog in my head bled away and I was left sitting, looking at a girl who –

gazed at her arm.

Where the tip of my finger had touched the black was a dead white patch like frostbite. It ached. And I had touched – nothing.

'The stars change,' she said in a small voice. 'Over the nights, they change. I watch them move in great circles.'

I looked again.

Deep in the blackness was a myriad of intensely bright sparks. They made a far distant spiral.

'They are stars,' she said, tiredly. 'When I watch I feel as though I arch above, mother of the sky host.'

A tired almost-woman, small, heavily bound in a coat.

'Like that Egyptian. Goddess. Thing.'

She rolled the sleeve slowly down.

'Something even wants me there.'

She looked at me. 'Are you going mad too?'

I stood unsteadily. My eyes hurt from being kept too wide. My jaws hurt from being kept clenched. The unknowing laughter all around was harsh and raw and all the flowering colours had died. I wanted a glass a jugful a flagon of sherry to bring back the sweetness, to drown all the hurting, to believe in tomorrow again.

'You are not mad. Please wait. I am coming right back. Not mad.'

I remember she didn't smile as I stumbled away. She stayed huddled against the wall, the upright collar of the coat at once frame and shelter for her pale forgettable face. I once knew a girl. Who?

I found my sherry. I drank too much too fast in a gay swirl of chatter. 'Who's the girl?' I yelled. 'A houri,' said Anna, 'a houri from the fragrant paradisiacal smoke.' And Michael simpered, 'Who cares, dear James? There are better things to do.' And Big Molly looked at me carefully before saying, 'She is one of my staff nurses. Sickleave. Nervous trouble y'know. You smitten?'

'No. Yes. I don't know.'

Molly smiled. 'Theresa Wyatt. Boards at Rossiter's. Y'know where?'

The sherry, the chatter, and inevitably, the nausea and the obligatory trip outside. When I returned inside, the girl had gone.

I went to Rossiter's in the dizzy morning after. Her landlady said she had not come home. 'Which I expect you know about,' she said grimly.

She never came home.

And here I sit, writing lines by a dead roach. I am doing it awkwardly, one finger swathed. I once knew a girl who –

the police believe committed suicide, jumped in the sea,

rendered herself bodiless.

Molly believes that. Her landlady believes that. Most times, I believe that. I meant to say, my dear, she was on six months sickleave *and* had gibbered openly about going to other worlds. So I believe that. I do.

Except when I take the bandage off my finger. My inquisitive forefinger. Where now, centred in the dead white like a strange intrusive wart, sits a tiny bluegreen jewel. I think. Staring at it.

I have wondered. If you sat among heartless strangers, with a universe within your reach, would you always stay, wallflower at the party?

Already the dark is growing round the jewel, and behind it in the depths of black the bitter stars wink.

HOOKS AND FEELERS

On the morning before it happened, her fingers were covered with grey, soft clay.

'Charleston,' she says. 'It comes from Charleston. It's really a modeller's clay, but it'll make nice cups. I envisage,' gesturing in the air, 'tall fluted goblets. I'll glaze them sea blue and we'll drink wine together, all of us.'

I went out to the shed and knocked on the door. There's no word of welcome, but the kerosene lamp is burning brightly, so I push on in.

She's pumping the treadle potter's wheel with a terrible urgency, but she's not making pots. Just tall, wavery cones. I don't know what they are. I've never seen her make them before. The floor, the shelves, the bench – the place is spikey with them.

'They've rung,' I say.

She doesn't look up.

'They said he'll be home tomorrow.'

The wheel slowed, stopped.

'So?'

'Well, will you get him?'

'No.'

The wheel starts purring. Another cone begins to grow under her fingers.

'What are you making those for?'

She still won't look at me.

'You go,' she says, and the wheel begins to hum.

Well, you can't win.

I go and get him and come home, chattering brightly all the way.

He is silent.

I carry him inside, pointing out that I've repainted everywhere, that we've got a new stove and did you like your present? And he ignores it all.

But he says, very quietly, to his ma, 'Hello.' Very cool.

She looks at him, over him, round him, eyes going up and down but always avoiding the one place where she should be looking. She says, 'Hello,' back.

'Put me down please,' he says to me then.

No 'Thanks for getting me.' Not a word of appreciation for the new clothes. Just that polite, expressionless, 'Put me down please.'

Not another word.

He went into his bedroom and shut the door.

'Well, it's just the shock of being back home, eh?'

I look at her, and she looks at me. I go across and slide my hands around her shoulders, draw her close to me, nuzzle her ear, and for a moment it's peace.

Then she draws away.

'Make a coffee,' she says brusquely. 'I'm tired.'

I don't take offence. After grinding the beans, I ask, 'What are you making the cones for?'

She shrugs.

'It's just an idea.'

The smell from the crushed coffee beans is rich and heavy, almost sickening.

His door opens.

He has his doll in his hand. Or rather, parts of his doll. He's torn the head off, the arms and legs apart.

'I don't want this anymore,' he says into the silence.

He goes to the fire, and flings the parts in. And then he reaches in among the burning coals and plucks out the head, which is melted and smoking. He says, 'On second thoughts, I'll keep this.'

The smoke curls round the steel and lingers, acridly.

Soon after, she went back to the shed.

I went down to the pub.

'Hey!' yells Mata, 'C'mon over here!'

'Look at that,' he says, grinning hugely, waving a crumpled bit of paper. It's a Golden Kiwi ticket. 'Bugger's won me four hundred dollars.' He sways. 'Whatta yer drinking?'

I never have won anything. I reach across, grab his hand, shake it. It's warm and calloused, hard and real.

'Bloody oath, Mat what good luck!'

He smiles more widely still, his eyes crinkling almost shut. 'Shout you eh?'

'Too right you can. Double whisky.'

And I get that from him and a jug and another couple of doubles and another jug. I am warm and happy until someone turns the radio up.

'Hands across the water, hands across the sea . . .' the voices thunder and beat by my ears, and pianos and violins wail and wind round the words.

The shed's in darkness.

I push the door open, gingerly.

'Are you there?'

I hear her move.

'Yes.'

'How about a little light on the subject?' I'm trying to sound happily drunk, but the words have a nasty callous ring to them.

'The lamp is on the bench beside you.'

I reach for it and encounter a soft, still wet, cone of clay. I snatch my fingers away hurriedly.

'Are you revealing to the world what the cones are for yet?'

I've found the lamp, fumble for my matches. My fingers are clumsy, but at last the wick catches alight, glows and grows.

She sniffs.

'Give me the matches please.'

I throw the box across and she snatches them from the air.

She touches a match to a cigarette, the match shows blue and then flares bright, steady, gold. The cigarette pulses redly. The lamp isn't trimmed very well.

She sighs and the smoke flows thickly out of her mouth and nose.

'I put nearly all of them back in the stodge-box today.'

What? Oh yes, the cones. The stodge-box is her special term for the pile of clay that gets reworked.

'Oh.' I add after a moment, apologetically, 'I sort of squashed one reaching for the lamp.'

'It doesn't matter,' she says, blowing out another stream of smoke.

'I was going to kill that one too.'

I take my battered, old, guitar and begin to play. I play badly. I've never learned to play properly.

He says, out of the dark, 'Why are you sad?'

'What makes you think I am?'

'Because you're playing without the lights on.'

I sigh. 'A man can play in the dark if he wants.'

'Besides I heard you crying.'

My dear cool son.

'. . . so I cry sometimes . . .'

'Why are you sad?' he asks again.

Everlasting questions ever since he began to talk.

'Shut up.'

'Because of me?' he persists. He pauses, long enough to check whether I'm going to move.

'Or because of her?'

'Because of me, now get out of here,' I answer roughly, and bang the guitar down. It groans. The strings shiver.

He doesn't move.

'You've been to the pub?'

I prop the guitar against the wall and get up.

'You've been to the pub,' he states, and drifts back into his room.

My mother came to visit the next day, all agog to see the wreckage. She has a nice instinct for disasters. She used to be a strong little woman but she's run to frailty and brittle bones now. Alas; all small and powdery, with a thick fine down over her face that manages, somehow, to protrude through her make-up. It'd look so much better if she didn't pile powder and stuff on, but I can't imagine her face without pink gunk clogging the pores. That much has never changed.

She brought a bag of blackballs for him. When he accepts them, reluctantly, she coos and pats him and strokes his hair. He has always hated that.

'Oh dear,' she says, 'your poor careless mother,' and 'You poor little man' and (aside to me) 'It's just as well you didn't have a daughter, it'd be so much worse for a girl.' (He heard that, and smiled blandly.)

She asks him, 'However are you going to manage now? Your guitar and football and all? Hmmm?'

He says, steadily, 'It's very awkward to wipe my arse now. That's all.'

For a moment I like him very much.

My mother flutters and tchs, 'Oh, goodness me, dear, you mustn't say . . .'

He's already turned away.

As soon as my mother left, I went out to the shed.

'You could have come in and said hello,' I say reproachfully.

'It would have only led to a fight.' She sits hunched up on the floor. Her face is in shadow.

I look round. The shed's been tidied up. All the stray bits and pieces are hidden away. There's an innovation, however, an ominous one. The crucifix she keeps on the wall opposite her wheel has been covered with black cloth. The only part that shows is a hand, nailed to the wooden cross.

'Is that a reminder for penitence? Or are you mourning?'

She doesn't reply.

Early in the morning, while it's still quite dark, I awake to hear him sobbing. I lift the bedclothes gently – she didn't stir, drowned in sleep, her black hair wreathed about her body like seaweed – and creep away to his room.

The sobbing is part stifled, a rhythmic choking and gasping, rough with misery.

'Hello?'

'E pa . . .' he turns over and round from his pillow and reaches out his arms. He doesn't do that. He hasn't done that since he was a baby.

I pick him up, cradling him, cuddling him.

'I can still feel it pa. I can feel it still.' He is desperate in his insistence and wild with crying. But he is also coldly angry at himself.

'I know it's not there anymore,' he struck himself a blow, 'but I can *feel* it still . . .'

I kiss and soothe and bring a tranquilliser that the people at the hospital gave me. He sobs himself back to sleep, leaning, in the end, away from me. And I go back to bed.

Her ocean, her ocean, te moananui a Kiwa, drowns me. Far away on the beach I can hear him calling, but I must keep on going down into the greeny deeps, down to where her face is, to where the soft anemone tentacles of her fingers beckon and sway and sweep me onward to the weeping heart of the world.

He stays home from school for another week. It's probably just as well, for once, the first time he ventured outside the house, the next door neighbour's kids shouted crudities at him.

I watched him walk over to them, talk, and gesture, the hook flashing bravely in the sun. The next door neighbour's kids fell silent, drew together in a scared huddled group.

'What did you do to stop that?' I ask, after he has stalked proudly back inside.

He shook his head.

'Tell me.'

'I didn't have to do anything.' He smiles.

'Oh?'

'I don't imagine,' he says it so coolly, 'that anyone wants this in their eyes.'

The hair on the back of my neck bristles with shock.

'Don't you dare threaten anybody like that! No matter what they say!' I shout at him in rage, in horror. 'I'll beat you silly if you do that again.'

He shrugs. 'Okay, if you say so pa.'

(Imagine that cruel, steel curve reaching for your eyes. That pincer of unfeeling metal gouging in.) The steel hook glints as he moves away.

How can he be my son and have so little of me in him? Oh, he has my colouring, fair hair and steelgrey eyes, just as he has her colour and bone structure; a brown thickset chunk of a boy.

But his strange cold nature comes from neither of us. Well, it certainly doesn't come from me.

Later on that day – we are reading in front of the fire – a coal falls out. He reaches for it.

'Careful, it's hot,' I warn.

'I don't care how hot it is,' he says, grinning.

The two steel fingers pick up the piece of coal and slowly crush the fire out of it.

It hasn't taken long for him to get very deft with those pincers. He can pick up minute things, like pins, or the smallest of buttons. I suspect he practises doing so, in the secrecy of his bedroom. He can handle almost anything as skilfully as he could before.

At night, after he's had a shower, I ask, 'Let me look?'

'No.'

'Ahh, come on.'

He holds it out, silently.

All his wrist bones are gone. There remains a scarred purplish area with two smooth, rounded knobs on either side. In the centre is a small socket. The hook, which is mounted on a kind of swivel, slots into there. I don't understand how it works, but it looks like a nice practical piece of machinery.

He is looking away.

'You don't like it?'

'It's all right . . . will you string my guitar backwards? I tried, and I can't do it.'

'Of course.'

I fetch his guitar and begin immediately.

'There is something quite new we can do, you know.' The specialist draws a deep breath of smoke and doesn't exhale any of it.

The smell of antiseptic is making me feel sick. This room is painted a dull grey. There are flyspots on the light. I bring my eyes down to him and smile, rigidly.

'Ahh, yes?'

'Immediately after amputation, we can attach an undamaged portion of sinew and nerve to this nyloprene socket.'

He holds out a gadget, spins it round between his lean fingers, and snatches it away again, out of sight.

'It is a permanent implant, with a special prosthesis that fits into it, but the child will retain a good deal of control over his, umm, hand movements.'

He sucks in more smoke and eyes me beadily, eagerly. Then he suddenly lets the whole, stale lungful go, right in my face.

'So you agree to that then?'

'Ahh, yes.'

Later, at night, she says, 'Are you still awake too?'

'Yes.'

'What are you thinking of.'

'Nothing really. I was just listening to you breathe.'

Her hand creeps to my side, feeling along until it finds a warm handful.

'I am thinking of the door,' she says thoughtfully.

You know the way a car door crunches shut, with a sort of definite, echoing thunk?

Well, there was that. Her hurried footsteps. A split second of complete silence. And then the screaming started, piercing, agonised, desperate. We spun round. He was nailed, piniored against the side of the car by his trapped hand.

She stood, going, 'O my god! O my god!' and biting down on her hand. She didn't make another move, frozen where she stood, getting whiter and whiter and whiter.

I had to open the door.

'I know it's silly,' she continues, still holding me warmly, 'but if we hadn't bought that packet of peanuts, we wouldn't have spilled them. I wouldn't have got angry. I wouldn't have stormed out of the car. I wouldn't have slammed the door without looking. Without looking.'

'You bought the nuts, remember?' she adds, irrelevantly.

I don't answer.

There are other things in her ocean now. Massive black shadows that loom up near me without revealing what they are. Something glints. The shadows waver and retreat.

They stuck a needle attached to a clear, plastic tube into his arm. The tube filled with blood. Then, the blood cleared away and the dope ran into his vein. His eyelids dragged down. He slept, unwillingly, the tears of horror and anguish still wet on his face.

The ruined hand lay on a white, shiny bench, already apart from him. It was like a lump of raw, swollen meat with small, shattered, bluish bones through it.

'We'll have to amputate that, I'm afraid. It's absolutely unsalvageable.'

'Okay,' I say. 'Whatever you think best.'

They say that hearing is the last of the senses to die, when you are unconscious.

They are wrong, at least for me. Images, or what is worse, not-quite images, flare and burst and fade before I sink into the dreamless sea of sleep.

I went out to the shed.

'Tea is nearly ready,' I call through the open door.

'Good,' she replies. 'Come in and look.'

She has made a hundred, more than a hundred, large, shallow wine cups. 'Kraters,' she says, smiling to me briefly.

I grin back, delighted.

'Well, they should sell well.'

She bends her head, scraping at a patch of dried clay on the bench.

'What were the cones?'

She looks up at me, the smile gone entirely.

'Nothing important,' she says. 'Nothing important.'

When she's washing the dishes, however, the magic happens again. For the first time since the door slammed shut, I look at her, and she looks willingly back and her eyes become deep and endless dark waters, beckoning to my soul. Drown in me . . . find yourself. I reach out flailing, groping for her hard, real body. Ahh, my hands encounter tense muscles, fasten on to them. I stroke and knead, rousing the long-dormant woman in her. Feel in the taut, secret places, rub the tender moist groove, caress her all over with sweet, probing fingers.

'Bait,' says a cold, sneering voice.

She gasps and goes rigid again.

'Get away to bed with you,' she says without turning round.

'I'm going to watch.'

An overwhelming anger floods through me. I whip around and my erstwhile gentle hands harden and clench.

'I'll . . .'

'No,' she says, 'no,' touching me, warning me.

She goes across and kneels before him.

(I see he's trembling.)

She kisses his face.

She kisses his hand.

She kisses the hook.

'Now go to bed e tama.'

He stands, undecided, swaying in the doorway.

Then, too quickly for it to be stopped, he lashes out with the hook. It strikes her on her left breast.

I storm forward, full of rage, and reach for him.

'No,' she says again, kneeling there, motionless. 'No,' yet again.

'Go to bed, tama,' she says to him.

Her voice is warm and friendly. Her face is serene.

He turns obediently, and walks away into the dark.

At the weekend, I suggested we go for a picnic.

'Another one?' she asks, her black eyebrows raised.

'Well, we could gather pauas, maybe some cress, have a meal on the beach. It'd be good to get out of the house for a while. This hasn't been too good a week for me, you know.'

They both shrugged.
'Okay,' he says.

'I will get the paua,' she says, and begins stripping off her
jeans. 'You get the cress,' she says to him.
'I'll go with you and help,' I add.
He just looks at me. Those steely eyes in that brown
face. Then he pouted, picked up the kete, and headed for the
stream.
He selects a stalk and pinches it suddenly. The plant tissue
thins to nothing. It's like he's executing the cress. He adds it to
the pile in the kete. He doesn't look at me, or talk. He is absorbed
in killing cress.
There's not much I can do.
So I put on my mask and flippers and wade into the water,
slide down under the sea. I spend a long peaceful time there,
detaching whelks and watching them wobble down to the bottom.
I cruise along the undersea rock shelf, plucking bits of weed and
letting them drift away. Eventually, I reach the end of the reef,
and I can hear the boom and mutter of the real ocean. It's getting
too close; I surface.
One hundred yards away, fighting a current that is moving
him remorselessly out, is my son.

When I gained the beach, I was exhausted.
I stand, panting, him in my arms.
His face is grey and waxy and the water runs off us both,
dropping constantly on the sand.
'You were too far out . . .'
He cries.
'Where is she?'
Where is she? Gathering paua somewhere . . . but suddenly I
don't know if that is so. I put my mask back on, leave him on the
beach, and dive back under the waves, looking.

When I find her, as I find her, she is floating on her back
amidst bullkelp. The brown weed curves sinuously over her
body, like dark limp hands.

I splash and slobber over, sobbing to her. 'God, your son nearly died trying to find you. Why didn't you tell us?'

She opens her brown eyes lazily.

No, not lazily; with defeat, with weariness.

'What on earth gave you the idea I was going to drown?' she rubs the towel roughly over her skin.

I say, haltingly, 'Uh well, he was sure that . . .'

(He is curled up near the fire I've lit, peacefully asleep.)

'Sure of what?'

'I don't know. He went looking for you, got scared. We couldn't see you anywhere.'

A sort of shudder, a ripple runs through her.

'The idea was right,' she says, very quietly. She lets the towel fall. She cups her hand under her left breast and points.

'Feel there.'

There is a hard, oval, clump amidst the soft tissue.

'God, did he do . . .'

'No. It's been growing there for the past month. Probably for longer than that, but I have only felt it recently.' She rubs her armpit, thoughtfully. 'It's there too and under here,' gesturing to her jaw. 'It'll have to come out.' I can't stop it. I groan.

Do you understand that if I hadn't been there, both of them would have drowned?

There was one last thing.

We were all together in the living room.

I am in the lefthand chair, she is opposite me.

He is crooning to himself, sprawled in front of the fire.

'Loo-lie, loo-lay, loo-lie, loo-lay, the falcon hath borne my make away,' he sings. He pronounces it, 'the fawcon have borne my make away.'

'What is that?' I ask.

'A song.'

He looks across to his ma and they smile slyly, at one another, smiles like invisible hands reaching out, caressing secretly, weaving and touching.

I washed my hands.

I wept.

I went out to the shed and banged the door finally shut.

I wept a little longer.

And then, because there was nothing else to do, I went down to the pub.

I had been drinking double whiskies for more than an hour when Mata came across and laid his arm over my shoulder.

He is shaking.

'E man,' he whispers. His voice grows a little stronger. 'E man, don't drink by yourself. That's no good eh?' His arm presses down. 'Come across to us?'

The hubbub of voices hushes.

I snivel.

'Mat, when I first knew, her fingers were covered in clay, soft grey clay. And she smiled and said it's Charleston, we'll call him Charleston. It's too soft really, but I'll make a nice cup from it. Cups. Tall fluted goblets she said.'

His hand pats my shoulder with commiseration, with solicitude.

His eyes are dark with horror.

'I'll glaze them sea blue and we'll drink red wine together, all three of us.'

We never did.

HE TAUWARE KAWA,
HE KAWA TAUWARE

There was no-one outside waiting for us.

So we stood in the dark and waited.

A child came to the half-open door and banged it shut. Open. Shut.

Waina whispers, 'They must be getting ready inside.'

I shrug. I feel excited and tense and the shrug takes an effort. I say, 'We've got a minute I think. Let's have a quick practice. Voices low.'

I struggle with the guitar strap. My fingers are numb. It's June in St Mungo's and there's frost on the ground.

Even singing quietly our voices sound clear and resonant and much sweeter than in the old hall at home. Does the dark make them sound sweet, the resonance come from the empty spaces of the night?

The child peeks out again, but shuts the door quickly.

Old Mrs Parker tugs my sleeve, 'Morrie, what about the dark? D'ye think they might have a thing about the dark?'

> Me, in my best lecturing manner: In the old days it was dangerous. You didn't know whether the other people were going to welcome or murder you, and they didn't know whether you were paying a friendly visit or coming club in hand. Even today, you don't arrive at night in some places. You time it so you get there in daylight, or go hide somewhere until morning. They were polite interest, shuffling feet, smoking, looking at each other and round the old hall.

'Na I don't think so,' I say to the old lady. 'This is an urban set-up, for everyone no one people in particular. Anyway they know we had to start late.'

'And travel three hundred miles.'

James is stamping his feet, swinging his arms hard against himself, muttering 'jeez 'kin cold, 'kin cold.'

'Just as well I didn't make you fellas get into maro and piupiu,' I joke.

'Yeah, some things'd be getting pretty crisp by now.'

I didn't like James before the group started. Greasy-haired Pakeha, forestry worker, big bike, drinker, trouble. Give him his due, he's come along every practice night full of noisy energy. He puts his heart into the haka, tolerates the singing, keeps his swearing to a minimum, and has grown a surprising affection for Mrs Parker. He leans over and whispers in her ear now, and the old girl giggles and switches her hips. Give her another moment like that and she'll break into a hula from her girlhood.

No-one comes out yet.

'They're taking their time,' grumbles Allison. Her spotty face looks sour in the electric light.

'Probably as nervous as we are. They're a new place, wouldn't have done this often.'

I hope she won't get on her high horse. It was her greatgreat-great grandmother that was the Maori princess I think. Might have been the greatgreatgreatgreat. Can't remember though I vividly recall the thirtyfoot scroll of whakapapa she brought along to prove it. All of us down on the floor following through the branching lines of dead people to Allison, a twig on the bottom line. She's proud of that whakapapa. As she's one of the blue-eyed white-blond kind of Maori, she probably feels she needs it, nei?

I shiver. My teeth are knocking. I try a quick chilled chord.

The child has the door open again.

'Hey boy, cm're.'

He does. He's got bare feet. He scuttles over the icy gravel like it's shagpile though.

'Are they nearly ready inside?'

He looks blank.

I look blank back at him. Then I think, They don't know we're here. The cars can't have made much noise, pulling up on a busy street. Maybe they didn't have anyone watching out for the arriving parties.

'Go tell someone we're here – look, you know Bessie Rongomai? The big lady with one eye? Yes? Tell her Ohaupai's arrived.'

He scampers inside. The door bangs shut again. Could hate that door.

On the second night, we made up our song. Ohaupai? asks James, I thought we were Bismarck Break. Not for this, I'm firm about that. In a Maori world you do things in the Maori way, and there's nothing more Maori than the marae. What do we need a song for anyway? he's genuinely puzzled, I thought it was all hakas and that. It's for after the speaking, the oratory, I say. The old people called it the kinaki, the relish for the food of speech. O, they all say, O.

'Everyone feel OK?'

Nods and shudders. Waina and Allison and Mrs Parker and Connie are the lucky ones. They've got their fancy cardigans on, natural wool with kowhaiwahi patterns across the chest. They come from our part of the world, I said, good as a piupiu for those people over the hill eh? We better wear bush-shirts then, says Steve, grinning like a fiend. You can always scrawl some of those fancy spiral things on them. Steve, the quiet Pakeha with the Maori sense of humour. He's shaking now in the thin red shirt I thought would make a good background for the women.

Connie had asked, Do we have to all wear the same? It looks good and shows respect, I said. We're a visiting party, part of the ceremony, the show if you like. She was worried. I've got this nice brown cardie, she said. We all knew she meant Tommo wouldn't give her any money for a new cardigan. Bastard, I'd thought. He's the one who should be leading this, not me. Big man's son from Gisborne, brought up by his grannies in the old way, Pomare Cup winner when he was at school, speaking the lingo like a native as my Dad used to say (because he was a native and couldn't't) – bloody Tommo. The group must have felt my tangled angry thoughts. Steve spoke to Tommo at the pub and got, 'I'm not having anything to do with your stupid mongrel group. Waste of time playing round with things you don't know about.' Then the offer of a fight. The women, however, got together and bought Connie her cardigan and black slacks, and somehow leaned on Tommo so he didn't interfere with her taking part. Five weeks, I'd thought then, just five weeks and already the aroha grows.

God, I wish I could warm my hands. Our breaths come in quick clouds. In the heartless electric light, we look as though we're steaming. Waina is trembling beside me. Is it just the cold? Or is she thinking her impetuous husband has got himself up the creek again? Don't worry about it all, I love you as you are, she'd said coming over. Reassuring Waina. But I do worry. For one thing, it's my first sole-charge job. Big deal eh. Bismarck Break: two hundred people spread over about two hundred square miles. One sawmill, one pub, one hall, and one sole-charge school. A dozen farms and half a league team and now ta-daaa! one cultural group. For the first time ever in Bismarck Break. That bigheaded new teacher's idea.

The door opens. Half a dozen kids straggle out.

'Quick, into line! I'll just go "toru wha – hope!" when we're ready, one chord OK?'

A big woman pushes through the kids, stands on the single concrete step.

'Hey you fellas, Bismarck Break, kia ora you fellas! It's just me and my black self to be your welcome. Haere mai, haere mai, haere mai!'

Waina shivers. Her voice rises in a beautiful quaver, controlled keening, as she karangas in return. But properly.

'Tena koutou, tena koutou' I can feel her wince, 'tena koutou e nga iwi o tenei marae, tena koutou katoa e . . . ee . . .'

Her voice trails away into the night.

'Ka pai, you did that nice,' says Bessie. She fidgets by the door.

Hey Dad, give us a hand. You must be able to remember something. I'm going to be the main speaker, and I'll have to teach Steve and James something in case they put up two or three.

He'd made a special trip coming up from the North, and we'd welcomed him with our song. Big hit, the old man. Showed us the right gestures, how to pace and turn – o, he remembered a lot more than he'd told me he'd remembered. Or he'd been taking a lot of lessons since. You'll be all right, he'd said seriously, nodding to each of us. You all do your best and the old people will do the rest. You'll have them on your shoulders when you go on, all of you remember that! Be proud, you are carrying your dead onto a strange place as well as yourselves. It is a time to be strong and very careful, but also a time to be very proud. Kia kaha, kia manawanui, kia u!

The gravel glints. The light blurs. I am furious to the point of tears.

They can't do this to us!

I thought of Waina, practising her karanga for hours out in the back paddock where she thought no-one could hear; I thought of James, giving up his lucrative Saturday night shift at the mill; Steve travelling thirty miles into town each practice night; Mrs Parker with her arthritis, stiff and hurt after a five-hour journey by car, but the old lady is here with us, standing there shivering in the dark.

I yell out, boom out, my voice fierce and rough,

'TORU! WHA! HOPE!'

and chord down hard.

The little group of kids claps uncertainly. I hope I'm strumming properly. My face is hot, my heart is burning, but I can't tell where my fingers are any more.

In our shock, we sound ragged, gestures ragged, we are all ragged beggars in the night.

> Ten weeks in the old hall. Ten weeks of learning, not just the things I tried to teach, but learning each other, helping each other, being fired by an idea that said
> In this Maori context you will be important and welcomed and accorded respect because anciently this is the way

things have been done. You are no longer lonely indi-
viduals: you have become part of something great and
deep-rooted and vital. Welcome!

'Ka pai,' says Bessie again. She slips into the shadow of the
door. 'Come in quick, it's cold out there eh? We got some
important people from Maori Affairs, surprised us eh, they're in
there talking now but we can slip down the back and have a
kaputi, get warm eh?'

And then you will hongi with each person in the welcoming line, manuhiri turning into tangata whenua, and some
person will call out Ae! Kua puare te tari o te ora! Haere
mai koutou! and we will all walk in together to taste the
special foods the local people have readied for us. Neat!
said Connie, her thin face glowing, and James and Steve
had grinned, and Allison said Ahhh! and Mrs Parker gave
Waina a hug and my wife smiled her secret touching smile
to me.

Someone shuts the door again. One of the kids, after Bessie.

We can't see each other's tears in the dark. We can only feel
them, swelling out of our hearts.

THE KNIFE AND THE STONE

Every morning before it was light, just before the alarm went off, she woke with a jolt. Not from a bad dream: it was as though her body had a prescience of pain and responded with a sudden hurtful wakening.

This morning was no different.

She lay quiet a moment, feeling her heartbeat slow down to normal.

It is today.

She sighed. Shuffled off the eiderdown, shuffled into her work-clothes. Stood a moment by her warm disordered bed, touching it with one finger, her mind a blank. Then, like every morning, she went straight to the lavatory. Her bowels never worked until after breakfast but it was her father's belief that everyone should empty themselves on rising. And her mother was listening.

She banged the seat. The noise echoed. She stood a moment, not thinking. Letting whatever was around imprint itself. The stink of Jeyes fluid and excrement. One hinge off the door ever since she could remember. The old map showing English ley lines. Ahh! said the Guests.

Hand-adzed walls!

Rain-stained walls.

She touched them, briefly.

Five minutes after she'd risen, she was stoking the range. Like every morning. The rata-chips caught alight: the coal dust flared. Ten minutes to boil the kettle. She hated the range.

She set out milk-jug and honey-jar, china spoon and tea-mug on the wooden tray while waiting. She hummed, automatically, a tuneless wavering no-song. 'You have no idea how much it means to me,' her mother had said, often, 'hearing you cheerful and busy at dawnlight. It's only then I know I have survived another night, that another day has truly come.'

She picked up the tray with care and carried it, still humming to herself, into her mother's lair.

The room is dazzling with lights her mother never turns off. It is crammed with boxes piled with scraps of materials, with large pots and huge pale dusty plants. It is foetid. Full of blood-stink, like old menses or meat on the turn. Incense-smoke eternally spirals, boring into the blood-cloud. Today, as well, there is the rank sweetness of lupins, bunches of them jammed into the Ali Baba pots.

She drew a deep breath.

Past the harsh stares of the bed-lamp, side-lamp, signal-lamp. Past the duelling flickers of the thousand fragments of mirror sewn into the canopy over her mother's bed. Concentrating on the intricate stepping needed to carry a laden tray through the maze.

The breath ran out by the bedside.

Her mother smiled at the sound. With her pallor and enormous grey eyes, she looked a nocturnal carnivore. Her smile menaced.

'My darling daughter.'

Never, thank you.

'You had good dreams, my bantling?'

Never, how did you sleep?

'Yes mama dear.'

Another smile.

'Alas, no visitors,' said her mother.

What a menace you are, Maeve! laughed the Guests. An Aldis lamp. Imagine if some ship sees your flashes . . . Maeve the wrecker!

Her mother answered dreamily, 'Imagine if some starship sees them, and we have visitors. . . .'

'Maybe tonight, mama.'

'The blind hope of youth,' said her mother and sucked at the mug of tea.

She put the tray down carefully. She thought, No more mama.

So charming, some of the Guests found it. How charmingly old-fashioned, said one, with a lop-sided smile. Natural word, said her father then. Better than you lot with your Mum and Mummy. Bloody old dead gyppos. He'd barked with laughter.

You can call me my given name now, said her mother a year ago, but o how I shall miss being your mama.

She waited for the next cue.

'Your father will be home soon dear one. Back from the wearying sea. Perhaps you could have something ready for him?'

My mother is mad. She knew that wasn't true. She sounded mad, with her artificial stilted language. She looked mad in her scrambled light-ridden den. She was frighteningly sane.

Today, she said

'I'll put something on for him.'

As I've put something on every morning since I was eight. Mainly the same sort of something. Last night's spuds, chipped and fried. Two fried eggs, two onions carved into rings.

And he'll say

'There you are,' said her father, and

'Good. Breakfast,' and

'There's about a case on the lawn.'

That last could change.

Sometimes he'd stamp in, snarl over breakfast, grunt after every mouthful of tea, then rush into her mother's bedroom and slam the door.

On that kind of day she could steal back into her room and strip off her work-clothes; have a proper wash in water now warmed by the range. Get rid of the stinks. Then, no sneers from whoever sat next to her. Gidday Fishy, how's it goin' Gutbucket? Life okay down on the dope estate, giggle giggle.

Unless it was Mark. If it was him next to her, he'd grin his hesitant badteeth grin and whisper, Today, your eyes are like *pure* Marmite. Or something equally fatuous.

Which was worse, she wondered, turning the eggs and onions and chips with precision, which was worse?

If there was nothing, They sulked or did something horrid. If there was a case, it was bad because there was time to process it but not enough time to get properly ready. Inevitable scales on her hands, a feeling of slime all over her. Yet the times her father came in jubilant, shouting Hey a dozen cases! Hear that! We're riiccchhhh! the rich sounding like coarse cloth tearing – those times were probably worst. It meant taking the day off, because a dozen cases took her hours. It meant her father could do the full round, paying something off the grocery bill, a bit off the petrol account, even some to the hardware store. But then he'd waltz into his favourite pub and drink his way into instant friendships. He never seemed to see the sly nudges, Could be on to a good thing here Mac, that she felt on her skin as though it were raw and they were hard knocks. And later, buying a crate or two of beer, a quart or two of vodka – 'Vodka my girl!' he'd roar. 'No congeners, remember that!' – he'd collect the drink friends and they'd all come rolling home. And he'd stand in the front door yelling You're Guests in my home, everything's yours my Guests! his dark face suffused with a purple wash, his lips loose and wet. And he'd take his dobro off the wall and twang it; sing old and pseud songs and the Guests would sing along. And some would vomit and some would wander curiously around, admiring or puzzled, and some would lie in a stupor on the livingroom cushion pile. And sometimes, her mother would limp out, swathed in one of her quilts, her face glowing, the blood aroma trailing heavily after. The singing would gather a mellowness, the bottles lower more slowly. She would have finished making tea for the drunker Guests by then. She would steal away to bed before her father noticed her, because otherwise he would come lurching and whispering God I love you girl love you girl, fumbling delving

The jubilant times were very much the worst, she decided, sliding breakfast onto the three plates.

Yet, some times, rare times, she would get safely to bed by herself, and wake, she never knew how much later, and hear the end of the party. Her mother's thin perfect soprano winding like a flute above her father's velvet baritone, the dobro a sure melancholy underlining third voice. The songs were real, unknown to her. They were beautiful. She would cry, at the way the good dreams had come to die, and crying, sleep.

She ate quickly, as she did every morning. About a case, waiting on the lawn. She picked up her knife and stone and went to meet them.

The stone was a wedge of fine-grit sandstone, white and worn. A gift, like her first knife. One Guest, reeled in like all the rest, stayed until morning. He watched her awkwardly using the butcherknife. He didn't say anything. But when she had finished half the case, he'd gone inside and brought out a tableknife. He took the whetstone out of his pocket and beckoned to her. Warily she came. Still not talking, he broke most of the plastic handle from the knife. He bound what remained with tartape so it fitted edgeless and easy in the hand. He honed the blade to razor thinness, razor sharpness, after snapping it in half. He showed her how.

He took one fish out and demonstrated the right way, carve, scoop, flick, slice. He was slow and deliberate. Then he handed her the knife and the stone, and went back inside to finish off the remaining crate. He was a noisy drunk but he never touched or spoke to her. She still thought of him with love.

She also thought, bitterly, My fifth knife.

In the case on the lawn they waited, their murky golden eyes bulging in the heavy deeps of air. The slime was running out of the plastic slats.

Think of us as a team, her mother had said two years ago, picking her words with care. Don't *respond* to those ignorami at school. We are an elite, a tiny chosen venturing band. Do you remember the Company of the Nine Walkers? No? She had sighed. I never understood why your heart didn't thrill . . . let it be. We are heart people, special, tied by love, supports each for the other. If Gareth had lived . . . she sighed again. Not to mind (a brave smile). We are the team. Your father fishing our daily bread and maintaining the house. Myself, labouring over these quilts for all our extras. And thyself my dear one the helpmate, doing the little things to assist each of us. *Being* the reason it is all done for.

Hi team, she said, to the knife and the stone. We're the

winning side, you know that? Couldn't be anything else because he always checks his nets even if he has to crawl to the boat. And look at the other side.

Flat, sticky, and already defeated. Among them, occasionally, a stargazer; rarely, silver-bellied eels, and most rarely, a glorious coral-fleshed salmon fresh run from the sea. But those he took care of. His ruined hands took infinite care boning them. He soaked them in brines of his own composing. He nursed them through the drying stage, gauzed against fly-strike. He travelled long roads in the battered van, selecting manuka and silver pine for sawdust. He hovered nervously while they smoked. He sold the beautiful results and bought records and grog. Any spoiled results he ate for breakfast.

She never ate fish, least of all them.

First cut, just below the belly fin, slip through a vertebra and sever the spine. Out the other side in one smooth slice to arrive just above another scarlet-edged fin, in line with the gill case.

She remembered little of before. Before she was eight. Before Gareth died. Before the close warm world fell apart. She did remember the night they brought her father in, howling, bleeding, cursing, bleeding. Drunken, he had lifted the outboard motor from the water. Drunken, he had slipped, knocking the gear from neutral to fast forward. Drunken, he had slipped further, and grabbed the prop. Healed to grotesque stumps and scars, he'd growled at her, 'That fiddly work is woman work. In the old days, that was the proper way. We men do the catching. You women clean it up. That's what you're for.' He'd handed her the boning knife and yelled at her until she had learned, clumsily, to carve up flounders. Second cut, quick flash to the anus careful not to rupture any sacs of roe. Then hold up the slimed thing and quickly slit down the other side to the arsehole again. Arsehole was Mark's word. Right in the arsehole from my old man, slight emphasis on the 'my'. His tall thin body twitching, as normal. The locker bay was crowded. They had their heads close together.

Why? she had asked. Why tell me? ,

Because. He had brown eyes too, but not as dark as her own. Because I know about you. His eyelids flickered, a similar beat to his twitching body. Now you can destroy me if you want, he said.

He shrieked out in a hun yell REVENGE. No heads turned. Mad Mark at it again.

The momentum of the cut and the weight of the newly-severed head made it fall, dragging the guts neatly behind it slop into the gut bucket. Slice: the lower intestine freed. Chop the tail off in one fluent cut. Throw the bloody thing into the wet bucket, ready for later washing.

I know it's not easy but we make do, crooned her mother. We're not rich in material terms, but we make do. We planned for this when we were not much older than you are now. O the sun and flowers of being sixteen! We planned a good place out away out of the corrupt system, a clean strong place for strong new people. If Gareth . . . her voice became throaty. But you're strong, she keened, fondling her daughter's arm, wiry but strong. And so rich in your mind! Far more rich than we were at your age, poisoned by the garbage they taught *us*.

She remembered hearing a Guest burst out, O you've given her such riches but you've sacrificed so much! Her mother had looked out the windows, over the beam of the Aldis light. We have riches too, she said strongly. Natural food and holistic medicine and freedom from city pressures. Strong Guestly murmurs of support. And we have a *good* child. God yes, said another one, you want to see my little monster fat and pasty and deathrays all day long and god the language! Yes! Yes! Yes! they top each other's monsters as her mother's smile grew wider, tighter.

Am I rich in my mind?

I have words for every colour under the sun. Weird gobbets of knowledge from weird Guests. I can hate. I can gut. I know all about dead and dying flounders. The fibrillation, the strange and beautiful fluidity of their rippling fins as they try to gain purchase on air. The mottling of their skins, mosaics of rust and olive-green and sepia on the back; mushroom and grey and terracotta and lemon-blotched cream on the underside. The pout of their lips as you hit their heads with the hammer.

She did that surreptitiously to the livelier ones. Her father sneered, 'Afraid they'll bite? You're bigger than them.'

She knew all about the occasional parasites, pinholes in the .

white flesh with black writhing cupheaded worms extruding. Sealice pecking away like bloated pink slaters. Colours, she thought, colours.

The pale yellow granular roe. Faintly blue gluey strings of slime. Grey blurred crabs in the anus tubes. Green fragments of annelid worms in the guts. Matt rusty liver. Pink veined coils. The delicately iridescent inner skin. The brilliant viridian of the gallbladder.

Today, she was halfway through the case.

It's not really work, said her mother to her complaint last week. You cannot, my sweet, truly call it hard labour now can you? I remember working twelve-hour days, on my feet all that time, waitressing for slobs. And your father, immersed to the heart in the gore at the freezing works, a sensitive singer breaking apart with all that pain. But we earned the money for here that way. That's work, my girl!

Now she thought,

Every morning for the last eight years. Unless nothing has been caught. Maybe a day a week. 300 days a year. 2400 days. Normally an hour of blood and guts, sometimes much much longer. In the wind. In the rain. In the frost. In the sandfly hordes of summer. 'Allergic to sandflies? But she was *born* here,' exclaimed a Guest, a hundred years ago. 'Surely she'll grow out of it?'

Not so far. The bright welts keep coming, each marked with a watery red centre. The sandflies know her hands are full. They feast with impunity.

Cover yourself with treacle, said Mark. They'll have a bloody hard job biting through that.

Then he said, I have a cousin who can get us out.

Her heart had seemed suddenly huge, forcing the air from her lungs.

I have a cousin with a fish-shop in Auckland. Don't wince. There is a restaurant attached, and a flat attached to the restaurant. I can cook in my poofy way. You can process. He will send the fare.

He said, carefully,

If you want, we can make it?

She whispered.

I can't hear that, said Mark.

I said, it has got too hard. And your teeth are horrid.

Long lean body, long lean hands, long lean smile, all suddenly beautifully still.

Tomorrow then, midnight eyes.

She had shivered.

Why don't your friends ever come? she asked her mother yesterday. She remembered the afternoon light fighting through the lamps: her mother's hands stitching polygon to polygon: patchouli incense at war with the omnipresent reek of blood. Her mother gave a high sharp bark of laughter. 'O dear heart, we are friends of all the world! The house positively *vibrates* with our friends. Our hospitality is acclaimed far and wide – my darling sweetsullen child, you must have noticed!'

Slither. Cut. Scarlet floods or slow upwellings or a cold dark ooze. Slice. Slap of body in the water. Heads with eyes unchanged piling up amid the coiling innards.

It was time to cleanse them; scrub off the outside blood and slime, and force out the inside jellied clots from the secret cavities by the spine. A final inner sluice. Marketable goods.

As on every morning, she came to the last one.

She looked at it a long time, not thinking of anything.

Then she staggered to the porch with the basket of cleaned gutted fish, left it covered with a sack.

She scrubbed down the gutting block and the fish case. Slow cold-drowsy blowflies lifted away reluctantly from the streams of water. She picked up the shovel and the gutbucket and went to the burying-ground. The tin banged against her leg: the wire handle creased her palm painfully. She dug the hole, emptied the tin savagely down it, stared at the mound before covering it over.

Then she hurried inside. Washed her hands, pulled comb through her hair. She watched her father pull off his boots, awkward and slow, and tramp into her mother's room.

She picked up her heavy schoolcase.

On impulse, she took the knife and the stone and slipped them into a side-pocket.

She thought, I don't have much to offer. A body and a baggage of words. A hate. A knowledge of how to gut things. But it must be better.

'I'm late,' she called to the shut bedroom door.

This morning, she didn't say goodbye.

WHILE MY GUITAR GENTLY SINGS

> *and the words drain into the music*
> *and the music drains silently, west*

There is dust on my guitar, thick grey deadening dust.

Dust, on my guitar.

You remember the day you came home with it?

'Hey girl!'

yelling up the path,

'hey girl, I got it!'

And me sulking out by the lav, wild because I've had to get the tea on, again; round up the boys for their baths, again; feed the chooks and the pig and the house-cow, again, and all the time I wanted to be alone and quiet down by the creek, listening to friendly water and wind.

I won't come in until you're inside, until you've skidded your shoes off your swollen feet, and are sitting down with a cup of tea Maki's made you.

'Hinewai,' you reach a hand, 'don't be sad. Now you can sing all your troubles away!' My big mother, throwing her head back and laughing at my sulks. 'Real joygerm eh?' she says to the boys, winking. Then she picks up the long box. 'My girl, here it is.'

And I take it in a grabby way, tear off the paper – then go more slowly, unpicking the Cellotape, because I can feel you've got something good, not a Woolworth job.

I look at you a moment.

And that was the first time I remember *looking* at your face. Not just seeing Mum. Your lips are curved in a thick grin. There are dark shadows under your eyes. Rusty grey hairs already at the corners of your head. Aue, my mama is not young, still unwrapping tissue tenderly from the box and then further thought is drowned in Aaaaa!

The varnish is rich golden: the wood like tawa, pearly-grained and blonde. The belly is some close heavy black wood, like ebony. Ibanez is the name above the neck.

'E mama,'

breathing hard, just touching the silver strings.

'Now watch her break it at a party,' you giggle, 'watch e Maki?' Maki is pouting because I've got the present and he hasn't, just for a change. You throw a pretend slap at him. Maki ducks, giggles back, and then Hone and Tara start in too, and I watch sneering, as you and the boys tussle on the floor.

I never did say thank you for my guitar.

E mama, taku whaea –

I am sitting in the dark.

Everyone else is asleep.

There is too much smoke in the air, cigarette and that other soft cat & pine scent. Kohatu they call it now. I used to say pot.

Somebody has spilt beer on the chair I'm on and my pants are damp.

I'm not drunk or stoned. I'm gone past that.

I'm wretchedly sober.

The blue and white telegram, there.

The dusty guitar here, ready to hand.

I am smoking again, despite the clogged air. The small red eye pulses, in breath, out breath. You remember that, first of all, you never smoked anything but roll-your-owns? Tasman Gold Cut, and Zigzag rice papers. And you had this neat way of being able to roll a thin tight cigarette without looking at what your fingers were doing.

I never could. I've tried with pot and tobacco and everything leaks out either end. But then, when you went to work at Smith-Bonds, you took up tailor-mades.

'Cheaper nei?' you said, laughing your deep gutty laugh. 'I don't have time to make them, just time to pay for them!' Another belly laugh.

And you smoked them, two packets and more a day.

I hated that. Your fingers always smelt of smoke, each time you touched me, or gave me anything. And your breath smelt of smoke, kissing me goodnight. And your long black plait of hair, fallen over one shoulder to tease my face, reeked. You went round in an aureole of smoke.

And it got so fast into your lungs. You'd wake up in the mornings with this smoker's hack, and any fast stuff, like running up the hill home, or rounding up Nig Horse, or wrestling with the boys – why did you never wrestle with me? – and you'd get this breathless wheeze. 'Jeez Hinewai, don't smoke, you get just like your fat old mother!'

Rocking with laughter because you never knew yourself as old or fat or breathless. I am nobly big, your eyes flashed, and just for this moment my lungs are playing tricks on me.

I only started smoking three years ago, with the band. I don't like it all that much. The taste can be as foul as the morning-after smell, but it keeps my fingers busy and after a while, my mind . . . stills.

Sometimes it must have been like that for you. Do you remember that night I woke up with period cramps and came into the kitchen, ready to groan and carry on and gouge some sympathy out of you? And stopped, because you sat so still in the chair before the fire. Your legs stuck out, propped on a stool. The only things moving were the flames and the smoke from your cigarette,

When you looked up, you didn't smile, you didn't make a joke. You said, so quietly

'I wonder where your dad died?'

And I forgot the ache in my young womb and crept back to bed. Because I swear to this day you spoke without opening your mouth. As though the thought that was always in your heart had grown to loudness out of the depths of your pool of peace and quiet.

We all wondered, time to time, what had happened to Dad. He was a possum-hunter and used to stay for days in the bush. But the last time, the days grew into a fortnight. After two months, the search parties stopped. Everybody said, 'He's great in the bush, Tom Kura, but nobody can last this long.'

Nobody even found his bones.

Not even his dog came home.

You wept. You stopped weeping. Went out and found your job, and worked days at the factory, nights round the house, weekends looking after the fences and the paddocks of our shrunken farm. And all the years it took us to grow up, you never wept again.

It's your laugh, e Mama. I keep hearing your laugh.

Loud, and so warm.

I always envied that great ability of yours to warm people. Shake them into smiles and laughter. Didn't matter their age. Some could be as old as blind Miratawhai, who was supposed to be a hundred and ten. You snuggled up to her the day she came to our marae, 'E kui, ka nui te pai nei?' Nothing specific, just isn't this good? And the old old lady's face, so laced and ridged with wrinkles, webbed out into a sensible smile. And her crooked hand crept into yours, and this creaky voice, made whispers by age, says 'Mokopuna.' Claims you as grandchild and she's never seen you before and hasn't spoken to anyone for a decade.

Some could be as young as that Samoan kid, Falasi. I never liked Fa'. Never thought of him as a brother. He was just this stubby heavybrowed kid, who never smiled at me, you brought home one night.

'E hine, look! They've cut him – look there. And there.' And you cuddled him, crooned over him, evening after evening, until his hurts healed and he would smile his dark slow smile as soon as he heard you yell from the hill path, 'Hey kids! Your mother made it through another day!' Raucous with laughter, roughing up the boys, grinning to me, 'Ah my Hinewai! You done all these jobs again!'

Fed the chooks and the pig and milked the house-cow and bathed the boys or harried them to the bathroom, when all I wanted to do . . . you knew it. Weekends, when I'd sneak away to the creek and play my songs, you never sent the boys to look for me, to rouse me back to the work. Just cackle when I mooned back to the house. 'Guess what fellas? The eels didn't get your sister *again*!'

He he he. Off I'd go, sulk into the bedroom, while the boys roared round the house and you roared right along with them. Fa' had fitted in by then. The boys protected him from the sneers – 'Hey coconut!' and fists at school until the stubby little kid grew so hard and solid and fast with his fists that it was a moot point who was protecting who. They never hurt him with words, just joked with him over his cloud of hair and his love of kilts and his hatred of the cold. Strange little brother Fa' grew stronger than them all. They still go visit him in Auckland. The last time I saw him was by accident, when I went bail for Colin, the drummer of the band. He was the constable taking down the details. He said, 'Hinewai. Sister. Kia ora e 'Wai,' in that heavy masculine voice of his and then, flatly, 'What is your relationship with the prisoner?'

Did you like it that Fa' became a cop?

Or that Hone is the newsworthy voice from Black Power in Wellington?

Or that Tara has a wife and two children in Christchurch, a child in Westport, a child in Gisborne, a child in Taihape, and twins in Porirua, and you've never seen any of the last five?

I know you hated it when Maki crashed his bike, from 80 miles an hour to a full bleeding stop against the side of the bridge in Whangaroa.

You and I were the first ones there, you cradling his bleeding head and me retching over the side of the bridge. I can't stand blood. I never watched when you killed the pig each year, but there would be the excited crowding boys all leaning over the stywall and drooling. 'E lookit that!' BANG! the old .270, and you always got them in the head (said the boys) so there was this thin trickle of blood from bullet-hole and mouth (said the boys) from the head that had a moment ago been alive and grunting. Maki sometimes says 'pig'. Most of the time, he drools. The nurses and attendants, you wrote in your last letter, say he smiles among the drool sometimes. So he might be happy, you thought.

That was your big thing, remember? That we all be happy.

I know you didn't like it when I said Whangaroa was too small.

That I didn't want to go and work in Smith-Bonds, packing stockings into bags or ironing them or sorting them or having anything at all to do with them. I said,

'I am seventeen and Whangaroa is the arsehole of New Zealand and I am too bright to slave away in that bloody factory, or just marry some farming oaf and have a tribe of kids.'

And you laughed till you nearly cried.

'*That*'s what you think of your mum eh!' Because you had been seventeen when you married my farming oaf father. Then you said, seriously, 'Hinewai, brains are important and you have a lot of fat in that head of yours. But heart is important too, and you think hard about all the good things we got in our place.' And you enumerated all the ones that were so important to you, from the marae at the heart of the village, to the bones, dead in the cemetery and live in every second house. 'Who do we know in the city?' you kept asking. 'Why do you want to go there?'

Because nothing here makes me happy, I'd snapped back, not even my creek any more. I want to make something of myself, I said, drawing myself up so proud, I want to be (first thing that came into my head)

a teacher!

Well, it might have taken one week of that first term e whae, one week for me to decide that I didn't want to be a teacher at all, but after all your work – talking to So & So who was president of the Maori Women's Welfare League, and to So & So who was in the Wellington rununga, and So & So who was with Maori Affairs – and after all your saving (overtime for my trainfare and new clothes, all the money you had in the bank for my first year's board) – aue! I couldn't back down immediately.

I quit after a year. But I didn't say anything to you. Not even when the train came to take me back, six weeks later after the holidays were finished supposedly. You hugged me and tangied over me, big gruff greying woman stinking of smoke and cheap lipstick. 'E, I'm so proud of you, my girl, so proud! We're all proud.' Then, throwing your big head back, the glint coming back into your eyes, 'Even those damn eels down in the creek are proud! You be happy, Hinewai.'

Easier said than done.

I worked in a downtown Woolworth's first; a Lambton Quay hamburger bar second, and a Cuba Street massage parlour, third. By that time, I was six months gone and neither knew nor cared who had been the father.

I've my mother's height, but not her strength or bulk. I hid the baby under my heart as long as I could, hid it all the glaring drunken weed-rotten nights, but it had to slip down, lower and lower. And sadly, it did not, she did not, stop outside my womb, but imperceptibly kept on slipping down, lowering her spirit back into mother earth. She lived 24 hours, tiny, hairless, yellowed.

E mama, I never told you. I could not tell you.

Hone came to Wellington and found me, at the end of a long bent trail from the Teachers' Training College. He was angry first, and then weeping second, and at last, practical and stern. 'You're eldest, tuahine. You can't live like *this*,' sweeping his hand round the tacky flat, messed with bottles, smeared with the sloth of grief, 'we won't let you.' He picked up my guitar. Play me a song, he ordered. And wild at him, sick of weeping, I played. And Hone grinned.

'I know just the band, the scene, the sound.'

And he did. Skilful little brother, two weeks in the city, already the big organiser, already in the know.

E Ma, did we chop up all your strengths between us? Tara has your fertility, your deep but easy love. Hone, your quick knowledge of people, your organising ability. Fa' somehow has got hold of your disciplined acceptance of life, your insight that 'this is the way things are, so I'll make the best of it.' Me, I have your music and way with mood and language. And Maki had your . . . who knows what Maki would have done, could have been?

It is strange.

Here in the smoke-stained dark, my hands have found my guitar. I am rubbing the dust, sweeping it carefully gently away.

Assuring the instrument that my neglect is not its fault. Pat pat stroke stroke and another little dustball fluffs away . . .

But I do know one thing Maki would have been good at, something you have great knowledge of – kawa. Marae protocol. The old people's way of doing things right.

I was never interested in the past, only what happens to me, now.

You remember that old witch Granny Hawe taking me out and whacking me because I pranced across some bloke's legs?

'You can't do that, you take all the mens power from him. He's no good if we take his power from him. And those mens in there, they're very high persons. We have to be careful eh?'

Wallop.

I remember the words and I remember the sting, and I still hate all that shit, men being tapu, and women being noa. Don't eat here; don't put your head there. Don't hang your clothes higher than the men's: never get up and talk on the marae.

'Our women don't talk out front,' you said. 'Arawa women speak only from behind their men.'

And you wonder why I went city?

But Maki used to love hui. He'd hang in there, listening with all his soul. He learned our whakapapa way before I did, and I have an ear that leads straight to my memory. He sucked up kawa – sucked up any kind of Maori knowledge. And then, and then

The second to last time I came home, you recall I wouldn't go to that hui? Aue, I know you recall. You lost your good temper and yelled at me all kinds of rude names and swearing, taureka and sloven, 'pokokohua and bitch. 'I spent months getting this together, all the old people who know the waiata! It's a big thing for us, a big thing for *you*, and now Miss High and Mighty you *thing* won't go! Aue, what did I do to have such a daughter?'

And I smiled back from my bed where I was lying, nestled in against Colin. I smiled a slow smile, a sneering smile at my big ranting mother, but my lips trembled. And you said then, quietly, painfully,

'E hine, sometimes I think we live in different worlds.'
Stopped a minute, shaking your head, rubbing your heart-place.
'You in one world, me in quite another. It's my fault, Hinewai.
When you were growing, I wanted a place of sun and water and
song. Not the mud and the bush and Tom's heavy silence. The
farm. The thick animals.'
My smile trembled to a stop.
'Different worlds, my Hinewai . . .'

It rings. Te ao tawhito, te ao hou. Different worlds . . . a slow
minor chord and suddenly the strings sing so softly, my fingers
play so easy – suddenly the stale smoke and the damp chair and
the crowded dark are another world away.

You used to wear this glistening lipstick of shocking red
that nobody had used for years. The last boyfriend I brought
back, last time, saw you dressed to the nines for another hui and
whistled at you. He didn't know then you were my mother. 'God
what arse! God what class!' he crowed, genuinely applauding.
'She's the only woman in the world could get away with
that!'
I was shuddering. There you were, six feet tall and nearly
sixteen stone, your eyelids lacquered green and your mouth
crimson and your nails varnished shellpink and your brown skin a
glowing background for this preposterous flaunting of colour.
And while your feet were swollen over the edges of those narrow
Pakeha shoes, you stood ebulliently, head thrown back, mouth
full of that generous warming laughter, because you liked him
coming straight out with what he thought and you were amused
by my shrinking response. Go broadside into the world, Hinewai,
you are grinning –

When Tara first rang me, I didn't believe him. He and his
Pakeha wife came round then, and like Hone years before, first
ranted then wept. There were no more bands by then. I grieved
now for my dead music, and I still grieved among bottles. Tara
said,
'You've got to come home. She's asking for you. We're going

in the morning so let's clear this up,' the same sweep of arm as Hone, batting savagely against the clutter and debris 'and we all go together.'

I shake my head numbly, whisper I can't.

'But she's crying for you,' says Tara.

E whae, it is your laughter, loud and so warm, your laughter I keep hearing.

When the telegram arrived this morning, I knew what it was without opening it.

I did not scream.

I did not tangi.

I stood a moment in hopeless greyness.

Then yelled

'I need a party!'

It became a chant, She needs a party, Let's have a party! Party! All the groupies and opportunists, the streetwalkers and trans-vestites, the city underbelly: my mates, my friends. Knowing the need, not needing to know what prompted it. Rowdily starting to make a party. The chant was the seed, and the seed grew and swelled into a roaring peoplemass that drank and sang and fought its way through all that day, and then, this night. Now, the party is dead. Someone is moaning in their bitter dreams. Someone else is snoring. And I am alone in the dark.

Different worlds, e mama. You are gone into the night, and I sit here, clutching the neck of my guitar, tears falling in tiny beads of sound. By now, you will have found Tom: by now, you will have met your secret grand-daughter. By now you will know all the disgrace and emptiness of my noisy crowded life. If I had any of your strength and generosity I would be packing up now, getting ready to catch the train, the bus, getting ready to hike, anyway back for the tangi. Doing all the proper things as befits the eldest child, as befits the daughter of my mother.

E Ma, I am sorry.

And you are sitting there, a tall slim woman with no grey in your hair, no lines on your face. Your arms are folded round your knees: you look at me hunched weeping in the dark and you smile a marvellous smile.

'Be happy, Hinewai. Sing for me, my daughter. Play!'

And I am.

A NIGHTSONG FOR THE
SHINING CUCKOO

I hear them singing in the hills, *kui kui kui, whiti whiti ora*. Rainbirds. I used to think, O hell, rain coming.

Charlie's strumming the guitar, humming the sad little nursery rhyme. The rainbirds set him wondering too.

I broke my back falling off a log. It was a nice log; I used it for crossing the stream between my place and the beach. At first it felt like I'd just sat down too hard. Then it didn't feel. Four hours later, a hiker chanced by, which was lucky, and pulled me out of the stream, which wasn't. I had plenty of time in hospital to moan about it. 'I would have died. I *should* have died. I'm gonna be a cripple. I'm gonna be useless.' I went through all the stages: self-pity; rage; why? why *me*? more rage; and finally, well, what do I do now?

There was one thing I wasn't going to do.

Sometimes in my old town you'd see them, blanket-lapped waists, wheeling through the streets. They sought a dark indoors, a drowning, to stay in gentle beer and gin. All the stares knew that beneath the blanket was maiming; bare scarred nubs, amputations. So they hid.

I didn't buy a blanket. I didn't hide. I didn't go back to my lonely beach. 'You're mad,' said the physiotherapist. 'You've never lived in a city have you? Why start now of all times? And I can't imagine anyone less like a shopkeeper, you old bush – ahh – person, you.'

I said, 'Not so old. I can change my ways. I have to, eh.'

I didn't say, 'Beneath the cage of ribs there's a bare scarred heart. My old life is smashed. I want a new way so different I won't have to think about what I was. In the city, I won't hear the sea, the bush-wind or the birds.'

'I'm looking forward to it,' I lied to the physio.

There's no future when your body has betrayed you.

They loaded me onto the plane by forklift, as though I was a container of freight. They loaded me off the same way. I'm strong in the shoulders and arms, stronger now than ever. I hauled myself into the back seat of the taxi; the driver folded my wheels into the boot.

'Where to, mate?'

I opened my eyes after a minute and looked at him. Would you believe Heaven, mate? Would you believe Hell?

But we went to the land agent's instead. The agent looked at me dubiously.

'It's got the space you required,' he says, 'but the area it's in . . . you're sure you want to – ahh – spend your money this way?'

Why don't you take a world cruise or join a Cripples' Home or retire somewhere out of sight, he meant.

The flat at the back of the shop could be altered to be adequate. The shop itself was the only dairy for five streets. The previous owners had made a mint, they said. You'll have to restock it, but it's a neat self-service operation ideal for . . . you. Particularly when you engage your assistant.

I nodded. In the glow of their figures, all profit no loss, I could see myself sitting smiling behind the counter, watching the till grow fat. I *would* get myself an assistant. I shook hands all round. I said I wanted to stay the night. I could manage until tomorrow when a carpenter would come and start changing the flat to meet my needs. They fussed. Then they went away smiling and left me staring at the present.

Bleak bare lights.

Spiders sneering from corners.

A nugget-black bug rollicked under the till.

Encrusted dirt I hadn't noticed until now.

Outside there's screams and a sound of breaking glass.

A dog goes yelping down the street Au! Au! Au!

Unholy, I can't do this all by myself.

There was a knock on my insect-freckled windows. I slewed the chair round. All I can see is a shadow watching me. Some bloody nosey kid, right, it's going to cop an earful, but by the time I get the door open, there is nobody there.

I wrote to Fraser asking for help, for the first time ever. Fraser wrote back. Fraser has priorities. He began,

> Dear Sister, good to hear from you. Glad to hear you up and about again. Sorry we couldn't make it to see you, but we are particularly busy right now. I've just shifted the hydrangeas, and trimmed the wisteria, and begun a new rockery.

The garden details went on for two pages, plumeria, saxifrage, lobelia, and the letter ended,

> Sorry we can't make it up to see you in your new start in life, but you will realise the need for us to look after our own property. Madge has just got over The Change, and doesn't like even the thought of travel. However, Charles says he'll come and see you, but I've never known Charles to keep his word in anything. Your loving brother.

We never were close.

Poor Fraser. You adopt a child and try very hard to mould him into an image of your prim restricted self, and he leaks out of the mould. Wild, I can hear you say. Needs discipline, needs pruning.

Poor Madge. You adopt a child, wince that he smells, has a runny nose, orifices, but try very hard until the first time he bites you. Then you retreat into The Change of Life and don't come out of it until the dirty kid grows into a wild young man and leaves home.

Poor Fraser and poor Madge. Now you can huddle together

in your trim tight garden, untroubled by further notes from
me.

I poured myself another wine. Its label said, standard quaffing
wine. I'd been quaffing. I raised the glass, Haere mai, Charlie,
come quick.

My nephew and me are close.

He strolls in a couple of days later, and stops and stares at me
chairbound.

'Jeez, are those radials?' I can't help a giggle.

Then he shakes, stretches, sighs.

'Bloody long hike, that.'

Comes and hugs me.

'Where you been this time? Commune? Nga Tama Toa? The
wopwops?'

'Scrubcutting. You know, the employment scheme thing. I've
chucked it in.'

'For here?'

'For a while.'

He's still got a wicked grin. At 19, he's nervous of the
maimed, but he can smother it under a smile. He prowls round
the flat, round the shop, a tall skinny fella in tight jeans, all cock
and ribs like a musterer's dog.

'You really gonna live in this thing, really work it?'

'For a while,' I echo.

'OK, let's make it sing.'

'What'd you mean, make it sing? It's humming sweet now.
More or less.'

'The less first.'

'Lifting and shifting stuff. I can do so much with my tongs, so
much with my muscles. It takes a helluva time to stock the high
shelves a tin at a time though.'

'So I can lift and shift. Anything else?'

'Noooo.'

'Meaning yes.'

'Well, I'm busy enough, and the trading figures the last
owners gave me were honest enough, but I'm not making as
much as I should. I've got a small plague of shoplifters.'

'What size shoplifters?'

'All sizes. A couple of desperate pensioners, trying to eke their dole out. Schoolkids doing it for a dare. One blue-rinse matron, really snooty when I caught her. I dunno what to do.'

'I'll kick arses, auntie. Or we could call the cops.'

'You kick, for a start. Or play heavy anyway.'

He grinned a mean grin.

'First one we catch tomorrow.'

Which was Bird.

I was sitting behind my new low counter when he crabbed into the shop. He stared. He has eyes full of the dark.

Charlie blinks in surprise when I cough.

I can see him thinking, That scarecrow? She means him?

I cough again, and nod. Charlie keeps his eyes skinned.

Now, over the past month, I've learned to watch people the way I used to watch whitebait. Keenly but not looking at them. Peripheral vision picks up things direct staring doesn't. Even so, I've never yet seen Bird actually lift anything. The stuff goes missing after he visits, but that is all I can swear to.

He has a routine.

'How much is that?'

'You got any money, Bird?'

'How much is that?'

'Too much for you, I think, fella.'

'How much is that?'

He can keep up the unanswered question longer than I can refuse to answer it. His thin hard cheep wears my resistance away, even though I know – oath how I know! – his routine off by heart now.

'OK, it's a dollar forty.'

'Oh.'

He shifts to the next shelf, limp and creak.

'How much is that?'

And so on. He's never bought anything yet.

Today, he stares longer than usual, his eyes flicking from me to Charlie, from Charlie to me. Bird, being Bird, can smell trouble.

But Charlie turns his back on us after a moment, and stuffs his hands in his tight pockets, whistles nonchalantly, starts rocking back and forwards on the balls of his feet as though he wanted nothing more from life than to stare out the window into the grubby street.

So Bird starts up his routine, and we play it through until the last 'Oh'. And then he shuffles towards the door. And Charlie blocks it, and holds out his hand.

'I saw you swipe a torch battery and a peppermint bar. Give.'

'I didn't take anything.'

'There's a mirror up now boy, and I saw you taking all right.'

Bird swivels his head to look back above the window, and Charlie follows the move, grinning in mean triumph.

Bird snatches the nearest thing to hand off the shelf, heaves it, and lurches for the door.

The nearest thing to hand was a pound tin of spaghetti and it thumps Charlie hard in the belly. While he doubles up ooof! he doesn't shift from the door, and Bird stops. When Charlie straightens, he's lost his grin.

'Jeez you little bastard.'

He snatches, collars, shakes.

'Hey Charlie.'

Yeah, I'm sick of being preyed upon; yeah, I'm sick of Bird ripping me of all people off, but I don't think I can stomach seeing him made an example of – there's already three curious regulars watching from out in the street.

'Charlie, let him go. Bird, piss off. Don't come in here again.'

Charlie is very quiet for the rest of the day. We close up shop. We eat.

'You like a wine, Charlie? Or a beer?'

He is brooding over the fire.

'Nope.'

I pour myself a glass. It's more of the standard quaffing.

Charlie says suddenly,

'What was it? That he's a cripple too?'

That was meant to wound, and does.

My turn to nurse a silence.

'Look, we agreed last night, we catch a few and warn 'em off, one way or the other. You called him out, I acted. He deserved thumping for that, let alone hanging one on me. You never used to be soft, Frances.'

Serious if I'm getting my name instead of the auntie label I detest. So I try an explanation.

'I haven't started to decay, Charlie. Look, you remember Ally Wang who came in late this afternoon?'

'The fat wahine, the one with the old lady in tow?'

He's frowning.

'That's her. She and the old lady and Bird were the first three in here. I was open at eight in the morning, brand-new paint, sawdust and fresh plastic smells, waiting. They wandered in about lunch-time. Not so much customers then, as dogs sniffing out a new tree. But hell I loved them Charlie. I was beginning to think there was a neighbourhood black ban on paraplegics or something. So I gushed a bit. Wanted to know their names, were they from the neighbourhood, all that kind of crap. And towards the end, when the boy had finally got himself inside, I asked, "And what's your little um, what's your child called?" Ally Wang looked blank. "Him? Bird. And he's not mine. I just look after him for my sister." And the old lady looked surprised. She said, "Bird? Tika?" Ally: "Kaore. Ko Te Pipiwharauroa tona ingoa." Old lady: "Kaore noa iho! Penei me te pipiwharauroa, ne?" And they sniggered. Your Maori good enough to follow that?'

'Nope.'

'OK, his given name is Te Pipiwharauroa. There's an old saying, Penie me te pipiwharauroa, which is a polite way of saying a child is a bastard, you know, a cuckoo's child laid in some other bird's nest. I followed all this with interest, and then made the mistake of looking at Bird. I can see how he looked now. I'll retain that expression of his while I breathe. But do you know what?'

'Nope.'

'He's made a game of that shame label. He calls himself Bird. He won't answer to his given name unless he thinks you're a friend. So that's one reason I wouldn't let you hide him. The other was his defence: I like guts and quick wits. I think if he had snivelled, I would have been happy for you to give him the message about thieving.'

'Frances, you haven't gone soft. You've gone bloody soppy.'

Have I?

Does city living eat away at your survival instinct?

Dunno.

The hard thing I find about the city is the dirt. I wheel out these days, down to the corner, back round the block. Not going anywhere, just getting acclimatised. Used to the filth. Greasy shreds of paper, dogturds, glass-splinters. People-spits, bird-shit, grey wads of chewing gum studding the footpath. Clogged air, and too many people to breathe it. Even the rain is dirty here.

Charlie left after a week.

He stocked the shelves, and said he'd be back in a couple of weeks to do it again. Said to ring 'Mike in Hastings' if I needed him sooner. I didn't think he'd come back for months if at all.

Bird came back in the shop the day after Charlie left. It can't have been coincidence. He must have been watching.

I said, 'Get the hell out of here', full of sour self-pity that Charlie had gone.

'How much is that?'

'Out.'

'How much is that?'

I sped my wheels round the counter and came at him.

'Out Bird, or else.'

He stood his ground. He switched from pointing at the goodies on the shelf to pointing at me.

'How much is *that*?'

I stopped.

There was a smile in Bird's eyes, not reaching the rest of his face, but lighting the night of his stare.

So the city's made me soppy. So what?

'Ally, why doesn't Bird go to school?'

She shrugged her heavy shoulders.

'Bird's simple, you know, retard-ded.'

'O yeah? Who says?'

'The Welfare. Like the social people you know?'

'O. I know.'

But I don't.

Bird stopped playing the How-much-is-that? game. Now I mainly talk, and he listens. Poised foursquare between sticks and caged ungainly legs, head bent, while I waffle on and on. The house I built myself. The white pine posts I used to cut on contract. Whitebaiting September through to the last day of November. Trickles, shoals, runs of bait.

More and more, try to stop it as I do, I talk about walking south to the top of the world, south to where the surf makes a high bright haze.

Bird doesn't say anything. He listens, then looks with those lightened eyes, and then struggles away.

I think Bird may be smart, smart enough to hide all he feels and all he knows.

Nights that are never fully dark, mornings that feel used by dawn.

Business is wearisomely good. The shoplifting spree has diminished to an odd time or two a week. I rise early and stock; serve through the day and early evening; balance; clean up, and head for the comfort of the bottle.

I had quaffed to blurdom the night Charlie arrived back, two weeks to the day just like he said.

'Who's there?' I asked the knocker at the door.

'Auntie? You OK auntie?'

'Hell, Charlie!'

I unlocked the door.

''E good to see you again,' I was weeping into his hug.

He is frowning at the tears.

'I never seen you cry before.'

'It's the piss more than anything, Charlie. No worries, eh. Hey, it's *good* you're back, man, so good.'

He looks more worried still.

'You've got thinner, Frances.'

'Liquid diet, eh!'

'Ah hell, auntie. This sort of life isn't any good for you. Look, why not go home? I'll come back with you. I could lay a path. Concrete slabs right the way to the beach so you could wheel there and back, eh. Widen your doors. Bring the sink down. Do up the loo the same as this one's done. make it so you can live properly at home. And I could –'

'Charlie, you don't know a shovel from a spade.'

'I could learn.'

'Yeah, yeah, yeah.'

He cooks tea in silence, but it is thoughtful silence, not sullen. After we eat he asks,

'Shop going alright?'

'Could use your help in some restocking. Otherwise, it's steady.'

'How's your shoplifting society?'

'About extinct. Well, what goes on now is tolerable. The business can stand it.'

He sipped some of my wine.

'Saw that Bird hanging round the shop door.'

'At this time of night? What was he doing?'

'Nothing. I clouted him, told him to push off home.'

My nephew grinned his lean wicked smile.

'I still remember that can in the belly.'

That night I dreamed, and heard the rainbirds, the shining cuckoos whistle in the hills.

O Charlie, you and your talk . . .

I can hear his easy snoring.

I can hear a distant siren.

I can hear a dog suddenly yelp, head away down the street Au! Au! Au! May be the same dog I heard the first day . . .

'I'll give it another month, Charlie. Stay at least that long, and see if I can't get used to it.'

'OK. I'll stock you up this week, go south next week, and be back before your month's up. Just in case you want to leave early.'

So much for your resolutions, I told myself. So much for cutting yourself away from the old mobile past. Because I'm feeling drunken with nothing to drink at the thought of a month-to-go. A mere thirty days of exile and then maybe . . .

Nothing like shopwork to keep your wheels firmly on the ground. Mundane, materialistic, matter-of-fact. Fraser, you would be proud of me as I scoot about serving, smiling behind the counter, really watching the till grow fat. I keep my books in order; I prune myself, poor Fraser, in a way you wouldn't understand. You would see it as the sprouting of florid sprawling tendrils of self-will. Wine, and late nights, and too much giggling. Charlie rears his young strong shoulders, holds my world steady. He cooks for us both, cleans most of the place. The shelves are packed with stock. He serves in the shop, when I can't hold the giggles down.

I am out the back in the bathroom, cooling my flush with tap-water. If I keep feeling this high, I am gonna solve the immobility problem, Frances . . . I am just gonna float away out of this chair he he, and then I hear,

'Why don't you want to go back to Auckland?'

'It's dark there.'

'Go on, they burn more lights down there than the rest of us put together.'

'It's dark there. It's dark where I am.'

'You live in a hole or something?'

'It's dark there.'

'Ah come on Bird. I heard you say that three four times already.'

'Don't you understand English, Ngati DB?'

'You're Ngati DB yourself, come to that.'

'It is dark though.'

Charlie hrrmphs in disgust.

I hear Bird creak away out.

I sit looking at the mirror.

Pain eats flesh. So does fear, and hate, and worry. Thinness is never a virtue. My legs are shrunk to skin and hollows, but I been warned to expect that. Hollow eyes too. Death carving a skull already. But I am past fifty.

I had never thought before how thin Bird was.

Dirty, yes. His pale hair is pewter-coloured, matted with

grime. But Ally is a sloven. Her bulk smells rancid, layer on layer of nightsweats. She doesn't take care of herself, let alone anyone else.

And I thought the dark in his eyes inhabited him, was not imposed from outside. You get some people born with that dark inside them.

Charlie comes through, whistling an odd little tune. He grins at me.

'Sober, auntie?'

'Yes . . . what's that piece of mournfulness you're mouthing?'

He grinned more widely.

'Something I'm going to sing that Bird before I go.'

'O yeah? Was that Bird in just now? You were talking to? You kissed and made up or something?'

'That was that Bird. I've been chatting him up . . . he! Whatchya do in Christchurch, Charlie? O chatted up a bird and that.'

He twirled around.

'He's cuckoo in more ways than one, eh? Heh heh!'

Heh heh heh.

Charlie tuned his guitar. Bird stood and stared. I sat immured in my chair. I was sick to death of that chair. Maybe my tiredness showed on my face. Maybe that stirred Charlie because he laid the guitar down before he played.

'You got a favourite song, Bird?'

'No.'

'You like Maori songs, Bird?'

The boy shrugged.

Charlie picked up the guitar again, but uneasily. He looked at me. I looked into my wine. The jokiness had gone out of the air.

'Come into the back, Bird.'

Charlie had said before, 'You going away soon? So are we.'

He winked at me.

'Got a couple of presents for you. Here,' handing over a torch battery and a peppermint bar.

'Free,' says Charlie, beaming. 'No nasty questions asked either.'

Bird took them. Then he repositioned his sticks, and stood without moving a muscle. I got the feeling then that Bird would take whatever came to him, had done so all his life. But like me, when I sprawled for four hours underneath the nice log, he knew that some blows kill, and you can be killed piecemeal.

He hadn't so much braced himself, I realised after, as armoured himself, frozen himself, against what was coming. If you don't move, you won't seem alive. If you don't move, it'll pass over you. So Charlie played and sang to stillness.

Pipi pipi manu e

I hadn't felt the dead half of me so heavy before.

Pipiwharauroa,

The break between living and dead parts ached.

E pi pi pi ana e

I wanted a knife of fire, to sever me, to free.

Mo papa, mama wharauroa,

But only my lungs hurt, taut and strained because I wasn't breathing.

Mo papa, mama wharauroa.

'It's a good song,' said Charlie sulkily. 'Good tune, good rhythm. And it's a nursery rhyme, for God's sake. It's not like I was singing him obscene words.'

He stuffed his last pair of jeans into his pack.

'I'll see you in May. Maybe.' He turned once on his way out. 'Frances, jeez it was a joke.'

I waited 'til he got out the door. Then I threw the standard quaffing bottle at it. Threw myself hard forward so the waist strap cut in and hurt something live.

Yeah, I know. 19's not man-size. 19 is boy growing into man, still capable of a child's casual cruelty. I knew some kids once who sorted out their baby sister, stuck her in a cardboard box, and left it in the middle of a busy road. They giggled like hell when two cars hit it. Jeez Mum it was a joke.

Go away frozenness. Go away eyes.

I had another dream with rainbirds in it, but this time they weren't haunting the hills. I was near my bright surf, and

I was walking, hobbling towards it. I was trying to kill it. I screamed.

> *I asked for riches.*
> *You gave me scavenging rights*
> *On a far beach.*
> *Now you have taken the rights away!*

Somebody laughed loudly.

Blessed are the people who expect nothing, for verily they shall get it.

I tried to ease my cramped chest by breathing crowd air. Wheeled myself four blocks down to the local tavern. A long distance sped by hands. The kerbs are murder, jolt the breakline, so I breathe hard. Doesn't undo the cramps, though.

The bar is ripe with smoke and noise. There are embarrassed edgings away from my wheels. I get a jug and steer towards a table. The crowd melts a wide hole round me. Now I'm one of the maimed, blanket and all. Like the tired old men wed to alcohol, their wives clasped in brown paper bags; left lonely in corners, dribbling in their love. I brood over the beer. Then,

'How yer gettin' on mate? Boxa birds, eh?'

'Boxa birds all right, mate. All shit and feathers, eh.'

He cranked a laugh out. Puffed red face. Full of the terrible instantaneous friendship drunks ladle out, I think. Then I see him groping round his crotch, unconscious he's doing it, and realise he's one of those weirdos turned on by cripples. He keeps on lipfarting away. Talk dull as dead cod eyes, thick as yesterday's porridge. I'm wedged against the table and can't wheel away.

I borrow Bird's defence and freeze. I don't notice when he goes.

Maybe the child's armour worked for him.

I say to Ally on my last day as a fat-till watcher, 'Bird sick or something?' Very casual.

'O me sister took him back,' says Ally, her face shuttered. 'Last week. Me sister got him then.'

'O yeah,' very casually indeed.
Bird sent back to Auckland, his smile still trapped in his eyes.

I hear them singing in the hills, *kui kui kui, whiti whiti ora.*
There's a young bird calling out, a shining cuckoo, calling
continually, for the father, the mother cuckoo. Rainbirds.
I used to think O hell.

THE CICADAS OF SUMMER

'Francis, I'm thirsty.'

'There's water in the jug.'

'It's got warm.'

'Get some ice for it then.'

'Can I have a coke, Francis?'

'No.'

'I'll go to the shop for you.'

'No.'

'Aw why?'

It is midday and the cicadas are crackling everywhere. It is a chainsaw racket, a nerve rack.

'Whoiiyyy?'

'O god.'

The bush is shrivelling under the sun and his head is getting tighter, shrivelling with the bush.

'Please Francis?'

He lays his head on the clutter of paper and dreams of deep cold pools. If he dreams hard enough the pools will seep in behind his eyes and flow gently out and maybe, maybe, that osmosis will ease the tightness in his head.

When she gets tired of his silence, she goes out to the Rileys in the back.

Mrs is saying, 'I heard the queerest thing about him hello dear.'

Hall Riley is bending cane as usual. 'Must be lunchtime, look who's deigning to pay us a visit.'

'I'm not hungry, I'm looking for a book. What's queer?'

'Nothing dear. Just someone saying that he used to live in Christchurch, same setup as here. Little place away from the house. Kept to himself except for the bowls. Never a drinking man, but a good enough fellow, for a Pom. Then he left one night same way as he arrived here, sudden. And then a week later they discovered this wee I shouldn't be telling this in front of you dear.' Mrs knows better than anyone in the world how to gaff a listener. She perks a grin at Gwen.

'Wee what?'

'What sort of book?' Hall snips a pale cane end.

'Insects. Cicadas. Wee what?'

'Would have thought your dad had everything in his library,' says Mrs.

'Only maths, and stuff like that. He doesn't have anything live.'

'Poor man.' Mrs swings round to her sink and rattles a pot, a lid, another pot.

Hall heaves himself out of his chair, and lurches, clicking, to the shelves.

'Try this,' he says. 'Bring it back when you're finished.'

'I always do.'

'Except for the twenty or so you've got stashed in your room,' he says tartly, and they grin at each other. He lowers himself heavily back behind his workbench, his legs snicking rigidly straight. 'Hearsay and gossip,' he says to his wife. 'Shall we all have a beer?'

They all sigh happily. The glasses are crystalled with cold; the deep amber brew cools throat and head.

'I don't like it,' Mrs frowns suddenly at her husband. 'Those hollyhocks, no more kits.'

Gwen knows what she means. The backyard lodger had arrived in the winter. The Rileys had been in the back half of the house forever, but when her mother died the outside dwelling, the shack the studio they called it, stood reproachfully empty. Fill it quick, said Mrs, and advertised for a tenant. They landed several, none of them staying for long. And then, late May, he had arrived, threadbare and leanly erect, all his belongings in an old vinyl suitcase. 'Nice little place, m'cottage,' he said of the shack, and secreted himself away until the sun came again. He emerged, splendid in bowling whites. He smiled at the Rileys as he passed quickly by them. He ignored Gwen. He seemed never to know about Francis. He was up early and away to the bowling rinks each morning, and they never heard him come home at nightfall. But he came back.

'I caught him pouring boiling water on that flax you know,' says Mrs grimly.

Don't mind d'you? he'd said to her with a tight smile. Make m'cottage just like home. The gaudy forest of hollyhocks towers over the sickly flax now.

'He's he's he's' Mrs can't find the word for what he is.

He is tall and thin and his immaculate whites gleam. 'Dunno where he washes them, y'never see them drying,' grumbles Mrs. Somehow the bowling whites lacquer the man. They cling to him in stiff plating folds. And he has leathery planes of skin which slide back to reveal his smile. His speech is clipped.

'I don't like the talk,' says Mrs in defeat. She puts her glass into the sink, bangs a pot onto the stove.

'You can't hang a man for talk,' says Hall. He weaves another cane into his basket. 'Or for killing a clump of flax. He pays every pension day on the dot. He's never a trouble. Remember Lanson?'

Mrs shudders. '*He* was just a young yoick.'

'So be happy we got an old mystery this time.'

'I'm not . . . tell your father I'll be bringing his lunch up in ten minutes, Gwennie dear.'

'Okay.'

She wanders out into the brilliant sun, into the click and shrill and rattle of the cicada hordes. The air shivers with their sound. Hall says it is unnatural, this side of the island getting such a long dry break. Hall says that's why the cicadas are so noisy, why there's so many of them. Hall says that's why they're driving people nuts. She doesn't mind it. It's the holidays and she can stay by herself in the bush as long as she likes, no rain to drive her inside. So what if some people are whiney and querulous, so what if Francis has turned into a whimpering shade of himself? As long as the Rileys cherish her in their dark cool back rooms, beer and business all round, she doesn't care.

She squats in the shade of the ngaios and opens the book.

Francis knows lunch will come sometime, doesn't need her to tell him. Besides he never eats it. Besides he is probably crying again. She stares at a page. A tiny whitish book louse hurries down a margin. She waits until it is nearly at the bottom before smearing it dead.

And then slowly, but with increasing power, the words draw her eyes to them, enclose her, stop her ears to the world.

She heard 'cicada' for the first time when she arrived home from school for the holidays. 'Bloody cicadas,' said Hall. It didn't mean anything. A day after, lying flat on her belly out in the yard, not doing anything just getting away from Francis' tears, she had noticed the thing. A brown hollow shell of an insect, appearing to be made of varnish. 'That's just a cicada husk,' said Mrs, and showed her what had come from it. The insect was immobile on the yard post, waiting for the sun to harden it, said Mrs Gwen stared at the three ruby studs on top of its head, stared until it flew away.

'Francis, I've found these. Exuviae.'
'What?'
'It's a good word eh? These.'
He looks. He doesn't see them.
'That's nice.'
'The singers come out of them. It must be like dying, coming out of your skin.'
'What?'
'It's their skins, these exuviae. You know, the cicadas?'
'Yes. Gwen, take this plate back to Mrs Riley.'
'But Francis.'
He has put his head down again.

She doesn't care that it doesn't interest her father. She has half a chocolate box full of the crackly skins. Tombstones on the way to noisy life . . . no wonder the adults are called singers, the singing birds of Rehua. She wonders briefly who Rehua was. Her singers, his birds, shrill and rattle all day, all night. They sing for joy in the sun and then they sing again, pleading for the sun to come back. Sometimes, waking before dawn, she hears them, a feebler clacking attacking the night but still loud above the restless sweaty movements Francis makes in the bedroom next door.

The Rileys' cat caught them, batting them out of the air. She ate the soft abdomen and left the brittle fleshless wings, the armoured chest, the hard rubied head. Sometimes the torn half-cicada crawled away. Francis found one such and stamped it to nothingness, stamped it so hard he hurt his foot.

Gwen, cuddling the cat to her chest, thought it was the first brisk movement she had seen him make since Briar had died; thought it was a pity doing something, anything, had hurt him. She looked at the cat. 'What did it taste like, Mica?' The cat blinked golden eyes and yawned, wriggled out of her arms. The book said the cicada nymphs were edible. So were the egg-full females. She went back out into the bush and began digging.

The bush looks a bit brown and some of the ferns have withered. Grass has grown huge and strangely pale; the black-berries have died, drupes withering to seed without truly having achieved fruit. She has to dig inches of warm dry earth before she comes to the damp soil where the nymphs lurk. She holds the first one in her hand. It curls its abdomen a little but makes no other move.

A year or so ago, a female had thrust her ovipositor deep into the living tissue of a tree. She knows those egg incisions, a strange and dangerous stitching for a tree already haggard from lack of water.

The egg hatched into a tiny nymph, and the nymph crept downwards, groundwards. It pierced with its probiscus, drew up the living sap, and grew. When it reached its full growth, for this body, for this life, it stopped feeding and constructed an under-ground chamber, therein to lie dormant while being transformed.

She knows some of them lie underground, dreaming, for three years; some for much longer. And while they dream they are at more risk than ever, despite the cunning underearth rooms. Beetles eat them, and some beetle larvae. That curious fungus Cordyceps is intent upon making them vegetable while they sleep. And there are people . . .

The dreamers are white-eyed, but their eyes change to coral

as the time draws near for them to dig to light. To die in the light. To live a singer. All that changing, from egg to nymph, to pupating dreamer; from the long cool silence underground, to the screeching bright sun. She notes that this nymph has coral eyes.

Tough, thinks Gwen, before putting it in her mouth.

'Francis, do we change when we die?'

That jolts him. He stares at her with narrowed eyes.

'I mean, do we turn into something else? Like the cicadas?'

His stare is frightening.

'I'm just asking . . .

'We rot.'

His voice is harsh; his hands crush his face.

'We rot.'

'Hall, when we die do we really change into angels and that?

Hall looks at her. He hasn't bothered putting on his legs today. He leans against the back of his chair.

'Some people say we do, Gwen.'

'What do you think?'

'Dunno. Haven't done it yet.'

Mrs bangs in through the back door. 'Heavens, it's hot . . . do you know what I just done?' She has a triumphant smirk on her face and her hands are covered with earth. 'Planted four flaxes, *four* of them! That'll show the old stick.'

Hall shakes his head, looking at the girl, looking back at his wife. 'It's the heat,' he says to himself, 'it's that bloody racket and the heat.'

The rain that fell in the nights was tired, was never enough. One morning, though, she found a cicada on its back in a puddle beneath the broken spouting. Its wings were plastered to a stone. It still clackled, each time more slowly. The sun didn't turn hot fast enough to free it. She watched it die.

When she looked up afterwards, sighing, it was into the bright bright eyes of the bowler, the lodger in his white armour.

'Hello m'dear.' He raises his white hat quickly to her, turns quickly, walks very quickly away towards the street.

'Francis, can I help?'

'O for god's sake. For god's sake.'

He is leant back from his desk, his eyes closed. His face looks grey, and sodden from all the crying he does, at night, and whenever he thinks that nobody can hear.

'Please Dad?'

There is the yard, and the neighbouring bush, and in the middle of the bush, the creek. She has finished with Hall's book, can chant 'Amphisalta cingulata, amphisalta zealandica, black and mountain cicada, green cicada and brown.' She knows the names for each joint in each leg, and all the segments of abdomen, and words she never dreamed of clack harshly in her mind – mandible thorax chiton tegmina. And in the yard, and the neighbouring bush, and all along the creek, the cicadas stridulate.

In the blistering days, she sickens of – it is not easy to call it a name to herself. The hard insect names interfere.

It is this, thinks Gwen. Everything coming ripe out of the ground. I've eaten a dozen. I've explored and pulled apart a dozen more. And they keep on hatching. Everywhere.

She hunches her shoulders furiously. If Francis would stop crying, it might rain. The dust might stop. *They* might stop.

The strident chorus continues in a mocking tattoo.

'For Christ's sake shut up *maun*dering on about those *bloody* hollyhocks!' shouts Hall.

Mrs throws her glass into the sink, where it shatters.

They are snarling at each other, thinks Gwen. They are really *snarling* at each other.

The coolness has evaporated from their cool dark backrooms. Hall and Mrs glare at one another and she can see the glittering sparks.

Mrs turns away. She pickes up the glass shards from the sink as though it didn't matter whether they cut her fingers or not.

'Christ, love,' says Hall, low and slow, 'Christ, love.' And long seconds later, 'I'm sorry.'

There is a deep and belly-satisfying side to killing. She

extracted a hundred nymphs and left them to fry, prematurely birthed to the sun. It was good watching, but slow. It was much better to disinter them and pull their fat bodies apart. But it was best to have a nymph exposed on the ground and smash the stone down. Have an unwitting singer full of himself in the sunlight and crush him to instant oblivion. Over the hot days she stalks the singers, pulps the nymphs. Coming home in the still dusty evenings, she listens. Is it less, that cackling song? Her fingers are varnished with nymph fat, and her wrists ache.

'Francis, how do you get strong?'

The charts around him are overlain with dust. His computer monitor has been frozen grey all the weeks she has been home.

'Get strong?'

'I been, I been picking up stones and things. They've got a, a certain weight you know?'

'Yes.'

His eyes are dry. He is quiet.

'I wondered if you you, *I* keep doing it, you get strong?'

'Why, Nen?'

And tears rise in her eyes and surprise her with their sudden onslaught. I haven't missed my petnames. She scowls around the darkened room.

'Just my wrists hurt. I *know* what any stone any old stone feels like? You know? They they fit in the hand. But –'

'You want me to find a ratio? Between weight of stones picked up in a week and muscle growth in a prepubertal girl?'

There is, at last, his olden laughter in his voice.

'Yes please Francis.'

He sighs.

'Later Nen. But I shall.'

I will kill them bloody all, she promises the dark. The lone cicada clakkclakkclakking by her open window stops a moment. It is a good omen.

It is a week later and the bush is full of the stink of smoke. There is a bluebronze corona round the sun and the cicadas crackle at fever pitch. Mrs said at breakfast, 'Jimmy Fast has shot himself,' and Hall sighed. 'Went to school with him. Was in the Railway with him, until.' She fills in for herself only, 'until I lost my legs.' She refuses a drink, and goes out the door, heading for the creek, rubbing her wrists. They don't ache any more.

She reels away from it. They don't *do* that. An ordinary pallid nymph, heaved out of its chamber, was threshing about on the surface. Its body bent at a 90 degree angle, skywards, earthwards. Do some of them feel it, dying, squashing, extinction, pain? She breathes hard. I don't care, I don't care. She picks up a pebble, hefts it judiciously, slants it, throws it, and the angular spasms stop abruptly. I don't care.

But o god there is so much waste in life. There is too much strangeness. And I got five more days. This won't do anything.

She hunkered back, leant against the nearest hardness, and tried to shut out the agonised switching of the nymph.

I haven't sucked my thumb for years . . . what's the shadow? Rain? My rain? sitting up fast and

'Good afternoon m'dear.'

His smile creaks. His eyes are fixed and cicada bright. His grip on her shoulder is screaming ironfire to the bone. His grip is irresistible. Come, he says, the creek is cool today. Come with me

'O god Mr Prendergast o god Francis wake up!'

His fingers splay off the keys.

'It's me, it's me Eadie Riley, don't look like that!'

'Eadie?'

'Please Francis that old bugger has gone.' She gags, whoops, catches control of her voice. 'The lodger right?'

'What?'

'She's not here, Gwen's not here, she hasn't been anywhere for hours. Do you know what I mean? And Hall is drunk and o god Francis!'

'She?'

'Gwennie! She's gone and she's not here and that old' and Francis hit the monitor and began to run.

He'll hit the bloody door – no he won't, I have never felt the streaks of tears, Hall has fallen over, I will go.

The ache spread upwards, paining her to her breastbone. The creek is cold and the world is a blur. As the mud pushes past her ears, she feels the hardness, push it away, a stone?

Her hand closed round the stone. All summer through she had practised
     and she knew
     the finite ways
     they squashed

It rains.

KITEFLYING PARTY AT DOCTORS' POINT

You said, write it all down, write it out, put it in writing.

Well, I will try.

It is not easy.

After years of marking essays, one is inclined to mark oneself. Teaching a craft tends to make one overly sensitive, and thus, ill at ease when handling it. One becomes a critic rather than a practitioner.

However, I will try. I will take it as it comes.

I am neither young nor old. I suppose I had a sheltered childhood, and have led a sheltered life. For as long as I can remember, I wanted to engage in an academic career. I have been a lecturer for some years, with some success. My career has not been meteoric, but it hasn't been a failure. I have been out here for three months.

You said to mention the physical details as much as possible. There isn't that much to me, physically speaking.

I am not tall, I am not beautiful, but I am not ugly. I look puffed, like swollen dough, yet my nose is sharp and my fingers are long and thin. This is a family discrepancy, I mean trait.

It had been a usual kind of night, that is disturbed. Fogged. Anaesthetized.

I will try to make it *present*.

The day is bright.

At least, outside the day is bright. In here it's the same as it is at night, dark and stale and still.

The doorbell shrills a high continuing summons.

I have been trying to clean up, ever since I heard the car sound the horn. The horn was a challenge, the blare a knight crusading might have made, outside castle perilous.

The clamour stops.

I open the door.

Half a dozen of them, and M and K and C and D, bright in their summer clothes.

They importune,

'Come with us eh!'

and the children dart round, flashy and venomous as tropical fish.

I suppose I look furtive and sleepy-eyed, but they don't seem to notice.

They chorus,

'It's a beaut day!' 'The weather's corker!' 'We'll have a neat time!'

'C'mon! C'mon!'

I can not get used to the way they truncate, abuse, alter the language.

'What?'

'We're goin' to tha beach!'

They grin collectively, they all smile, they exude friendliness.

'It'll bring you out of your moodiness,' murmurs K. 'Chase away those blues eh?'

'Moodiness? Blues?' I disclaim them, but the demon children latch on to the words and hurl them back at me, Moody blues! Moody blues! Moody blues! and their parents don't take any notice.

To stop it I say,

'I'll come, of course I'll come.'

They cheer loudly. 'Great!' they holler.

They are laughing at me of course.

The road twists, unreels in strange ways. There is a peculiar feel to it, as though it had only just decided to turn here itself and is surprised by the direction.

It arrives at an unexpected beach.

'Where is this?'

'Doctors' Point,' says, C, smiling. 'The kids love it.'

I had dreaded crowds; noise; loud hilarious people straining for fun. But it is a bare beach, featureless, a dreary plain of sand. The wind tears at its skin.

I am afraid of the wind, and linger inside.

Everyone else surges out of the car.

They unwrap mysteries, parcels like stakes, parcels like heads. The children dance in rowdy circles and are sent to explore the sandhills for the sake of peace. Bottles are broached, fires coaxed. There is laughter and secret conversation.

It is cold, watching them.

This is the physical point: it is very cold, even though the sun is shining.

I walk over to D.

'Can I help?'

He smiles, shaking his head. 'Have a glass,' he suggests.

He means, have a drink.

I try to sneer at his usage – he is a grammarian after all – but my head aches. The result must look like a lame, a timid smile. Another lie on my face.

I am tired of trying to give the lie to my face, to the mask Nature made of my face. I surge with torment inside, but to view?

Calmness. Composure. Plumply pallidly placid.

Do my eyes ever show agony? Life, even?

The dark is everywhere inside, the chase of shadows.

Nobody can see it by looking at me.

The sand on the beach is fine and white, like talcum powder. When I step on it, it squeals.

Unreal sand – for a moment I imagine I have fallen into a dream. I think there is nobody watching, so I accomplish experimental broadsides, producing crescendos of squeaks.

'It's the size and arrangement of the particles,' offers M.

She is crouched down by the sandhill to the left, ringed by avid-eyed children.

'O?'

She smiles softly. She looks down at the thing she is putting together. 'We're just going to put this kite up . . . do you want first go?'

The child horde is choiring, 'Me first! Me first! Me first!'

Shaking, I shake my head, No No No, walking away on the tormented sand.

The beach is littered with dead krill.

They appear to be the same kind here as at home, but I have never seen so many of them driven on to a beach before.

They are stranded everywhere, mounds of them heaped and ghostly, decayed to pale plastic shells.

Why have they died in this amount?

Possibly because the baleen whales kept the krill in check. The factory ships destroyed the whales. 'A whale dies every twenty seconds.' And then there were no more whales left to die. Now the krill breed to superabundance, spread an insidious red tide through the sea.

This is possible, although I don't know whether it is correct. I haven't read newspapers, watched television, listened to vain talk for many months.

The sand is squealing hideously under my moving feet.

I try to walk stealthily, silently, tiptoeing, but the sand chitters triumphantly with every movement.

I sit down in defeat amidst the holocaust of krill.

I remember thinking in one of the northern cities, just after I had arrived there, 'Courtenay Place! What a ridiculous name! Place Place!' I chided myself immediately.

This is a new land, a new chance, a beginning. Ridicule has no place here.

I have a cousin called Courtenay.

He is presently unable to continue his research in genetics owing to nervous exhaustion. That, of course, is neither here nor there.

M has the kite aloft now.

It is a blue delta shape, batwinged. It looks like a cruel unnatural hawk as it sways on the end of its strings.

M pulls the left string. The kite dips. She pulls on the right string. The kite loops down to the sand, its white plastic tail whipping circles in the air.

The children are scrambling wildly round it. Their shrieks carry to me.

O why?

Is it triumph over the descent of the kite? Or have they found an ally? For the kite is a bird of prey . . .

I look at the sand, my eyes filling with tears.

Through the mist I see it is not stark white. That is a trick of the sun. It is really pale fawn, a dun colour. Though there is a mica-glitter, a light rash through it, that helps the sun's disguise.

One of the children comes trotting past.

She wears a garish t-shirt covered in scarlet and yellow blotches, and poisonous green shorts. Bare arms, bare legs, bare feet, all in defiance of the wind, the cold. She shies as she passes me, but turns to grin shyly. Small white needlepointed fangs.

My lips curl in reply. Suck off bloodimp.

Her smile wavers.

She trots away faster.

There were two things about the child; her whole air of sly friendship, defiant friendship, friendship that is not real, that snares, that entraps – that was one.

The other was the fact that she had a birthmark on her forehead, the port wine kind, and she seemed unconscious of this deformity. She did not hide it, or show herself ashamed.

I have thought about these things a lot. They troubled me: they trouble me still.

Then there was the uncomfortable feeling about the vividness and inappropriateness of her clothes.

Do people not feel the cold out here?

My dress was linen, plain, neat, covering. I felt ridiculous among the shorts and jeans and casual shirts of all of them.

But I am presently self-conscious about my clothes.

I had been sitting in my office with the door open, and I don't think they were aware of that.

D had said loudly,

'Holy Christ, have you seen her latest number? Sort of trimmed horse-blanket and the kind of necklace even my aunt Gertrude wouldn't be seen dead in!'

Throbbing laughter from them all.

I closed my door very quietly.

I am tired of living a lie, the lie that is my life. Though it is better to appear dully normal. Better to be considered old fashioned and slightly eccentric because of my sane normality.

Let them be amused. Let them laugh. Let them sneer behind my back and smile falsely to my face.

It is far better that they do this than get a glimpse of the chaos within.

But I am tired of lying.

The girl child is a long way up the beach now.

Her curling floss of hair, her thick glasses, the stain on her head, all hidden.

Her garish clothes are easily visible however.

I have a theory about deformities. People are either fearful in the company of a monster, or they will worship it. Any other reaction is rare.

For instance, you are familiar with the giant stone Olmec heads?

Did you know the Olmecs worshipped were-jaguars? That their race was subject to a scourge of birth malformations, deformed children with warped skulls and squashed-in faces? Some of these mutations may have lived. Olmec heads seem to me to represent a deformed mutant with a protective head-covering. A were-jaguar born to a mortal woman. A fit subject for worship!

For my own part, I think all deformed monsters should be painlessly destroyed at birth.

The pain they cause to those who are closest to them is unbelievable.

The wind is blowing harder. To sit still is to shiver uncontrollably.

So I walk along the sea-edge.

There are pieces of krill, of crab and weed, swinging in oozy decay in the water's rim.

All that death . . . the sand feels unclean under my feet. It is unthinkable to rinse it in the sea. All the oil, all the mercury and phosphates and waste, and the brooding atomic foulness crated in leaking concrete: no wonder the sea is dying.

And I can see huddles of krill in scarlet encrustations round the bases of rocks in the sea. Doomed, because the tide is going out. Doomed to join the dead masses on shore. Some are already stranded on the sand, unmoving, cooking in their armour.

My eyes sting with tears again.

This is silly, silly.

Why cry for crustaceans? Why cry for an inevitable end? I mean, who cries for me?

The beach is narrowing. Rocks block the end. They look rotten, fractured dark-green rocks, knobs and specks and splinters of them, in higgledypiggledy heaps.

But they have real shade and real shadows, and the wind is thwarted by them. Even the searacket is less. And they build in unsteady blocks, higher and higher. Vaults of them. A crooked cathedral.

The fire is fine damp sand. The sea has retreated from here. It feels peculiarly clean.

The walls are greenly wet, almost translucent, like chrysoprase.

The seanoise is muted. The air is still.

I love this kind of peace.

If I could shush the voices, shush the sounds, the last whimper, the talk and recriminations and my own drawnout anguish, still the noise of the badgering living, the crying of the dead; if I could make a cathedral of peace, a retreat in my head . . .

But I am aware that withdrawal is madness. You don't have to tell me that.

When I open my eyes, having rested a little in the cool of this cave, I see there are swarms of mussels on the wall. Crusts of them, blueblack and shiny as though varnished.

There is the occasional stranger mussel in their midst, pale green, like a wraith of a mussel. Pallid, obvious, vulnerable. There is never another palegreen mussel closeby for company.

The different, the abnormal, the alien, the malformed.

Who – or what – selects a person for the torment of difference?

Do you know the sensation of pondering deeply on something – and suddenly falling into nothingness?

Something tickles the back of my neck.

A fly?

Suddenly they are everywhere, hordes of kelpflies, a monstrous swarm rising from the walls descending from the roof swirling in humming spirals everywhere. I batter my hands against the buzzing air.

I may have yelled.

K asks,

'All well?'

His voice is deep, concerned.

My breath catches in my throat.

'Of course.'

He smiles, a ready compassionate smile, a little too smooth to have come from the heart.

'Of course,' he answers.

He draws nearer.

'I've come to see the caves. And you?'

'I had come to see the caves.'

My voice is cool and steady, a pleasure to my ears.

'Good,' he says. 'They're a neat set of caves.'

He draws back again and disappears round the seaward end of the cave. I hadn't realized the cave went further. There is a conical thrusting rib of rock, at the far end a flying buttress carved by sea and wind. Beyond it is water, stirred by the tide.

I go forward. The seanoise beats on me, and the wind pierces my smile.

There is nothing but a shallow eddy of the incoming tide in the next cave.

In the third cave, K waits.

He grins from the rock he is perched on. He looks bulky and cramped on top of the rock.

'Well, do you like our caves?'

'Is this the last of them?' My voice is still cool, still steady, despite the ache and the waves in my head.

He waves a hand vaguely south.

'There's another one beyond, same sort of thing. Besides, you can't get to it now. Tide's too high.'

He bends his head, his smile lost. He doesn't appear surprised that I didn't answer his first question. The seanoise seems somehow louder however. Then,

'Are you all right?' he asks.

Do you know that inane joke, Are you all right? No, I'm half left? It skips through my mind but I say,

'Pardon?'

'You've seemed a little, ahh a little, *tense* these few weeks you've been with us. I've been wondering if something's wrong?'

It is the inevitable. The invitation to tell. To betray.

O, I know they must have gossiped back in the staff room. I know the year gap in my record must look peculiar. I have been prepared, almost, for this question ever since I arrived. But to have it put now, not in the clean bright confines of a university office, but in a shadowed cave with the sick and dangerous sea running close by!

I cannot see any way out.

I say my lie, quickly and finally:

'A very good friend of mine died in sad circumstances. It

upset me a good deal. I was under a doctor's care for some time.'
It doesn't work.

'And now?' asks K.

I am silent.

'And now?' asks K.

I press my hands together as hard as they can go.

'And, now?' he questions yet again.

I don't want to. I dontwanto, it blurts out, it's not me.

'O God I didn't mean to, it was puerperal insanity, she died by
her own hand.' A small eternal silence. 'I mean, we had lived
together happily for years, and then she had to go and have a
baby. It was, it was, it wasn't born right. She killed it. Then she
killed herself. They said it was puerperal insanity.' I am shaking
again, my voice is shaking with my body. 'It was a long time ago,
nearly two years, but it comes back to me. I am sorry. I try. I
shall never get over it.'

The wind drops slowly, its voice moaning down to extinction.
The sea is conspiratorially silent.

His head stays bent. He remains on the rock, stolid and still.
He says at last,

'I am very sorry. We knew there was, ahh some tragedy, but
we had no idea you see?'

'It is past.'

Only my hands are shaking now.

'You have had help?'

'Yes.'

'And you think you can get over it?'

'Yes.'

He climbs down from his rock and I step back. He will touch
me in sympathy and I

but he says

calmly

'If you need someone to help, anyone to talk to, I am here. We
are here,' softly, impulsively, compassionately. More compassionately than anything I have ever had said to me in my life.

Then he walks swiftly round the rocks into the other caves.
A wave rushes over my feet.
The tide is coming in fast.

It is nearly all lies of course.
I have been alone for most of my life.
And those nine months were horror afterwards.
Why do I tell this expedient set of lies? Why do I live a lie,
portray a lie, many lies?
Because the chaos, the turbulence, the shadowhorror is too
terrible a ruin and reality to inflict on anyone. To tell the truth
about – NO!
If I explain with an acceptable melodrama, my frumpiness
becomes an ally, my pallid composure a refuge. My alien self, a
focus for pity and understanding.

UNDERSTANDING!!!
I rage. The rage shakes me harder, harder, harder,
harderharderharder then convulsively to stillness.
If there had been a long period of peace and stillness after,
nothing would have happened, you see.
The physical point to mention at this stage is, not only was I
still very cold, but also I was so tense that if someone had
dropped me I would have exploded.

There's a moon pale as gauze in the blue noon sky.
On the barbecues, the steaks drip fat. The fire smokes and
sizzles and spits. Rustle and confusion as food and utensils are
laid out. Clink of bottle to glass, and the laughter grows louder.
The bloodstained paper that wrapped the meat lifts and shifts in
the wind.
They talk casually, staff scandal and academic gossip. I am
kindly included. The looks are discreet; the assumption, I will
prefer pitying silence.
I am safe, for a while.
I nod, and I smile.
I know my nod is stiff, and my smile frosty and distant.
They are all sure they understand. The very air reeks of

sympathy. It sifts through the talk like the burnt offering smell from the charred steak, which we are forced to inhale.

Why should I be so contemptuous?

They did their best, invited me out, invited me in. It's not their fault I don't fit.

And as for understanding . . . I don't understand.

I gave up understanding after the terrible gush of blood, after the final silence, after the weakening into darkness when all I could think was an internal gibberish.

The deed accomplished and my hands incarnadine have wreaked their mercy and all the sick sea shall fail now fail now fail now, this last pollution original sin and worst.

I gave up understanding after the wailing 'Owhydidyous?' had chanted themselves into quiet oblivion, after the slow slow settling back into a kind of normality. A normality of chaste lies. The mask face and the shadow chase of lies.

And I still don't understand.

I go for another walk on the beach after lunch, trying to feel warm, to feel at ease. I wander the high tide line of the beach, watching the sand, gazing at the sea debris. Snail shells. Giant cockles and clams – do they call them quahogs here? Bleached bones and things so worn by time and sea they could be anything. The broken husks of crabs.

And everywhere the krill.

The laughter of the others is very far away.

I look back once.

They are gathered in a group at the far end of the beach.

I cannot see what they are doing.

I turn back to my perusal of the dead and the broken.

It began as an uneasy feeling, as though something unfriendly was watching the back of my neck.

I couldn't understand why I should feel this disturbance.

When I looked up I understood.

It was the kite.

It is the kite, high above my head, a hard electric-blue intruder. A threat.

It sways easily on the end of its strings, as though it knows it could be free of them at will, free to hunt and kill.

Did not the kites feast on the flesh of the dead?

Did not the Parsees build the Towers of Silence to invite the kites to their feast?

The sand squeals risibly, a sharper tone than I have heard from it before. I glance down. The shadow sleeks by. The tail whips past my cheek.

I have crouched, my hands shielding my head before I am aware I have done so.

Before I can rationalise it, and think, 'It's all right, it's just the kite that's fallen.'

It had stopped so fast!

And already it is back in the sky. It swings back and forth in an ominous aerial jig.

I am pinned for a moment, still crouched, like a rabbit under the scream of a hawk. Then I straighten slowly, my heart athud.

The kite above me wavers. Then it dives, striking the ground inches from my heels.

I look at the fallen thing, plastic and string. I look along the beach.

A child holds the distant ends of the strings, standing there gaudy as a toadstool, poisonous in its laughter.

The adults are laughing too, I know.

It is like being an automaton. I can approach them freely, smiling, can joke even, with equanimity.

Smiles all round, and a lot of heartiness and high laughter and backslapping.

They invite me to take the strings, and make a game of it. And I am still smiling as they scatter up the beach, all of them, the toadstool child as well.

They rush into kite territory, eager prey.

The sun has wheeled round a little. It is late afternoon.

The sky is still a striking blue, though black clouds lower over the rim of tamed and manbarren hills.

It is the lowering clouds that make me feel that this is an arena. I am minded of plays, of theatre. Of a starkly-set opera involving gladiators and death.

The sky is painted blue.

The hills are fake.

The wind comes from a machine.

And we are protagonists in an ancient and misunderstood drama.

Yet now, holding the kite-strings, I am exultant. I didn't know I could still feel this alive. My blood has secret fires, and they are soaring, spiring through me. The kite has a voice, and it is speaking.

I can feel the sand sinking under my feet, the hem of my dress whipping the backs of my legs, and my teeth are so chilled the fillings in them ache. But these things are immaterial. They cannot dim my rising ecstasy.

I know the lethal bird above me is really insentient plastic, frail fibreglass rods, lengths of string.

I know that, and it doesn't matter. It isn't real knowledge.

The truth and beauty is: the vibrant strings are my hands and the way I now look, out of the kite's eyes.

Down there, they are dancing, M and K and D and C, and all their mocking children. They think it is their game.

I am laughing, I am laughing, laughter that has been absent for a year. For all my life.

I am the beautiful killer. The strings are tingling sinews, and I am singing through the kite.

I know I can dive down through any one of their dancing brittle skulls.

We dip and soar and wheel and skim.

We drive them in a frantic scattering pack.

We sleek over their heads, and they dive screaming joy to the sand.

They applaud our skill wildly.

We whirl and we spiral. It is effortless. Coming near, speeding up and away amid all the gay retreating shrieks; sweeping down and brushing by with a smirking kiss of death.

With the forty-mile push of the wind, a fibreglass rod turns iron beak, and plastic and string make a griffin's skin.

And there she now runs giggling, the toadstool child. Hair an innocent halo, shining in the sun, and below it, the dark mark flaunted indecently . . . we swoop, and she shrieks with delighted laughter.

Ascend
    steady:
and we stoop.

Struck between the shoulder blades, she falls.

And then it is black night and we are breaking apart forever.

There are shouts and cries in the distance, and people running.

The dark clouds spill over, and the air is suddenly full of fine weeping mist.

I am numb now, so cold, so dulled.

They have grown strangely silent, along there, but I cannot let go the dead strings.

The silence grows with the fog, blotting out even the whimpering wind.

The sea is holding its breath.

The krill are dying, dying.

The hopelessness of the pallid mussels forever cloistered apart.

The endlessly crying sand.

And ah, my dark dark room . . .

Have I told you anything?
Has it meant anything to you?
Or is it all just writing?
All just words?

UNNAMED ISLANDS IN THE UNKNOWN SEA

[*The Contents:*

damned dear. In the last crazy hours before you died, I saw sights through your eyes, sealions tombstoning, albatrosses with weary hearts, eggs with pink yolks. Now I am myself alone again, I must balance what I saw with what I know surrounds me. This reality before the next.

1: the overhang. It juts like the prow of any ship but is massive. It broods over me. One day it will fall but I do not fear that. It has anciently hung here – remember the bones? Moa you said, and I believe that. They were old old bones, so old the rats hadn't bothered them.

2: the pile of seaweed at the left end. I have rewoven it, more tightly. It makes a ragged screen.

3: your sleeping bag. I washed it, beat it against the rock until all your sweated pain & foulness fled. It is nearly dry. I have rolled it, so it serves me as a backrest. I am undecided whether to sleep in it tonight. I think I might.

4: the rocky floor. It slopes towards the sea. Did it never strike you as odd? The roof rears heavenward and all our floor tries to slip away from us, downwards, outwards, away.

5: the fire – o yes. I haven't let it go out. Even if I go swimming, I want it there to look back to. I feed it dried kelp butts, and twigs from the mikkimik and detritus from the moon, feathers and sundried bladders and a piece of polystyrene float.

6: twelve mussels in their shells. They are placed in an arc by my feet. They make small popping and hissing sounds, as though they had minute mouths that cared to suck air. Kissing sounds. They are tea.

Then there is me clad in my despair & wet clothes; my raw feet; your weatherbeaten seabattered notebook. My notebook. My pen. I hope to God it doesn't run out.

(As you were ultimately your last clear analytic words, so I shall be these pages. And maybe they will be found by someone who doesn't understand, who doesn't read English even, or just can't be bothered reading such stained and faded script, and so burns them. As I burned those poor brown remnants of moa, which had maybe stored all the song of its living in those bones. Did moas sing?)

I have eaten the mussels. Thin meat, mussels. Even the peacrabs don't add much more than crunch. And I used to love them, mussels succulent on a scrubbed shining navy shell, topped with garlic butter or richly robed in melted cheese –

Better to remember Day 2, my feet already butchered by those bloody rocks, and me despairing because you couldn't keep the mussels or limpets down and that was all I could gather. And suddenly the waves flung a fish on the beach. It flopped weakly, one flank deeply gashed – a couta you said. I managed to hit it on the head – indeed hit with a savagery I didn't know inhabited me.

Cooking mussels and limpets had been easy – arrange them carefully in the embers and let them toast. But that red cod? Easy, you said. You sounded very tired, and you were huddled over. That seaweed, that bullkelp? Get some thickish fronds off it and split them and stick the cod inside. Never mind the guts.

You kept down the soft flesh. But it wasn't enough. Maybe it worsened matters.

I can't remember the order of days after Day 2. It could be as long as 9 days I've been here.

Sometimes during the nights – 10? 8? – sometimes during the nights we saw lights far out at sea. Distant ships perhaps, though some grew at a strangely fast rate and others stayed abnormally steady, beacons through the night, winking out at dawn. *We* saw lights? The only time you showed awareness of any of them was that night the waves danced, alive with phosphorescence. Porotitiwai, you whispered, porotitiwai, and I never thought to ask you what that means.

Do you know I have always been scared of the sea? Don't laugh. It is remorseless. There is no humanity in it.

You would have laughed at that.

I am cold and smoked and damp and so alone that I feel all the rest of the world has deliberately gone home, leaving me in the dark. I miss your laughter. O God I miss the way your arms felt either side of me as you paddled. A jaunt you said. Only thirty k to that island, and look at the sea. Flat as a pancake. I can get us there and back between dawn and dusk, hell I've paddled Cook Strait! And to my demur you said Think! No-one's set foot on that island for bloody years! Now that's a story! And then added, your eyes full of a wicked glinting glee, That's if you came to get a story and not just see me.

I said very primly that I Am A Journalist Albeit Freelance, and a story was what I came for, and writing about scruffy field assistants cutting transects won't sell *anywhere*, so lead on MacDuff. McLeay actually, you said. From the whisky actually.

This is pointless. The rats'll eat it.

Who's going to come looking for a freelance peripatetic journo?

I don't want to say what bottle I have sent out on the waves –

I used to love reading about islands as a child. Being ship-wrecked on one would be heaven. You'd use the materials from your wrecked ship, and feast on the island's provender, and finally when it was getting a little boring, you'd light an enormous bonfire which would hail a passing cruise ship and you'd sail happily home a better and a richer man.

God knows when I heard the plane I tried. I grabbed anything I thought would burn and a piece of smouldering kelp and rushed out on the halfmoon of gravel that is the only beach. And the drizzle made everything sodden. The fire was only smoke and a few sullen flickers of flame. Desperate – o how *weak* that reads! – *desperate!* I would have burnt my hair had it been longer, I would have fed my clothes to those flames if they hadn't been wetter than the driftwood! I raced back under the overhang and grabbed my sleeping bag and folded it round the smoulder. I prayed. My feet ached so much from the running I cried. The plane droned away and as it got further and further towards the horizon the sleeping bag suddenly flared into a glorious bonfire. Nobody saw it. Just me.

It has been silent since then, if anywhere near the sea is silent. There were silences before. You would say something, mainly a coherent few sentences –

'Do you know they shake penguins out of their skins before they eat them? Catch them underwater and surface with them and shake 'em so viciously quick that the bird flies out of its skin. Then the leopard seal dines.'

Up until these few days ago I had never *heard* of a leopard seal.

I wanted to ask more but you had closed your eyes and there was another silence that lasted all night.

The days are silent too, mainly. At least, the first few – 3? 4? – days. Your belly blackens. The haematoma spreads up to your collar-bones. You bleed to death inside but it all takes silent time. At least, mainly silent.

You start to curl up, going from sitting-up huddle, to lying-down hunch. And as you curl slowly into your beginning shape, you want me to see some other island. You talk against the unremitting pain.

It was a harsh place, this island you loved. A bleak volcanic terrain, sere and disordered. Some subantarctic place where the waters teemed with whitepointers and the winds never ceased.

There was mist around our island, closing the world down to just our size.

It was either cliff or swamp, you said, but we had hardwood-plant tracks and so could walk through the headhigh tussock. We could walk past the peat bogs. But if you went off the planks you got quickly lost in the draco . . . and you'd come to a cairn where there was maybe a body underneath, as though the cairn called you. Or arrive at a still inland tarn and there, deep in the water, was an unrusting tripot. We'd been there, people had been there, lots of people, but the land felt *unlived on* and somehow, it wanted people living on it, people as well as the elephant seals and the sealions and the skuas and the albatross.

This Godforsaken rock, *this* island is lived on. It doesn't want us. It already has rats and shags and the mikkimik. The rats live on the shags and each other I think. Presumably the shags live off the sea. They aren't nesting at the moment. The adult birds shuffle but they shuffle faster than I can limp. And the guano burns my feet horribly.

You said weakly, The wind is in my ears.

It is so still outside. The mist hides even the sea.

There is always the wind you say, and nearly always the rain or the snow. 90 knot winds . . . I used to worry about the birds. And how did the cattle stand it? That small shotabout fearful herd – did they crouch into the gullies, die finally in the peaty bogs?

It was then your breathing changed.

Between gasps you say, 'Sometimes there is an unnatural quiet, a threatening calm, as the wind holds still for an hour, deciding its next quarter.'

O God he can't have spoken like that. It got hard. The blood on his lungs. I can do nothing, could do nothing. Collect limpets and mussels and stew the juice out of them and have it ready in the thermos flask so when he is ready he can sup soup. The mist pools on the rocks. We have water. The mist makes it hard to breathe. My own lungs are husking.

But your lungs are heaving in and out harnh harnh every hard intake, the sound pitching higher and higher until you are screaming –

I stay outside for the screaming –

remember thinking, But I screamed too. I screamed, What was it? What *was* it? We lay in a tangle a crush in the froth on shore. You had just laughed and pulled the right side of the paddle down hard. 'Landing!' you yelled. And then the sea lurched. Something sleek and bulky and sinuous, a grey fast violent hulk punched into the kayak punched past me into you fled past us into the onshore surf. I screamed What *was* it? until you had caught your breath. You grunted, 'Leopard seal. Wanted to get out to sea. We were in the way.' You grinned. Your last grin. 'We probably scared it to hell.'

None of the kayak has washed ashore.

I can do nothing now. I fold myself beside you and hold your hand. You say, the screaming finished, the breathing nearly finished, you say in that tired hoarse whisper,

'At new moons there are bigger currents than normal. Huge shoals of fish are swept close inshore. The sharks feed hard. Sometimes they will get in amongst a group of Hooker sealions that are also feeding hard. And then you will see the sealions tombstone – bodies rigid in the water, heads sticking straight out, while the white pointers circle and threaten and crazily decide whether to take one or to take all. They can't take all. Islands don't work like that.'

And somehow I am behind your eyes and I see the cliffs that arrow out of the grey seas to terminate in mean blade edges. I see the sheep, feral Drysdales gone surefooted like goats, gaze fearlessly down on climbing humans. I see the albatross effortfully trudge over a ridge down to the hollow where its chick roosts safely out of the wind. I see it feed the chick. I see a skua pluck a pink-yolked penguin's egg and then hungrily cruise on. I see it take the albatross's chick, a limpnecked vulnerable downy sac. I see the albatross halfway down the ridge, watch; then turn and stagger back up to the top of the ridge and launch into the wind.

And then suddenly the shags outside wave their snaky necks and shoot stinking excrement onto the rocks.

And there is no-one behind your eyes.

But you did say, watching the sad lumbering albatross, you did say, because I heard you there behind your eyes,

'Don't be afraid. We are all islands but the sea connects us, everyone. Swim.'

And I had enough heart and mind left to laugh at a swimming island as you died.

I gave you to the sea. I rolled you down the sloping floor onto a quartermoon of gravel and let the sea take you. The waves toyed with your beautiful black hair, the waves toyed with your scarred strong hands. Then they too rolled you over and swam you out of sight.

I have given my message to the sea, my bottle, my message. It is unbearable.]

[*The Notebook from the Unnamed Island off Breaksea Sound:*

It is a standard field notebook, issue item 1065, 18 cm × 13 cm, black elastic closure band, 46 double pages lined each side, and divided by a midpage column, with red, waterstained, covers. The standard issue pen is missing from the side holder. The last 10 pages, and the first 2 pages, have been torn out.

The notebook was found inside a plastic sandwich container (Tupperware, item CT 106), which had been wrapped in a light down sleeping bag ('Camper,' manufactured by Arthur Ellis, Dunedin). The sleeping bag, which had been extensively damaged by rats, was found tucked in the far corner on the overhang described in 'Contents'.

There was no other sign of human intervention or habitation on the island.]

[*Conclusion:*

Many people have speculated on the identity of the writer of this notebook since its recovery by two crew members from the fishing boat 'Motu' (Dunedin registration 147 DN). The unnamed 'you' may be Jacob Morehu, a field assistant employed by the DSIR on Resolution Island during the recent blue penguin (Eudyptula minor) counts. Two possible indicators for this identification are:
Morehu was employed during the '84 season on Campbell Island (by the DSIR), and
Morehu disappeared shortly before the now-infamous Skinned Body corpse was discovered at Goose Cove. (Morehu is not implicated. He was an ardent kayak enthusiast, and his kayak vanished at the same time. The area round Breaksea Island is marked 'reputed dangerous' on all charts, and this pertains to the unnamed small island beyond.)

However, it is much more probable the notebook is an obscure joke perpetrated by a person or persons unknown. The indicators for this conclusion, which is that of the Department, are:

a] *nobody else* was reported missing from the *entire South Island* at the time Morehu went missing;

b] the 'Skinned Body' was almost certainly murder, and is thought to have been committed by the eccentric gunship shooter, Mike Corely, who fell into the notorious giant eel tarn in Fiordland National Park two days before the body was discovered;

c] nobody has explained satisfactorily to me why two sleeping bags should be taken on what is described as a *day-trip* in a kayak. A plastic container of sandwiches, yes, but two light sleeping bags suitable only for indoor use?]

STATIONS ON THE WAY TO AVALON

The City

In late autumn, when the sandglass has been set and polished, the pigkiller comes. May is always pigkilling time.

They thunder up the covered way, trotters beating a sharp tattoo.

'Don't kick them, you'll spoil the hams.'

They are already food. But they keep on going, stumbling up the planks, complaining, snorting, complaining.

At the top, the pigkiller waits, with weighted shovel knife.

'Tickets from Wellington, all tickets please.'

He stops by me. I knew he would.

'You just got on mate?'

'No, you collected my ticket as I came in the door.'

He doesn't believe me. They never do.

'Can I see your ticket.'

'Yeah, here it is. That's your punchmark, right?'

He sneers silently, smart arse, banging his chrome puncher on the seat edge before turning away.

The drop opens again. The pig carcass falls.

The drop opens again. The pig carcass falls.

The drop opens again. The pig

Kaiwharawhara

Walking in the city sunshine . . . or is it suburb sunshine? Somewhere sunshine, weak, pallid, breathless. I mean, I can never get a decent breath of it. I gulp in great lungfuls, and they are somehow less gassy. What gas? A satisfying gas. A necessary gas. It isn't here in the city. Lacklife city.

There's another white dropping. Do they feed the dogs on

bones alone? There's another stunted tree. The leaves are gasping.

I'll soon come to the long driveway. Start another day. Or night. Sitting in the director's seat. Placing stopwatch, cigarettes, and script in line. The vision switcher's got a sniffle, the t.p.'s got a cold.

I massage my forehead and contemplate the bank of bare, bank of blank screens.

O the hams are always juicy, pink, saltsweet.

We hang them from the rafters – not to add to the smoky flavour, but because they have always swung there. It is the custom. Season in, season out, the hams will swing on. And as the end of autumn draws closer, we start to eat the sweet pink meat. Reach up and carve me a wet slice, m'dear, and I'll have it here with my soup.

'Okay, all lined up and ready to go.' The t.p. sniffs thickly.

'Thanks Mike. Can I have a midshot on three . . . who's on three?'

'David here.'

One and two chime in, 'Mary on one', 'Evening Robert, Trev ready and waiting on two'.

'Hello Mary, David and Trev . . . okay, midshot three please, exclude his belt buckle if you can help it.'

I talk too much. I know it. It's deliberate though. I believe in keeping a barrage of sound going over the cans. Linking everyone with my words.

I'm glad to learn it's evening. For a minute, walking, I wasn't sure. You know how it can be, sterile Wellington streets with their calcified dog turds and stunted trees.

The time gets away.

The time gets away.

Adrian is efficient. She should be the director, not me. She even prompts two of my cuts. Still, we get through. That's the main thing, getting through. Surviving it. You see, it's the tension. It never lets up in the control room. You can swivel round in the plastic padded seats, you can smoke until your throat is burned, you can gnaw your nails to the elbows, but it never lets up.

I don't think so anyway.

I don't know.

'I beg your pardon?'

'What?'

'Well, it's hardly an answer to say I don't know. I mean, you either know you're going or you know you're not. Or is it contingent upon some dire possibility?'

Smart bitch. She should be the director, not me.

Have I said that before?

Ngauranga

There are one hundred, thirty, and nine steps up this particular flight to the Terrace.

Each one of them would prefer I didn't stand on it.

The ferns some inept council worker has planted are dying from windburn. There's planty of weeds surviving. Thriving. Trust weeds to thrive in the city though.

There is nothing in my mailbox. The dead cat is still lying outside in the gutter. I expect it will stink soon. It's been there for three days now, and no one seems to know what to do with it.

The woman in the flat next door has her eye to the crack as I go by. The house is full of bad gas and must and something damp. It chokes me.

I wave to the crack.

I think it must be late.

Today I found a slater. Nothing odd in that, not in damp flats, but this one had been crawling round about the polished cold steel bottom of my saucepan. I wonder how long it seemed before all the pale legs gave out?

I was going to make a Chinese meal. I have the real noodles, and imported mushrooms, a genuine soy sauce, and a collection of vegetables. Now I don't feel like eating, so watch a sunbeam trail across the wall.

Petone

A young lankhaired man goes past, blowing on his fingernails – he has nicotine stains on his forefingers – and eyeing me sideways. It's not that late yet, is it?

And I do know it's not a working day. It's my weekend now, the way they split and carve our weeks. I know for certain. I could hear the woman in the flat next door clapping as the news finished. I mean, she claps the end of every programme, for praise or relief or something, but the difference was that the news was coming over. I sometimes direct the news, when a production officer is shortlisted, and if the news came through . . . where was I?

The news did come through today. And I have a letter from my love, wrapped in oilskin and sealed with the impress of that well-known ring. I saw her first in summer, while we were gathering the cutty sand, and we lay down in the long grass at the back of the hill. And she said, 'Lie with me. Run your tongue down my honey length. Flick and needle me, wheedler you', closing her eyes. Bronze lashes quivering. The cream grasses quiver, sway in the wind. The bed is whitened yarrow, rank, rank as a wet dog, but sweet to me now.

And the sea then was as variable as an opal, aquamarine and ultramarine and a strange pale lucid cream, with a bloom dark as a black grape near the horizon. Then a cloud shifted, and the colours flickered, shark green now, and thick blue, and a far colour near primrose.

'All tickets from Lower Hutt, tickets from Lower Hutt please.'

He stops by me. I knew he would.

'Ticket please mate.'

'You punched my ticket at Lower Hutt.'

He doesn't believe me: they never do.

Sneering again as he goes away again.

Or is this today and I'm imagining a past?

She did say, 'When winter comes, and the hunt begins, we will hunt together.' She *did* say it, for I saw the light spring from the sea and the whole turn diamond clear.

'And what luverly sight do I see? Him, casting his tea out in the sink. Sick as a cat . . . what the hell happened to you last night, Robert?'

'Me?' laying out the stopwatch, the cigarettes, the script, 'I wasn't on.'

'According to Ken you were on all right. Adrian had to take it through. There wasn't another bloody director around.'

'Look, I'm positive I wasn't on last night. I know . . .'

'What the hell, we haven't got time to worry.' Turning to Jan the switcher, 'We can manage fine without the wanker anyway.'

They think I don't hear.

'Give us the word when cameras are ready, Mike.'

They are running a strange film down from telecine. It flickers through the preview monitors, and I can almost see the pictures coming up before they come up. Do you know what I mean?

It's like being able to focus each eye separately on two different screens, each screen showing the same film, but say the left eye, or screen showing it about forty frames ahead.

'Robert, the presenter is wondering when the hell you're going to cue him . . .' Hisss. I hiss back. 'Ta Adrian . . .' (louder) . . . 'Three, tighten that MCU to a closeup, aannnd cue!'

There are two drunks on the late train home. I hear a cleaning woman at the station say, 'Imagine what it does to me, coming in every morning and seeing all this chunder lying round.'

Morning?

Melling

As soon as the bar opens, I go in.

I don't keep drink in the house. I think the woman next door has a key to my flat. I have carefully put pencil marks – o they're so fine, just skimming a needlesharp pencil across the very edge of the label so she couldn't notice them – on the bottle, and I can *see* quite clearly that she has been having a drink. So no more.

I am a careful drinker myself.

The amber green, and green solo, and the tawny: a hundred pipers and a pirate, and a serene white horse. Trinklets glint. Salt crystals on my chips throw light, and stranger drinks throw stranger lights. Rely only on golden drinks, golden light. Bronze light, to be specific. The nearest colour I have seen to it, is that glimmer you get in land octopi eyes.

We have finished the clean-up of the Far Block, and there is a drove of octopi, squatting, all wound together, by the fence. Their eyes are round, and that golden. Almost golden, and their leathery sheeny skins have a golden lustre. Almost golden. Soon the clubbing will start. It's a pity. I mean, I had an octopus as a pet when I was a child, and it was as tame and intelligent as any dog. But their beaks are poison for the pigs, and besides, there is some kind of alliance between them and the great sand dwellers.

'Another? Yes pleassse . . .' Then I really must get something to drink. I mean, eat. I haven't eaten since my Chinese meal. The one with a slater in it. There was a slater in the pot.

The Settlement isn't far away.

There's a small earthquake going on, but they happen all the time in this city. In this sick pale greenygrey slum of ill people and smoke and dusty memory. But how can they expect to get well if they can't breathe properly? I know. I ache for good air, and no-one lets me breathe.

The Settlement is full. I was meeting someone here? O yes, Adrian the production secretary . . . I said the other night I'd be coming. But I don't think I can push my way in here . . .

Up the 139 steps to the Terrace, then.

An old woman mumbles by the gutter. The child cries next door. The dead cat's gone. The night is cold, foreboding frost, and a dog pisses by the lamp post, sour sharp sting of smell and hiss and yellow for the frost to bite and turn to a solid treachery of a puddle . . . like ice melting, slipping into nothing, the child's crying dies. The old woman snivels. She's mad as a meat-axe, they say.

Why do they say that?

A meat-axe is a razor weapon, generous in its flaring shape, honed and well-hafted. I have one in brown paper now, in my cupboard. Its sheathed keenness is a comfort. This hallway is too dark you see, and I have never been easy about eyes that watch from cracks. If only the smell weren't so old! If only a freshness, of flowers, of cleaning, even the breath of the wind, would sweep away the stale stale stale air, and we could all breathe.

Ava

The stations are brown . . . is it fumes from passing trains? The sickness of the oily air? The railway track is brown as well, and the dying trees that sometimes line, they come and go in flashes, sometimes line the way coated with brownness.

'Hutt . . . all tickets from Lower Hutt please, all tickets.'

He stops by me. I knew he would.

'Your ticket, thanks.'

'You've checked it once already.'

He doesn't believe me. They never do.

Why don't they believe me? He fingers the ticket like he'd like to break it, or break me, or just break a window, or derail the train. He nearly throws it back.

The main Tower block has all the windows drawn on this, the sunward side. Now that the frost has melted, it's turning a ripe warm day.

Where am I on? O yeah, quite a good set-up. Edit half a film, rather watch an editor do it, and then upstairs to suite three and get it dubbed. 'What did you think of the earthquake last night?' I'm quite pleased I remember that. It makes for conversation.

The editor peers round at me.

'Earthquake? I didn't feel any earthquake last night . . .'

I shrug.

'Probably the day before.' The booth door opens.

'Ken wants to see you when we've finished this.'

Very efficient, Adrian, but she does have this tendency to look after everyone else's business.

Not like my melting bronze lady Kareth du Vree as the frames flicker faster and the sound gabbles sighs.

Woburn

I set out again on a bright cruel morning.

And here I set out cigarettes, stopwatch there, script *here*.

Ken says coldly, leaning over me so I can smell his peppermint breath,

'You are twenty minutes late. The crew has been waiting for twenty minutes. They were all on time. I will see you after you have finished. And for Godssake stop fumbling and get started.'

So I roll a tidy wooden show while all their eyes flicker secrets, back and forth when they think I'm not looking. So I stop looking. I stopped looking consciously at the dog-droppings and surprised myself this morning by noticing they had vanished. Been ground to paste by the frost and washed down the gutters by the night rain, I suppose. But now, in place after place, there are flattened wads of chewing-gum glued to the asphalt. And on Woburn station someone dropped and trampled their fish'n'chips to pasty white greasiness.

'Lose it', mechanically, 'standby theme, ready on one?' a slight juggle onscreen, she's ready, 'roll theme and cut!' Jan has cut just before I say it. 'Fade to black,' and what the hell.

Adrian lolls back in her chair. She picks up my packet of smokes. 'Shit, it's your last one . . .'

'Take it. I've got a headache.'

She smiles, eyes down.

'I'd have one too, if I were you. Ta for the smoke,' grabbing her bag, and heading for the door.

I would weep if I could.

But she despises tears. When I wept for the throat cut so young so young to die a struggling red gush and shower but winter must be brought in, she, she turned away. She reached a hand to my neighbour, slipped it under the fur of his sporran. He shivers, then laughs. The gold vine leaves pinned to his cloak clink with his shivering. I know those cold busy hands, but think, but think: feeding liquid gold to living vine until its cells suffocate, its veins run sluggish slower blocked forever . . . they looked only briefly at me, long at each other.

Ken's door is still shut, and it is dark outside.

Waterloo

'Your tickets from Hutt, Lower Hutt, ladies and gentlemen perlease!' Warm and cheery to emphasise the cold. The humorist.

He stops by me. I knew he would.

But it is as if he were changing step. A brief halt, and then he swings away up the carriage.

It muddles me all the long climb home. He has obviously mistaken me for someone else. That someone will be asked for his ticket instead. A bad mistake for all concerned.

The door closes softly, but the eyebeam was there.

I am glad I hid my blade safely. Tucked behind the switchboard, where snoopers cannot spy it. In case, in case.

Epuni

We have lifted the last haulm of potatoes, split and salted the last net of herrings. The work of the seasons is done. All is in readiness, and winter is brought in.

You can hear their moaning on the distance at night now. A deep pitch of sorrow. They talk as they travel the sand, an unfathomable language of tears.

The dogs that meet on a Wellington street are noticeably nose to nose. They share their breaths and so survive on a diet of air. We have stopped handing out the bones.

It is cold, cold, cold.

The trees shrink further, huddling in on themselves as the frost wages war on sap.

I have a scarf that touches my lower eyelids, my hat over my ears, gloves to muffle my fingers, and I wish for a cloak.

'I wish we wore cloaks . . .'

'I said, your ticket *mate.*'

He doesn't mean friend.

And my god ticket . . .

'Urrr.'

'Eighty-one cents', hard hand out. His eyes are shining are avidly shining under the visor of his cap.

My stomach hurts. I can hear rustles and furtive giggles. Everyone is looking. The carriage windows steam as they hide back behind their papers and their books and their hands. I give him a dollar keepthechange *please* keep the change. But he sorts out cents and more cents with slow gloating deliberation.

And each stop after he comes past me and slowly smiles.

And midway through, on air, there is pop! and a blank black screen where two's scene should be.

And juggling shots to no avail, two's blown a tube/I need one for the credits/standby one/wide three shot god lose the lights! ok just a bloody three shot then/start panning three/ready one and cut/the cans are thick with chatter with swears and we have the presenter gawping like a fish before he's cued again and even then no credits.

And we apologise.

And we apologise.

The t.p. says coolly, 'Robert, I think you had better go home.'

'I don't feel well.'

'I think you had better go home.'

The miles of corridor, orange carpet, green carpet. Miles of silence.

We gather the mushrooms of celebration just before dawn. It is quiet and gentle, looking over the hills. No sand, and no moaning, for the hunt is a faraway tomorrow and it is a dawn of peace today. Silent walking, and amidst the sunlit spunglass fantasies of spiders, fungi like white brainlobes convoluting on the ground.

But she is holding his hand. I don't understand. She did say, by the late summer sea, that the hunting would be done, would be partnered by me. She said, she said.

Somebody has deposited excrement on the footpath past the steps.

I step in it.

Somebody had a quiet shit under the stars.

I step in it.

Somebody crapping here, careless as to who sees, who comes.

And I step in it.

Naenae

Nobody sees me on the train.

I offer him my ticket as he brushes past.

He doesn't see my hand.

Nobody sees me in the Tower block.

Nobody sees me in the Settlement.

A bowl of soup, and a coffee, all my poor hoard allows. Ersatz chicken soup, chicken-flavoured glue, and the coffee is luke-warm. The guitarist plays Recuerdos d'Alhambra when I whisper the name but I have no money to give him and cannot look in his eyes.

There are eyes all down the hallway and they are watching carefully. I smile.

My lovely blade is in peace, and no one sees where.

But when I open the door, the air is full of smoke and burning. . . but I didn't leave anything on? The mat is intact, there are no black walls . . . where is the fire?

Wingate

You're maybe standing on one, or be walking in the middle of a herd. There is nothing to show, nothing to see but the endless stretch of the sand. And then the sandwhales loom, serrated spines and vast hump heads and the far wraith flukes. And unless the axe is sharp and your swing exact your eyes will hold forever their sad terrible eyes softly glowing as you are overwhelmed. But sandwhales have people's faces. And they bleed like us, head and heart and hide.

'I'm sorry?'

'I said, you did want to go to the city?'

I sigh.

'The train stopped you see, and I got off before he came round. Because I think I can join the others even if she isn't partnered with me, you see. I know how, now.' I laugh a little because that sounds odd. He looks at me sideways, then slides his eyes away.

'Yes, the city', quickly.

He shrugs.

The black highway is rushing faster and our stillness doesn't matter. For the breath that remains in me is enough to get me home. It is enough to wield a steel swing. It is enough to shut my outside eyes, to stop the screen that shows the flickering city.

It is enough to reach through a door and still an eye, dry my heart and disclose the island of apples, the island of glass, the island of dreams.

Avalon

In winter we hunt sandwhales, and we keep our axes sharp . . .

A WINDOW DRUNKEN IN THE BRAIN

After seasons of leanness and disquiet
all the world has filled with stars you breathing and the rushing
sea and your taut adorable fingers closed in mine all you, next to
me
Pathetic
cliché
what can I say, what else? Moon and June and spoon. Everyone
has tried every word before. But o my dear it was your closeness
and the salt and the starlight . . .

and hopping home in the early morning in a kind of drunken glory
of giggles

_____

o man gone, where are you
man, gone?
no hand hold

and death
the skeleton
that skeleton hold

travelling travelling
down the grey roads
leading nowhere
going nowhere
world's end

no more handhold
man gone, gone
from me in shadow
no day no night
no tomorrow

The words sit dumbly on this page. I cannot read their meaning. I
do not believe I have written them. Who else would have written
them, in my hand?

'O you're home dear.'
'I'm home.'

Painted all the rooms white, ceilings, walls, skirtings, floors.
Papers everywhere to shield the pallid green shagpile. Painted
the cupboards white. Wished to paint the mirrors but didn't dare
close their eyes. Painted the doors. Whited sepulchres ha ha.
Tomb quietude. Playrooms for errant light, limitless rooms.

He laid the pauas in the fridge. Their gluey black feet, sucking
pods, shrunk a little in the drying cold. Wincing. They curled upon
one another's shells for comfort of a kind.
He shut the fridge door, quite gently.

'We'll make the pewa into sauce.'
Pewa?
'You'd say stomach, no, shellfish rectum.'
You know the silly joke my honey? Teacher to Johnny/what'd
you do in the holidays dear? Johnny to teacher/Stuck a cracker
up a frog's arse my it were fun when it went off! Teacher to
Johnny/you don't say arse dear you say rectum. Johnny to
teacher/Rectum? I'll say, it fucking near killed him
O dear

The cold kills the pauas' love, shell for humping shell.
He slits each one quickly out of its glory and gropes out the pewa
a fat green bow of an organ and slices out the thin toothy radula
and beats hell out of the maimed shrinking fish with the back of a
butcher's cleaver.
Then he dips each mutilation into egg, renders it steak, flings it
into crackling oil. Half a minute this side, half a minute that side,
and then whip it out and leave it to drain a little while. And then eat
love the fruit of the reef. And it is sweet and succulent and tender
beyond meat. And I trust, dead now.

I eat four rich paua steaks. Protein-bloated. Energyfat.

And then it is a tangle of beansprouts tender and delicately green.
Harmonious dressing; a thin oil and scraped ginger and crystals of
seasalt and a sliver of garlic. Tangy, crisp, living.

Then it is carrot sticks and slender cuts of celery stalks and long
slices of tender raw french beans and florets of broccoli washed in
bright salted water. And as he promised, pewa sauce, the green
fluid squeezed out of the sac and mixed with wine-thinned sour
cream.

Then it is a bluish spirituous grog I have never tasted or seen
before. Fiery and cool. Fierce on the tongue then insinuating
itself cool and assured of a welcome down the throat into the
stomach.

Then, at last, it is a peach. I drip the juice. The juice floods me.
The juice is both sweet and cunningly acidic. He licks the juice
off me, he licks it off. I finish the peach and suck long upon the
stone.

_____

We all know menus that are transports of lust/to love

_____

Eye to eye while the mouth swallows oysters and the minds
envisage other swallows wallowings lushness

_____

Have you ever drawn a stickman over a naked man's nipple
in champagne? Ran a lazy tongue over to erase it? Slopped
champagne onto the sheets and rubbed them heated them dry

_____

Robbing the reef by starlight. He is waistdeep in the foaming
cold. I am eeking but quietly by the snaky bullkelp. He
is silhouette and darkly wet. I am shivering and gathering
each sopping paua into the sack. Rough then gluey in the
hand.

_____

Those limy trails are worm-homes, he says. If they have not been
quick, you are standing on their eyes.

_____

Think:
a thousand times on the sandy beach, and I never once ventured
the reef

_____

Snakeskinned chiton and corroded wave-battered limpets
You can eat those too,
he says,
soup.

_____

O man long gone
snakey man

I do not write bluesy drivel/I write treatises, theses, I know all about Geotria australis, from ammocoetes to macrophthalmia to velasia to pouchy sexually mature adults

---

'Home early, dear.'
'Yes.'

The bitter clear green water.
Stark starlight.
The raw and salty seafood.
White rooms. White shells
You do not need the connotations made so clear.

Do I note here, the rough soft warmth of a homespun cloak? Who spun it for him? What spider woman? What spider man? The lichen colours of it: the broad bands ochre and yellow-orange and rusted brown and light green. How he drew off very carefully a single hair fallen from my head. Do I note the strong hands? The blunt nails? The ragged deliberately raggedly cut hair? The smirk, undisguised, proud, inviting. The full and beautiful lips. The taut buttocks, cleft outlined, the washed denim. Do I pander to your imagination? This is my farewell, my particular fenestration.
Drink your own.

I drink with my eyes. I am a sot with my mouth.

Once on the interisland ferry, I watched a man with a halo of black frizzly hair crooning to his baby, sucking baby, milky baby, literal baby. He held cradled the soft young skull in broad & kind & capable hands. He was so drunk he kept skating from foot to foot stumbling each time as he stood straight. His baby smiled and bubbled at him. Totally safe. Truly safe. I kept waiting for him to fall over. He kept crooning, stumbling.

Have left open a window. May the sunbeams skate in and lighten me, lighten all. That is trite. Sometimes, through the tangle of toitoi blocking this window light *will* filter through

I said I had never touched such things before, those sly teeming nuts in their wrinkled cosy pouch, and you grinned said softly 'Balls.'
Touching another body. Touching another being.

Life is made real by sudden surprises, sudden illuminating delightful surprises. A man who smiles at you in the dusk, smiles at you & your early wrinkles & indoor pallor. Who takes your hands and leads you out onto a new reef full of danger, full of crevices that hold shocks and creatures that suffer cringe retreat become your tucker. A stranger man, confident, wistful, dangerous, strange. Whose smile is momentarily real, suddenly familiar, whose mouth is sweet and full of memory. For you. Memory from the buds of breasts reaching to those flat wrinkled dugs you shall presently behold. Witchery.

'That you, dear?'
'Who else?'

He did applaud the white-out. We sat on the carpet, and drily quietly drank champagne extra brut. I even felt at home. Wondering why he should like my whitewash, my message about tombs.

Crude jokes. Farts in bed and smothered giggling. Will yurr stop yurr tickling Jock? Leaving behind a tight narrow she. Leaving behind also a shoe in a rockcrack and hopping back with lightheart laughter to flat I never came to before. Spending a giddy bountiful night before hopping home, dour dutiful little brown bird. Strait home. Neat papers, stacked. Some printed. Lampreys yet. Silence & emptiness & no light.

_____

I was really tremulous with laughter a million bubbles of laughter.

_____

The other said with no smile, 'Another bottle of moselle?'
'Why not?'

I may catch another glimpse of the crooning man and this time I will bubble and smile and hug to his breast and the seas will crest over us and the paua snuggle us home.

_____

You permitted me to twiddle that little tag of flesh between your cheeks, you greased my explorations, encouraged my play
whereas here
here and now
it is mere insertion, weary reception, lifeless and little spilling of seed.
Why is my boldness limited to this one extraordinary one night affair?
And how you whispered deep in my ear, last, sweet,
'There is no tomorrow and there is no turning back.'

_____

What is a gap in the brainstalk but a chance for the light to come in?

_____

The words sing numbly. A dull continuing necessary whine.
My words? Who else writes day to day in my daybook?
Is it acceptable to the review committee?
Does it matter beyond these pages?
Of course not!

And I write,
She could not believe their meaning. She did not believe she had written them with intent. Seasons of leanness and disquiet indeed. A degree *and* a degree. Where are the fat paua of yester yester year? And the days of wild free roaming, and calculated cuckoory, where?

It fades, it fades, it washes like saltshadows off the skin under cold shower water.
It dies, it dies, and you are left a hungering gap, no surcease.
'Pass me that bottle o my dear . . . o you're home?'

White rooms and green plants long way away from the rolling sea.
Do you still stalk the white surf fringes?
Do you still wait on your black reef for lonely women walking in the evening, crooning sad songs lost lullabies to themselves? I hope you do and I wish you luck and I wish them luck and may your next paua be full of worms.
The wine is sour.
There are more shadows in that corner than I would believe. I have gone a hundred times to look for you. The beach has changed. The reef is lonely. The pauas flourish in an arrogant way.

We eat brown bread and brown rice and brown beans. We eat brown sauce o yes *cheese*-flavoured brown sauce and brown cake and sometimes brown meat. He has a theory about the virtue of carbohydrate. My tongue has forgotten its oily childhood joys. It has forgotten tangles. It has forgotten the velvetfat skin of muttonbirds. Smoky yellowsweet kumara. Broiled cress, dark green, dark green. Golden syrup and rewena bread Mrs Maki used to make. Honeysugar kiekie fruit my daddy brought me once.

'I'm home.'
'O.'

I had not been in a sea-garden since I was a bareleg girl making slippery sandals of the kelp and tormenting snails into closing their doors. I had not hugged anyone since my wedding, all those drippy noses and soft wrinkled skins. It is a different, a reticent, a rigid world I inhabit. By choice. Cool and quiet and ordered and shadowed and tidy and sane. Not a sniff in sight.

Our house. Bare clean furniture. No ruffles, no curtains, no frills. Carpet everywhere. Tiles in the bathroom, everywhere. He would have tiled the loo seat if he could. No decorations beyond two stark paintings, pure washes of pale colour. Not a squiggle anywhere. Never a florid plant. Dust is non-existent. My last joke, a year ago, was 'We do not shed skin cells here.' He agreed.

Your flat. Dustballs, slut cobbles, fluff everywhere. Egg varnish on old plates. Piles of fatty knives and forks. And clothes hung on the floor you ape. O man, don't wiggle your hand like that, I ooze, and that's untidy . . .

A short season you promised, thick-lipped, thick-voiced, a short season of sacred lust you understand. I do, I did, I do
And then home you go
to your old man
o man gone
I went

Echoes of songs. Echoes of past warm laughter, past mastering laughter. I won't prolong the agony. I won't go down to the beach again, the lonely beach and the sea, and all I want is a tall man and a randy man a handy man and me

I look and I do not believe I write this.
Consider.
The supra-oval laminae in the velasia stage vary in number and
may be used as an identification when
identify identify identify
indemnify the past. Sheer utu

I bathe my tongue in champagne. I bathe my palate in chablis.
I bathe my oesophagus in claret. I have run out of seas.

And he touched his broad pink tongue to the tiny pink tongue and
the baby gurgled to him and I felt my thighs wet, in sympathy. Is
that too much to ask? Is that too much to understand? There on
the heaving ferry: the wavering man, the secure burbling babe,
and me, with a window drunken in the brain.

Travelling where?
The grey safe way and the grey wary way
o long gone man
nowhere
    give me a hand

I asked for a light and
he gave me his hand

'Why are you crying in the dark?'
'I forgot to turn the light on.'
'O. I see.'

A clear lens that has grown slowly, tumourlike, a third eye
such as the tuatara owns, becoming clearer the more drink
I down, an inwardlooking secret hole

and I weep for what I see now, the hollow and the clearness
Man gone, man gone,
bone hand unheld
no travelling
quietude and old man sorrow
a way unravelling
alonelyment
man gone.

_____

You could come with me.
Lips against my skull. Words vibrating inside my head.
O no I haven't finished my doctorate I have
You *could* come with me.
No wait a moment this is too sudden no not yet not
Lazy lazy regard as you stared me up. And down.

_____

Huddled into my own arms some afternoons after teaching
earless beginning scholars full of their own thoughts, dispassions,
cares

_____

With a bottle as baby naturally.
This could read pathetically. Do not. I am happy with thickened
tongue and numbed lips and blankened windowed brain and
listen!
'I'm home my dear.'
Mhmn.

_____

Man gone

A DRIFT IN DREAM

Bright lights. She had forgotten the harshness of their flare. And noise. Too much noise roaring at her, beating on her. And the way people bustled past, some looking at her queerly but most blank-eyed, hurrying on somewhere else. She thought about closing her eyes, blocking off her ears with her hands, but then she would be more conspicuous, and shrinking away from pain or hardship never stopped it happening.

She stands there on a corner, wrapped in a long dress, a meek grey long dress, of good cloth. She also wears a jacket with broad padded shoulders. 'Good cloth,' Soeur Hildegarde had said. 'I wore this when I came in.' She had fingered the cloth thoughtfully. 'It will keep you warm.'

The cars snarl past. The people rush and push. She stands shivering.

> I am 36 years old. I am considered steady. I am considered wise.

The shivering is becoming convulsive. She wraps her arms round herself, holds on tightly.

'There is something the matter?'

One of the harsh bright noisy people has stopped by her. It is a man, she thinks. It has long hair drawn back from a highboned face. Slanting green eyes.

'You tripping?'

The voice is mellow, the note in it one of warm concern.

'I, I, I,' voice convulsing with her body. Panic has cramped her throat.

> I am 36 years old. I am Marie-Clare de Vraiencourt.
> I have been in the world four hours.

If he could, that is how he would always remember her, the
way he first saw her; a small slender woman with shocked brown
eyes, standing trembling in the middle of the crowd.

He makes a pot of tea. In all that he does, there is a fluid
beautiful grace.

'Sure and you'll feel better in a moment. Sit down now.
There.'

There is a – sack? cushion? a large cloth mound: the cover is
stencilled with amber and purple paisley patterns. She stares at
them until the intricate lines blur.

> I am considered strong. Remember the winter when
> your feet cracked open but you still walked the frosty
> ground, leading your sisters in laying the concrete blocks
> for the new dormer? All the while laughing when laughter
> was needed, because the pain was nothing beside the
> love burning in your heart? I am considered strong, I will
> not faint.

'Forgive me,' she whispers. 'I am not used, used, used to
people. Crowds. People.'

He folds himself neatly to the floor at her feet, a cup of tea in
either hand. Fragrant steam enhaloes him.

'And is that a sin now, not being used to people?'

She lifts her gaze, startled.

'Sin? What would you know of sin, young man, to joke so
lightly?'

> O insufferably school-marmish M-C, such a retort to this
> gaudy angel who has rescued you from the mob,

but he is grinning. He has white and beautiful teeth.

'More than I'd be telling . . . come, take the tea. It is mixed
with peppermint and is good for terror.'

As she takes the cup one of his long lean hands touches her
wrist, briefly.

'You've been a hard worker.'

The reddened roughness: the blunt ugly nails. Her last
duty had been the washing. She had been Laundress for three
years. Washing boards and cold water and hard home-made
soap.

She looks round the one-roomed flat. A perfumed smoke is stealing up from a bright brass buddha. The gas heater hisses. Long disorderly plants cascade from a dozen different shelves and levels. Strings of jewel-like glass beads surround the one light and scatter crimson and emerald and cerulean gleams.

'I am dreaming,' she says. The steam rises from the cup. She feels dizzy. Her tears fall.

'I must be dreaming.'

The young man groans.
He is lying on the floor beside the bed, wrapped in a padded kind of blanket. He had refused to let her sleep on the floor, despite her unsteady telling of how she was used to sleeping.

'Sitting up now! Sure, and I've heard of such things but never in this day and age. Enjoy that old bed. It is not soft, you'll not be spoiled. Warm though, and you need the warmth.'

And after he had turned the light out, his strong voice golden in the dark:

'Marie-Clare de Vraiencourt, do not be afraid. I am Liam Finn McConnell, and bad though I can be, I do not have it in me to rape a nun.'

Cloudily she thinks, But I am no longer a nun.

Not since four o'clock yesterday afternoon, and the signing of the stiff, strangely white parchment; not since the removal of that worn circlet from her heart-finger, thin, silver, and plain. The sadness in Mother's eyes, and the grieving absence of her eleven sisters, and the stiff politeness of the Bishop's black-clothed representative, there to see all was done aright. And the door closing with soft finality behind her, trapping her wedded name in the poor concrete walls, no longer Soeur Bonaventure, Marie-Clare again, no longer participant in the pleasures and pangs of God, dull laywoman again. Because, after twelve years not only did the human fire in her body flare as high and as discomfiting as ever, but the love she had for God, had died. The burning love had all burned away before that unwanted and urgent need for –

For what? Joining with a man? I have never tasted that. I need . . . to hold. To be held.

Her thoughts stray.

The young man groans again. In the dawn light, she can see the shine of tears down his cheeks.

'We must be practical,' as he sips another cup of tea.

In the morning he glows, long blond hair tidied into a plait, fair skin lambent with health. His green cat eyes are full of knowing kindness. 'I sing. I am good at singing. I trade. I am good at trading. Your skills are?'

She smiles, weakly.

'Washing.'

'Seriously now.'

'I was a teacher before I entered. Of English and French.'

'And you want to return to teaching? There's money in it they say.'

'I would rather play the piano.'

Afterwards, she doesn't know why she has said that. The memory of his tears at night or the pride in his voice as he said, I am good at singing –

'D'ye hear that, a fellow musician!' He is rowdy in delight. 'I knew it was a good deed to stop by you, and its goodness has come home already. Marie-Clare, do y'know you looked terrified away from your wits, but now you look like salvation to me? I *need* an accompanist.'

I am old enough to be his mother, she thinks. Remember, old enough to be his mother.

The afternoon is spent in another one-room flat, this one poorer in colour and lacking in plants, but seemingly half-full of piano. It is owned by a friend of Liam's; it seems Liam has many friends. This one is blear-eyed and sways as he stands by the door, waving them in, Course Paddy, yeah mate, do anything for you, help yourself. Got any gear?

'There it is, go play,' says Liam, but gently. He smiles to her, turns away.

The piano is dust-covered, but surprisingly well-tuned. Her rough fingers feel stiff and awkward. She is precipitated back into long-ago afternoons and the stern remorseless beat of the metronome; the stern voice of her mother; the stern sunlight that marched with the beat into the darkness of the room and raised clouds of motes, berated the shadows, frowned at the stern frowning portraits of her ancestors looming on the walls . . . Maman, why did you cart them along with you? They would have been much happier on the grim hall walls you left behind . . . the gay French. She had never felt gay. Just lost. But something is happening to her fingers in this smoky room: the stiffness is oozing out as the smoke grows, the stiffness is the smoke? where did the grim sunlight go and why is she laughing? But her fingers are truly supple now and she is learning that you do not easily lose twenty years of music and playing.

Liam is standing proudly beside her. She cannot ever remember at which note his voice blended into her music but suddenly it is as if her playing has created a gloryfilled highway, the path for a golden and enchanting voice to wander along.

'Shit, like wow. Shit.' The friend of Liam stands shakily before her, holding out to her a smoking finger. 'Wow,' he says into the silence while the magical smoke curls into her smile.

The night is full of subtle dreams. She remembers rainbows round plants, and strange sustained notes that bell out from her words, notes that linger on long after they should have died. And Liam making her more tea before she slept.

'Is that just tea?'

He laughs, and his laugh is a glittering cascade of bell sounds.

'O my dear to be sure!' pouring it from a vivid packet into the pot. He is slim and straight and golden, boy still growing into man, and she is serene and calm and younger than she has ever been. This night is full of music. Even the tea is singing.

'And why did *you* leave your home?'

This morning, Liam looks grey and subdued, the glow gone. The floor is too hard, she thinks guiltily, I must go today . . . but the conversation begins with her morning cup and flows on, and she has told him all her dull history, and now wants to hear his.

Liam frowns.

'It is not a good tale. Mainly I left because it was a bog of a castle with old grey men grumping in the corners. What could keep me there?' His laugh is short and hard and his vivid face has clouded. 'I will tell you, this once. My grandfather, may his soul rot a thousand years in torment, my grandfather laughed at my mother's funeral. Sure and that doesn't seem to be a big thing does it? She was a thrawn woman, gone in her mind, had been since I'd been born, so why shouldn't the old man laugh? That laughter though, just as her coffin went down . . . his palpable bloody relief, thank God the bitch is gone, now there's only her whoreson left . . .'

His shoulders are jerking and his face has grown both too young and too bitter for his eighteen years. The jerking and the bitterness would frighten her if she wasn't considerably more frightened by abruptly seeing somebody else's lives through someone else's eyes. A long season of grey and fearful pain it had been, the unwanted daughter-in-law stumbling back to her dead husband's home, with her unwanted son in tow, and the old and erstwhile powerful man reduced to corroding their grey little lives . . . ha! how he stamps and snarls, each stamp shaking his anguished bones, each snarl twisting back through his mouth into his throat and tightening there, clamping down as the woman whimpers and dribbles and the growing boy learns and practises sabotage and hate . . . and how did he manage to set the fire in the ancient beloved hall? How? I was sleeping there, a moment, a moment after the bitch was buried and suddenly there is smoke and burning Ha! stamp it out! and smoke . . .

She is lying on the floor in Liam's arms while Liam stares at her.

'O you know?'

'I do know' and her surprise shakes her voice.

It took time for her hair to grow back. She wore a scarf until its raggedness grew long enough to be trimmed to a neat crop. No-one remarked on the headscarf. One of Liam's friends had no hair and a tattooed pentagram spidering across his brow: another, who sang to herself in a tiny gnat-like voice all the time, had decided to braid her auburn curls into corn-rows a year ago. She had not washed it since. All that Liam's friends were interested in was music, and dreams, and sex, and how you wore your hair took zero place.

She smiles to herself.

And I had thought all worldly vanities eradicated this long time since.

She sips more wine. She has grown to enjoy this wine very much, a pale green brew bought in bulk by one of Liam's Antipodean Crew. They are a rudely merry crudely merry lot who gulp down Liam's voice and her playing and Liam's dreams in vast uncivilised quantities. Come south, come back home with us! they urge stridently, and Liam smiles his cat smile and she, she laughs now.

But when they had first rushed in, a roaring mob, she had hid in one corner and cried. Liam had brought her cup after cup of the still greeny wine, had held her and murmured to her, had held her and sung to her as though they were alone and the lusty crowd around had all gone home. And he said proudly next morning,

'We outdrank and outsang them all my lovely, and that is no easy thing to do with Down Under.'

She smiles to herself.

It is fading, it is fading, but it was the night to remember, Liam risen from the floor and knelt by her bed.

'I have truly waited,' he said. His voice was muffled.

'As have I,' she answered.

She sips more wine.

I shall soon be 37. I feel buoyant. I grow younger all the time. I must have been an ancient child.

O it was the stuff of legends, Liam told all his grinning friends, I have taken God's bride and she is more pleased with me.

Which was not wholly true.

Some grey mornings, after Liam has bounded from the bed, she feels an ache in the middle of her chest as though some odd hollowing had taken place. Then, she prays. Not the long uncluttered plainsong she had used for a dozen years, not the simple patter of set prayers. She holds the rosary that her mother had owned, her dowry rosary that the Order had held in trust and returned to her on departure, the rosary of jewels and gold that she had always wanted to hold as a child and had never been permitted to – she holds the rosary and cries softly, intensely, for the pain in the world, for her happiness, for something she doesn't know, for something she doesn't know what, for something she doesn't want to know what.

And over the next year, she watches small lines etch into Liam's pale and beautiful skin, round the corners of his mouth. He is never even brusque with her, but once, at a jangling screaming party, she watches him kick a woman in the stomach. She remembers too often that he tried to murder his grandfather with fire. When she cries over the violence in him, and goes to leave him, he insists on brewing them both a final cup of tea –

'Remember the first, Marie-Clare?'

and frozenly, as she drinks it, she does. She wakes two days later, distanced, detached, heady.

And he charms her fear away with songs, newly-coined for her, and with his serene sinuous lovemaking.

And she, who has always craved gentleness and fire, dreamily wonders why she wanted to go away from him who is every light beat of her heart.

'But aren't you bothered about getting pregnant?'

She is a scruffy little girl, 14 or 15, a friend of a friend of Liam's, overnighting in their haven. She had laid her foil circle of Pills proudly down, when all three went to bed for the night.

'I am too old,' says Marie-Clare calmly. 'Besides, Liam and I have been together for over a year now, and no-one has resulted.'

And as she speaks, feels a pang different from any she ever felt.

'You are lovely, my love, more comely than Deidre and whiter than Etain.'

She turns to him frowning. Her body glimmers at her from the mirror, small breasted, neat-buttocked, slender at the waist and wide at the shoulders.

'Do you see anything?'

'Perfection.' His eyes are as limpid as any lough, deeply green.

'You should see more than me.'

Her accent has sharpened. For a wayward moment, she wonders why she has never spoken French since she entered the monastery.

'Who can we tell?'

He has gone from shouting spinning ecstasy to this wondering whisper.

'Nobody except ourselves again.'

'It is strange,' he lies back on the floor with easy grace, 'we come from decayed families and have no proper parenting, you orphaned early and me with a mother who wandered in her mind for years and a father dead before I was born. And here we are, the odd couple, starting things anew.'

He asks, a moment of silence later,

'Do you wish for a son? Or a daughter?'

'I never thought of myself as a mother. Either . . . amazes me.'

He came back from Ireland gaunt-faced and angry. She stood away from him a moment, shocked by the fear that maybe he has tried the rainbows and enchantments of his trade-bag, maybe he has fallen at last for the sugary brown cakes, the jewel-like capsules, the powders that glitter like surreal snows. 'People need these dreams and I am happy to provide them but o my heart, we have our own enchanting rainbows and don't need to trade their golden pots for this – crap.' He blarneys, hamming up his lilting accent often and then deflating it with a word that could never be an Irishism. It is odd to hear his words from a year ago echo in her head while staring at this new and terrifying face.

Then she held her arms out and he entered their circle and wept on her shoulder.

Later he said, harshly of himself, that he was a fool making the fool's mistake. 'You can never go back, mo chridh, you can never go home once you've left. I thought four years might have . . .

mellowed the old man. He has become more of a grey monster than ever. Sure, only a monster would attempt to have his own kin imprisoned, now wouldn't that be so?' His bright sudden laughter arrowed through his tears and grimness. 'Even if the aforementioned kin had tried a little incidental . . . murder?'

Later still, their bodies cradled together, he fits a heavy gold signet ring onto her thumb. 'It was not empty-handed entirely that I was sent away. That was my father's, and his mother's father's and maybe others' before them. It was my inheritance and is your wedding night gift. For with this ring I thee wed, and with this body I thee endow, and with *this* heart I thee shall love all the days of my life. We have only each other, my own Marie-Clare, but we have each other.'

She thinks amid her glad tears, He has practised and practised those words and I love him for that as well.

And she thinks, I have him and he has me, but I carry a passenger.

She was not surprised by the two officers, or by their piece of paper. She was honestly surprised when they asked for Timon Padraic McDonnagh and her honest surprise disconcerted them. They left without looking through the flat.

It was as though she was floating with the passenger in a watery secure world. She smiled placidly through the gentle waves at the rush and the flare and the noise out there, aware that none of it could touch them, because none of it was real. The sun in Spain was . . . the sun in Spain but the water world was dark and cool. She remembered flakes of a conversation, ominous drifts of halfheard words, someone dying or left dead, a wallet?, and the tightness of Liam's mouth until they left Nepal, and the harrowing note that had crept into his songs. But she knew how sound was distorted when heard underwater, and his smile was as steady as any smile could be viewed through a shadowy sea.

Nothing frightened her, particularly not cities and crowds and particularly not this sprawling seaside Antipodean city and crowd. A delicate arch of bridge in the harbour and an opera house in full sail. She clasped her hands over her belly. It would be a good place to unload the passenger, a good place to . . . she frowned to herself. Come up for air? She could feel the child kicking in time to the pulse of the waves.

'There is more travelling,' he says. He kneels with neither pretence nor shame and clasps his arms round her bulk. 'I know it is near your time but I need you with me, and I shall be going over this ocean . . .'

Her fingers stray onto his head, play in his hair.

'So?'

'So I have found a man and a woman who come from where we are going, and he is a mariner and she is a midwife. *That* is not chance, or if it is God organised it.'

She smiles. 'So?'

She listens to the thin mewing sound. She feels the lift and sway of the deck underneath her, the sun crusting the sweat and tears on her face.

Is this really me, really Marie-Clare?

The other woman finishes with the pad between her legs and begins to wipe her body down. She is swift and professional. Her smile is swift and professional too.

'Well, how does it feel to have a son and heir?' The woman's voice is nasal and her vowels are flat. She holds out the baby with tender ease. It is scrawny and red and wrinkled, its face bunched round a wideopen gummy mouth.

She doesn't answer. She gazes at this sticky screaming stranger, tiny yet loudly alive. One of her breasts is oozing a thin creamy exudate. She is aware of the men grinning down at her, aware of Liam's face flushed with a furious pride.

'Here, I'll just finish cleaning him up for you,' says the woman, and at that moment she feels another spasm deep within. O God, I cannot be carrying twins? Ah no, of course, the passenger's life-raft.

The ketch rides her anchor under the high summer sun. The bay is narrow and bushlined and full of screaming gulls. 'Kakapo

Sound,' says Liam's mariner. 'We'll be back in an hour or so.' The men leave for the one small hut she can see, perched on stilts by the water-edge. The other woman spreadeagles, stretched and tanned on the deck.

She is glad of the awning Liam rigged for her. Her baby lies against her heart, mouth still cupped round her nipple. Six days old and already you are an international traveller. Fine blond hairs shine on his gently-pulsing skull. So in that matter you'll follow your father. An instant later, his eyes open and as she stares into his blank blue gaze she thinks she can see a hint of green.

And what will you have of me in you, small stranger? What does it matter? I am 38 years old and I have a mate and a child and I have forgotten you, God, entirely.

The lilt of Liam's speech has crept into her own as surely as the lilt of his life has become the rhythm by which she dreams and lives.

Liam hails her across the water and she looks up and her smile is full of the sun.

If he could, he would like to remember her like that, a small strong vivid woman with the shadows off her at last, the baby cradled at her breast but she ready for him as ever.

He looks at the morphine waiting in the glass tube. He looks forward to the sting of the needle and a momentary quiet.

We had each other, we had the good life.

He is shaking with anguish and impotent rage.

The car is sleek and exotic and he delights in its speed.

'Belt up,' he says, grinning at his mate. She does. His son on her lap grins back up at him. At nearly two, he has enough teeth to make a real grin, but he still doesn't talk. Which bothers them not at all: he walked at ten months, and is alert, highly responsive, and good-natured, a smiling child of the sun. When one of the parents at the local playcentre had commented on his silence, Marie-Clare had said, calmly and seriously, 'He is perfection. He is like God in my heart,' but Liam had become angry. An attendant intervened swiftly. 'Some take their own time, eh? Now, *my* son didn't talk until he was almost four and do you know what his first words were? "Turn off the telly please mum." Bit of a surprising mouthful mmm? That's him over there,' nodding towards the budding genius who is teetering on top of a pile of tyres and yelling his head off for all youse other kids stand away I'm descending *now*. They both smile back to the big brown woman, who turns to chat in Samoan to another mother. Liam is sure they are talking about him, the youngest parent there and the only father who turns up every session, but who cares when her eyes are full of that lambent dreaminess and his child is giggling as he wrestles with the genius and there is ninety thousand dollars in his bank account, a house in Remuera that is his own, and an ocean-going ketch for his business and this Citroën for his pleasure?

'And now I'll belt up,' he says, and this time Marie-Clare grins back.

Ahh GOD if he could remember her like that!

a slow cartwheeling through endless sky braking hard on black asphalt that scours him forever stripping the skin from his hands and back and arms a shocked realisation that *that* is a piece of my skin *that* is some of my body fat and all the time the thin high screeching of his son somewhere close and worse the crackle of flames and the searing heat and the searing screaming that will not STOP

The child, three months later, is a stranger, brittle and thin-faced with haunted eyes.

Sure and I am a stranger to you too. And to myself. I look into the mirror. You look 102, lovely Liam.

It is because of the constancy of the pain. It is because of the breaking of a rare piece of silence. When the child says softly, questioningly,

'Maman?'

he swings round catches hold of a hand a throat and shouts as he bends 'Don't talk of her! Don't talk of her! O God a life for a life is fair but not her you have him the grey man under the Himalayas roof you have me now that's fair for I watched the pulse in his throat flick and die under my thumb but not her don't ever talk of her!'

He says to the gagging huddle on the floor, 'For the fire of God has got her and shall come for us all.'

As he goes to arrange for another voyage, the needle slipping under the skin of his arm, he says for his own ears, 'the fire of God got her,' for that is the only way he can remember her now and forever and he weeps thinly, into the growing silence.

TE KAIHAU
THE WINDEATER

Lies & Reflections

There is
a sandbank somewhere at the end of Earth where ocean stops and welkin stops and the winds of the world come to rest. They are chancy beings, like their cousins the Fates, and prone to sudden inhuman boisterousness – which stands to reason; they have never claimed to be human. Indeed, they affect to despise us and almost anything to do with us. Someone got under their guard though, once. They became aunties.

I thought I'd begin like this rather than by saying, I was born and now I'm dying. That's so commonplace, and we know everybody does it. What I want to do is lay before you the unusual and irrational bits from my life because they may make a pattern in retrospect and, besides, they are the only bits that make sense to me right now.

For instance, I made the mistake of asking my granny on *her* deathbed whether her best story was true. Her best story went like this:

> 'There I was, not quite sixteen and your mother just due to come into the world and all alone, because your grand-dad had gone across the river with a barefoot horse and the river had flooded and he couldn't get back. I was greatly in pain and terrified that I wouldn't be able to help myself and maybe the babe would die before it lived . . . at the worst moment, when it felt like your mother was going to be jammed in me forever and I could do nothing about it except sweat and scream, at that

moment there was a light. Now, you must understand that we didn't have the electricity and it had been early afternoon when I began to labour and my labour had gone on deep into the night; I had lit no lamps and the range had long gone out. Today I'd say someone switched a light on: then, I thought the moon had come to visit. As well as the light, there was a sweet low voice, a man's voice, saying "Not to worry, girlie, she'll be right."'

My granny would shake her head in wonder at this point.

'How did he *know*, the man with gentle hands? That it'd be your mother coming into the world and not some boy-child? Anyway, my pain all went away and your mother came smiling into life. And I saw that the light in the room came from the glory round the man and though he said he was a horse-doctor, I knew him for one of the Lordly Folk and wasn't this proved when the shawl he gave the baby for a welcoming gift melted away when she turned a year old?'

Well, I never had an answer for that question, never having seen the shawl (or much of my mother for that matter). I grew up curious about granny's story though, because she never had another like it – just dour little morals ill-disguised as tales. So, I asked her on her deathbed, was it true? Lordly Folk and shining faces and that? And she frowned, and whispered huskily, 'What would you tell your man when he came home distraught and found you cleaned and peaceful and the baby wrapped in a silken shawl? What would you tell anyone? The terrible truth?' Then she sniffed, and died.

That has always been my trouble, you see. I have always asked the wrong questions and I have always got answers. Now I would ask her, Did he have redbrown skin faintly luminous, like the moon shining through a carnelian? Were his eyes so black that you only saw the lightning crackling in them? Was there some small thing malformed about him, a finger too many or a discolouration of skin?

It is four decades too late to ask her anything. You could try a question in the next couple of hours, though.

Behind Every Wayward Action Stands a Wayward Angel

I was a plump happy baby. I smiled at my unsmiling mother and chuckled wetly and merrily when she cried. I smiled at everybody, I smiled at the whole world. I thought life was a whole lot of fun. It was just as well I got smiling over and done with then.

The first thing I remember is something everyone says I shouldn't, because I was too young – eleven months old and just starting to walk. Nobody was keeping an eye on me out in my playpen on the lawn, nobody thought they needed to keep an eye on me. My mother was in the kitchen or wash-house, keening to herself (probably); my Dad was knackering another unfortunate horse (probably), and my granny hadn't come to live with us yet.

Now, the lawn was comfortably warm and I was chewing happily through an earthworm. I remember, vividly, the gritty brownish insides and the moist pink skin and the wriggle. Suddenly, there was a shadow and two cool redbrown hands and a marvellous trustworthy voice (you bet your life eleven-month-old babies know a trustworthy voice when they hear one) saying 'Ka kite te taniwha, e pepe?'

Well, that meant buggerall to me but I drooled earthworm charmingly and nodded hard, indicating I was all ready to go or whatever. All I recall next is strong gentle dark arms carrying me through the sunshine, bringing me to a waterlit place. 'Titiro!'

Can water both sink and burgeon at the same time? It was waterspout and whirlpool, a great green helix of live water, anaconda parading through its own massive and vibrantly-splendid coils, spooling and rising and falling, spooling and rising and melding

'He taniwha, ne?'

said the beautiful trustworthy voice, just before the gentle arms opened and dropped me in.

Looking Like a Looking Glass

I don't remember anything else until I was ten or so. The rest of my childhood might as well have never happened. I am told that I stopped smiling. I grew into a large overly-toothy blundering child who lurched through life inviting adult snarls and blows until a teacher discovered I was legally blind.

Whoa back. Legally blind is not at all the same as the real thing. While I was an eye-cripple, unable to recognise people or hills or my own hands at the end of my arms, as soon as I got glasses I could see, more or less; I could make out what adults meant when they maundered on about birds or views (or light-bulbs, for that matter). While it was a nice surprise to discover such things at the age of seven, it had two curious effects on the way I looked at the world. One was, I never quite believed what I saw.

For instance, if I look in a mirror I see someone of average height and twice average weight with cloudy no-colour eyes and pale brown skin. As for my hair:

Granny: 'Your mother had fine silky seal-brown hair and I had fine silky seal-brown hair and your grand-dad (God rest him) had fine silky seal-brown hair so where did those corkscrew red things come from?'

(Give her her due, she never looked at my father when she said this, who had fine silky coal-black hair anyway.)

But the person in the mirror isn't me as I *know* me. Many people have this feeling. If you look in mirrors, reflections is all you see . . . true, but my feeling carries beyond mirrors. I look at a mountain I have looked at a thousand times before and think, Did that peak always look like that? Wasn't it a little sharper last time? And hasn't that bluff shifted slightly to the south?

The second effect of the belated discovery of short-sightedness was this: I know what I see (I think) but I'm quite prepared to acknowledge and believe someone else sees the same thing very differently – and that a third party sees some-thing else again. Seeing is not necessarily believing: seeing is a matter of faith in sight.

If you look in mirrors, you might see someone else.

Moonshickered

The house we lived in (until my granny died there, and my Dad and me moved out) was old. It mumbled to itself on dark nights. There were places on the back verandah that were dangerous for even a child to walk on, and none of the doors would shut because the joists and rafters had sagged. Outside, there was a garden as old as the house, and as well looked after. In fact, telling where the garden ended and the scramble of bush and swamp began was difficult. Two things helped: whoever had planted the garden had loved redhot pokers, and a rough perimeter of them resurfaced each spring; close to the creek, was an orchard, unpruned and lichenous but still producing fruit. A child told not to go into the bush could find helpful patterns of apples and pears, rotten or ripe, defining boundaries. A child was frequently told not to go into the bush. Granny did not like the bush. Maybe it arose from the fact that my grand-dad had wandered away into it and never reappeared. Maybe it was because she had spent most of her life helping to hack farms from the bush, and she thought it resented her, and hers. Whatever the reason, my granny had unpleasant ways of ensuring a child did what it was told, so I was grateful to the orchard and the kniphofia. Particularly to the former one memorable evening.

I was eleven and had been in the bush all day (I'll tell you why later). Come moonrise, I knew I was late getting home and that my granny would have searched the garden. I knew she would be waiting. I knew my Dad wouldn't be home.

Thinking back, from the vantage point of 30 years on, it was an uneasy light. There was the red hugeness of the moon swelling above the trees. There was the rotten-ripe air of the evening. There was my fraught state of mind. So the boy standing in the shadows swishing a stick through the air and matching its whistle with his own may not have necessarily been there (except I saw him plain as in daylight). I remember him as tall, with broad shoulders arrowing down to a slender waist, and I remember thinking it was the hunter's moon that made his hair and eyes both so black and so bright, and his skin so palpably red.

I looked warily at him and he tossed the stick to me and

whistled, and tossed an apple to me and whistled, and I frowned at both for a moment until, in some atavistic corner of my brain, a thought formed, an old old thought.

Next moment I was excitedly gathering a skirtful of grub-rich apples, and *next* moment, hurrying home.

Incidentally, 'unthinking' is the only word I know to describe that state of atavistic *knowing*, but 'moonshickered' fits pretty well what happened next.

When my granny said coldly from the back verandah, 'Well madam, where have we been and how are we going to explain it?' I giggled. I sat down ten feet away and fitted an apple to the stick and flicked it and it sped with bruising force to spatter squashily all over granny. Her howl of outrage was matched by my squealing laughter, her movement towards me by two more speedy apples. I kept up a barrage of apples and laughter and she retreated into the house.

O that cider smell fizzing in my nostrils! And laughter rising in pitch to become ululation as twenty thousand wild and battle-happy ancestors rose out of their dark and joined me hurling apples and jigging under the bloody moon.

When Dad came home, there were shattered windows and apple splatters and smears everywhere and his mother-in-law cowering pale-faced and shaking inside and his maenad daughter raging redfaced and shrieking with laughter outside.

My granny and I declared a truce thereafter.

The old old thought I had was called 'atlatl', but that's not as helpful as 'moonshickered' is it?

Jokes of Gods and Whims of Ancestors

My granny finally died when I was 18. She took a long time about it. She had a stroke (unfortunately she was making porridge at the time and dropped onto our coal range) (Dad found her) (I found Dad) that disabled her from doing everything a human does, except talk. There was another question I asked her on her deathbed: Where do you come from? 'I'm a Celt,' she replied with an ancient and unknowable pride.

Well, her accent was odd, could've been Irish or Scots or maybe anything else. All in all, she didn't tell me much at all. (Of course, now I'd know to ask who her mother was, who her father was . . .)

My Dad wasn't much help with the matter of ancestry either. When asked about his mother-in-law to wit his wife to wit my mother, he said, 'Dunno much except the old bloke came from Cornwall.'

It was a bit tender to approach my Dad on the subject as to where *he* came from, who *his* parents were, because he'd been brought up in an orphanage. He knew he was part-Maori (so did Granny, who made sour snide little comments about that), and at some time during his orphanage years he'd been taught the language. He didn't tell it to me – or rather, he told an infinitesimal amount to me.

Because when as a 13-year-old, newly gone to high school, I finally plucked up courage to ask him, 'Dad um, about your Maori side, our Maori side, *my* Maori side . . . ?' he smiled tightly and said, and wrote down for me so I couldn't mistake the answers to my questions Who are You and Where do You come from?

'Ko Pakatewhainau te iwi, no Wheatewhakaawi.'

I made the mistake of saying that out loud out proud at school.

All the Smiling Faces Lonely People Keep on Walls

Photographs make up a large part of some people's lives. They will grin at old photos, weep before portraits, relive days so long ago they are turned sepia and curly at the corners. They keep their friends on the mantelpiece and their relatives in albums that would smell musty, only the leaves are turned so very often they smell of sweat and finger-grease and tears.

They prefer to talk to pictures because you can make the perfect answers back.

That doesn't quite apply to my father.

He is largely a silent man and I think I have conveyed that he couldn't care less about dead family. I think he loved my mother (who left him just after I was rescued from seeing the taniwha). I know he loves *me* which is not as reassuring as it might ordinarily be.

You see, he is a knacker, a horse butcher. Somebody has got to do the job, sure. My father is, I understand (never having seen him at work), gentle and dispassionate and thoroughly efficient. No horse, I understand, ever goes terrified to its death in my father's yard; no owner of a horse has ever made a complaint about the way my father treats the dead horses he sometimes has to collect. In fact, most of them hand him photographs of their beasts in their heyday, ears pricked forward, eyes liquidly ashine and alert.

If the owners of the horses he kills, or retrieves, don't give him a photograph, he takes one himself before the creatures are dead or are seen to be dead. He lives in two rooms above his knackery. The walls of the rooms are covered with many thousand photographs of horses. He is surrounded by horses, equine sad looks, equine glad looks, equine sighs and equine laughs.

My father loves horses much more than he does humans but I rather hope he will put my photo in some small spare space soon.

An Episode of Bagmoths

I spent as much time in the bush as I could as a child because I was looking for rare insects, maybe ones no-one had ever found before. O the sadness when I found one . . .

Now, when you're very shortsighted, you only see what is immediately in front of your nose. I early became aware of things that writhed oozily or scuttled away on a fringe of legs. When I learned to read, I read voraciously – but only about insects. They were my fascination and comfort and path to future fame (I thought).

We have many splendid and curious small creatures, from giraffe-weevils to astelia moths. There is such a range with so many bizarrely-beautiful life-cycles, that I should have grown up into a happy-ever-after entomologist.

I was 12. I had a collection of moths that would make a

lepidopterist sweat with pleasure but it lacked something that, while not in itself a rarity, was very rare in an undamaged state.

Are you familiar with the work of an Australian cartoonist, Mary Leunig? Her art is generally macabrely, bitterly, funny, but there is one where the humour is relatively gentle. It shows a young male moth with gaudy wings standing by a suitcase and looking at his watch. On the wall behind him is a skinny bagmoth case – his own. There is also a fat wriggling case – the woman, of course, late as usual in getting ready you think, and grin before turning to the next page. The real joke is that the woman in this case will never finish getting dressed because female bagmoths remain forever in their cocoons. They are wingless grub-like creatures: to pull one out of its silken home is to kill it.

Male bagmoths pupate and emerge winged and ready for action. There is one slight problem. Bagmoths tend to live way apart from each other, munching their way through the bush, dragging their cases behind them. As in everything else, the race is to the swift – first come, first serve so to speak – so off flutters the male in feverish haste, battering himself against twigs and branchlets and ruining himself as far as I was concerned. The only thing to do was to make a collection of bagmoths, hope there was a male among them, and anaesthetise it as soon as it came into the world.

I scoured the bush for bagmoths and found a thousand and 33. I converted my wardrobe into a bagmothery and reaped manuka by the armload to feed them. They all reached maturity and *none* of them turned into beings with wings. At least, not the proper Oeceticus omnivorous wings.

I was looking at them disconsolately one afternoon, one thousand and 33 fat bagmoths hauling their homes around as they got stuck into fresh sprays of manuka, or snoozing, the mouths of their cocoons drawn shut. And suddenly, I saw it. One cocoon was contorting into s-shaped bends. It was wriggling frantically. Bagmoths did not do this in my experience, even when attacked by parasitic wasps. A male moth was hatching, late but at last!

I took off my glasses and leaned eagerly close to the switching case. In one hand I had a killing bottle. Any moment now . . . something began to emerge from the bottom of the bagmoth case, very slowly at first but then with awful swiftness. Insect legs, insect abdomen, glorious? red! wings and a tiny head. With teeth. It looked like a human head. With human teeth. It was grinning at me, its minute black eyes viciously bright. The grin lasted a very long second. Then the thing dived powerfully into the air and sped past my goggling eyes out through the door and away.

I didn't touch or look at or even think about an insect in any entomological sense ever again.

Incidentally, if you're wondering how bagmoths female and male get it together in real life, why not keep a couple and see? Hurry, though. There's not much time left.

Never the Same Wind Twice

There's only one thing I've ever discovered since, that I enjoy as much as I enjoyed the world of insects and believe you me, I've tried more than a few things.

It's breathing.

Ordinary day-to-day breathing is fine, having the charm of novelty inasmuch as every lungful is slightly different, and deep breathing alright for some situations, and meditational breathing okay if you like meditation, but what I am talking about is the awareness of breathing.

Some mornings I'd wake up very early and grin with delight as I drew in that first conscious chestful of air. It tasted better in my lungs than wine ever tasted on my tongue. It was ecstasy, it was *sweet*, air soughing in and all my little alveoli singing away with joy and oxygen-energy coursing through every space and particle of me. I could feel my heart in its cardiac sac swell and float, held down only by ropes of veins . . . it flutters against those ties, wanting to soar in free air as a great luminous pulsing living balloon . . . hey! grab another breath! This time'll do it!

You've heard skylarks duelling for space, each pegging his own sky-claim with frantic song, making a chestburst effort to keep every other dueller fenced out as they quest higher and higher into the blue yonder? Sometimes I'd feel like their song on ordinary everyday air.

I *love* breathing. Damn, but am I going to do it hard when I stop.

Granny's Revenge

I cried just after my granny died, not for her though (she was far better dead by that stage, and I hadn't liked her much while she was alive). Remember I said the old lady had spent most of her life helping hack farms from the bush? Well, we had always understood that each new farm had just about paid for the last one, and that when my grandfather was lost to the bush, my granny was left destitute. But no: she had twenty thousand pounds squirrelled away and she left it all to me. My Dad grinned faintly when he learned that. He gave me good advice. 'Buy a small house and invest the rest girl,' and then he shifted quite happily into the loft rooms of his knackery. I did what he said, bought a solid little house on the edge of town, right on the beach, and put the rest away to work for me. If I lived fairly frugally, I'd never have to work for it.

Boy, the old lady must have hated me a lot. She'd obviously never forgotten those apples.

The Early Sown Skulls

We were one hell of a gang on the beach.

There was Elias, who lived closest to me, quarter of a mile away, bright and gay and very knowledgeable about drugs. He was discreet but indefatigable in the pursuit of new lovers. There was Pinky and Molly and Chris, an oddly-sexed trio who were indefatigable in pursuit of each other but rather liked others to watch. There was me, independent and alone and indefatigable in pursuit of any boy or man who would help me explore more of myself as a woman.

Don't yawn like that. I'm not going to tell you any of what

went on except to say that I learned a lot about myself and others and enjoyed most of the learning very much for the three happy years it went on. At least, I think I did. What with the drink and the smoke and capsules that Elias handed round with gay abandon, I can't remember much of the detail.

I do remember the young pothead who staggered to our bonfire one night, drawn by The Smoke amongst all the other.

'Could smell it a mile away,' he husks, and coughs throatily. He's a stocky youth with an oddly-gaunt face, and raggedy-black hair. The firelight dances on his bare chest and shoulders, on his teeth as the joint passes to him and he smiles slowly, 'maaan, that's so sweet,' cupping his hands round its ember end. He sucks and sucks and sucks, an inhalation into the deeps of his belly down below his belly down past his horny bare soles maybe, and the joint grows ash and shrinks and shrinks to a sickly stickily-yellow roach that he finally takes away from his lamprey suck and looks at admiringly. An nth of an inch left, just nippable by nail, bong fodder only. Without breathing out, not seeming to be breath-holding, not even looking distended round the cheeks or chest or eyes, he passes the thing on. Pinky was next, and dropped it, and we couldn't find it in the sand.

The young pothead smiles his gaunt slow smile at us, and it seems to have too many teeth now. None of us grin too widely back. As I recall, he never did breathe that toke out.

By the by, Elias and Pinky and Molly and Chris lived long happy lives by the standards of a couple of centuries ago.

The Beach Arab

When I didn't know what I know now, I said that the Beach Arab was the pothead's cousin. I was only half-joking, for while he was tall and thin (but full in the face), he had a similar slow smile and the same raggedy black hair. He never wore anything but denim shorts and his skin was a rich reddish brown. If you were on the beach, you generally heard him before you saw him because he played a fat little flute made of bone whenever he was alone. He came shyly to our bonfires at first, always eating whatever food was handed round with his fingers, even when it was a salmon mousse the fastidious Elias had made one March evening. He came less shyly as time wore on and he came to know Elias, then Chris and Molly, and lastly, me. Soon after that, I left the beach forever – but that's a story to come.

He had a strange sense of humour, the Beach Arab (no, he never told us a name).

There was one afternoon I recall in bright detail: three American tourists had invaded our bonfire and were talking loudly, heartily, amusing themselves with the local natives. We were quiescent under more sherry and smoke than usual, smiling dreamily and politely at them when their words gonged more harshly than ordinarily at us. The Beach Arab trailed in, a little after the voice of his flute.

And presently one of the Yanks said gushily, 'And what do you Mayories eat?' Chris who was Danish from Dannevirke looked at Elias whose parents both came from England, and Elias looked at Pinky, a strident Glaswegian, and Pinky in turn stared in astonishment at Molly who blushed all over her Coast Irish face. She didn't look at me, and while I was thinking out loud 'Uuhhh . . .' (what the hell did my father ever eat that was different, except horse?, and that didn't seem too Maori to me), the Beach Arab smiled and bowed and swept off a rock and away scuttled a small crab and the Beach Arab dived on it and put it in his mouth, chewing and smiling while the Americans gasped and went Mygahd Dan do you *see* that? and the little legs (half of them) tweedled on his lips until he swallowed the first bit and sucked them in.

They deserved it. I mean, did you ever see a brickred Maori? Okay okay okay, so did I, so have I.

Birds of a Feather

It was a three-quarter moon, waxing, that night. We lay together just beyond the rim of the firelight, listening to the others talk. Later, when they had gone, the Beach Arab played his bone flute: rather, he talked into it and the words came out intelligible music.

His round face looked both very dark and very oriental under the moon.

After we had made love, I smiled at that moon. I had a house; I had the kind of life that suited me down to the ground, and I didn't have to work to enjoy it; I had friends who were warm good fun, and here I lay satiate, gently held by a young man's strong arms, gently held by a lover. I went happily to sleep and dreamed of taniwha.

When I awoke at sunrise, he was gone, but not far. There he was, down by the sea's edge, naked, washing himself. I ran gaily down to help.

I remember thinking, I must have something on my contact lenses, he can't have feathers on it.

I remember saying, hesitantly, 'hey that looks like fun?' but then his upright ure wilted and the shining bronze-green feathers tucked themselves down tidily round it.

I remember looking at the flat silver sea, watching the water suddenly shiver under a passing breeze.

I remember his smile, o yes. I had seen that same smile on too many different faces, a whole flock of them.

I remember running home and locking my door and *never* going onto the beach again.

Funny thing though: I don't remember feathers on it under the three-quarter moon.

Home Is Where The Heart Is

My solid little house has four rooms; bedroom, wash-house, kitchen and livingroom. For three years I kept it immaculate. For the next ten years I – grew things. Don't get me wrong: it was comfortable enough. I had some pet slime moulds in the wash-house and a live & let live policy with any other agents of decay. There were umbrella toadstools on a dish-cloth that I recall fondly, and something phosphorous in a bedroom corner that I never touched. Once a month, when the local liquor store delivered my crate of gin, I gathered up all of the tins I had strewn around, put them neatly into rubbish bags and left them out for whoever takes such things away. Someone did. Just as someone delivered the tinned food I ordered.

I'd've kept on that way until my liver gave out except for a series of accidents.

Dry Horrors

About four one morning I awoke with a throat-aching thirst. This was usual and so was my remedy, stumble out to the kitchen and get water in a glass and gulp it. After the second gulp, I remembered something.

Now, I'd had contact lenses for 12 years, ever since long-ago Elias suggested they'd be a better idea than glasses. He was so right: I had got to love rain, and swimming was fun; steam, whether from showers or just-opened ovens or body-heat, was no longer a blinding hazard, and I never once sat on my lenses.

I'd just swallowed them, though.

Remember breaking your lens-case yesterday? Remember putting your lenses into that glass just before you stumbled off to bed? Yeah, you remember alright.

I thought about an emetic.

I thought again.

I whimpered until dawn.

In desperation, I rang my father. He sort of snuffled. 'Um well,' he said, seemingly unsurprised to hear from me for the first time in two years and with such a subject too, 'yeah well. Flax'll make you run, y'know. You can always stop it afterwards with little koromiko leaves.'

I wasn't sure whether he meant to use the koromiko as a cork and I wasn't going to ask.

'I'm not scrabbling round in my own shit,' I said shortly.

'You could always have a good meal of, say, scallops, to make it easier?' He openly snorted.

Conversation between a knacker and a drunkard isn't an easy matter, even when they're father and daughter. He did promise to take me to my optician's however, and three hours later, there he was, spruce and grinning on my doorstep. He sniffed a little at the fungal smell and looked sideways at my puffy face and gin-bloated body. He always did think people should go to hell in their own handbasket however, so made no comment at all, merely guided me into a taxi and out into the optician's and back home again.

'Take care,' he said then, and that was the last I've seen of him. You'll gather we weren't ever close. I should have been born a doomed filly.

Until my new lenses arrived, I lived back in the world of blurs. I couldn't go outside because I couldn't see who or what was coming – and for the first time in a decade, I wanted to go outside. Being returned to a condition of childhood had the odd effect of making me, well, not a child, but in some way renewed. The half-empty crate of gin was left untouched while I engaged in warfare with heat (you ever tried to pour boiling water from a jug you can't see into a cup you can't see?) and retaught myself to see with my fingers.

When the new lenses arrived, I put them in and realised immediately that was a mistake.

They melted into my eyes and I could see perfectly but not only what I wanted to see.

They Have Made the Moon a Skull Who Was my Lady

It is three sober days and nights later. I am walking back to the cleansed house under a thin frail fingernail edge of moon. I am breathing deeply and with joy for the first time for years and frankly don't care if there are creatures with feathered penises in this world.

There are two people swaying together at the bus-stop. She is short and stocky, almost squat, and she is tall and heavily-built and they are twined. The stocky one is muttering, They have made the moon a skull now, walking on it, she is a skull now, while the tall one is singing sadly about some lady lost, some lady gone, and the words run eerily together, mutter and song. As I tiptoe past, they stop singing and muttering and stare at me. Their eyes glow.

I look hastily away and see that the grinning moon really is a skull, the fingernail edge a highlight on her bare jawbone.

They Have Exits And Entrances Galore

Someone or something has started using my print as a getaway route.

It is a reproduction of George O'Brien's *Dunedin Harbour From Flagstaff Hill* and every so often, just as I've stopped looking at it, a particle of intense light swoops into the water past the wharf on the lefthand side of the picture. Three seagulls flying in an isosceles triangle mark the spot.

The oval 19th century print doesn't bat an eyelid at this intrusion, not even when a similar (identical?) light sears *out* of the water (aft of the steam vessel making its way across the harbour).

There! I caught one out of the corner of my eye doing it again!

The Constancy of Roads

I discovered today that, during my ten years self-immurement, my optician's clinic had burned down and she had shifted to the North Island. I had walked down to the clinic, my courage screwed to breaking point, to have her test my strange new eyes.

Walking back, I can't find the bus-stop.

Denying the Mouse

I can hear it. Every night for the last week.

Clink of chopsticks on foodbowl as it creepytoes across seeking morsels, leftovers, bits I've missed. Everything gets gnawed by its tiny defiling teeth.

I've left out tasty poisons for it, in neat dishes. One night I heard it chuckle over my latest cunning trap.

The experts advise setting baits in its own run. How? Mouseruns are the most secretive of paths. They go winding in and out of my walls with no sign, not even an exit hole. Entrances in deep shadows, exits elsewhere.

I can't believe I have a mouse problem. For one thing, in all the years of sloth and mould, neither rats nor mice showed up. Why should my bleached clean house draw them? For another, the thing is way too smart, and there was that chuckle. Maybe a mouseman? A minute anthropomorph, complete with basket of pottery droppings to scatter or stick in strategic places – what better way to disguise your predations than under the guise of another pest? and somehow, I can't see him/her/it raising narrow buttocks and squeezing out an instant turd. Nah, a little factory where they manufactured guises in silence.

In my walls.

Come out! I know you're there. If I can only see you once, I won't kill. I won't even try to kill you. I'll stop setting traps and I'll put out little dishes of good food. Come on, play fair.

Tonight there are two of them and I can hear their thin voices singing 'We'll Meet Again.'

Even Barnacles Have a Swimming Phase

I had a choice; stay, and drink myself to death, or, leave and try and find a heart somewhere else.

There was an eager buyer for my house the first day I put it on the market. He was an ordinary-looking fellow, thin and pale with nondescript hair, so I let him have it for five times the price I had paid for it.

His smile lit up his mirrored shades.

Next Time, Leave it Lying There

At first, I spent a lot of time on the Cook Strait ferries. It was soothing, watching the waves from the safety of the deck, and I liked the food. I stayed one night in Picton, the next in

Wellington, and I could have gone on living like that for the rest of my time except I got noticed after the first year, and turned into a celebrity after the second.

I gave in and bought a motor-home and set off round the North Island first, never staying more than one night in any place. I had no pictures and the van was mouse-proof and I never looked for bus stops or at moons.

I did pick up hitch-hikers – I liked to talk and there is something wrong about telling stories to your own ears.

I had been driving around for a year when I picked it up.

There was a young weary man slumped at the side of the road. He lifted his head and gave me a tired one-sided smile when I stopped. He didn't say anything while I talked, just stayed with his head bent, long felted rastafarian dreads swaying as we sped round corners. I thought one side of his head looked . . . odd, as though the skull was slightly dented and the skin darker and oilier there, but he was quiet and tired with none of the jolty energy or lightning smiles that I knew and dreaded. He didn't say a word until I said, 'Taumarunui, mate, I'm stopping here,' when he said 'Ta, mate,' and slipped out the door before I'd pulled to a stop. Tired he might have been, judging by his bent head and the way he sloped in his seat, but he was exceptionally agile. He did a speedy little dance as he hit the road, never a slip or a stumble, and then trudged slowly, heavily, away. The van spun up a small whirlwind as I drove into the town.

It's Better Never than Late

Nemesis shouldn't look like this.

Forearms on the table, head on clenched fists, I study the thing.

It lies in a pool of light, in the one-eyed glare of the lamp.

It looks like a slender rectangular tube.

It is a dull leaden colour, but is partly wrapped in what looks like finely-plaited sennit.

The sennit is darkly gold and ends in a snood as though it were hook.

It is three inches long and half an inch wide and half an inch high.

It weighs nearly forty pounds.

I *know* that is impossible.

When I picked it up off the seat it felt warm. I swung round to look for the young rasta but he wasn't anywhere around of course.

It is now very cold. A thin splay of ice crystals creeps out all round it.

I touch it with a tentative finger. A shining bead leaks out, bleeds out, like freshmelted solder or particularly viscous mercury. It lies there, glaring up at me.

The finger I touched it with aches.

After a while, I pour myself a gin. Then I pour myself another gin.

In the morning, there are little silver words on the table.

WHAT IS RAISED WILL BE SUNK.

And the tube is snugly ensconced in my aching left hand and I cannot let it go.

Mules Are Stubborn Creatures

I caught up with him many many months and miles later, on a marae in the far north.

He was lolling next to a very old woman and he hadn't bothered to change any of his shape. He knew I'd get to him when the time was ripe and he was ready.

I stood cradling my hand which had become inhumanly swollen. He stares openly at me and I stare openly back. For all his illdoing he is utterly beautiful, red and black and white perfection.

He is smiling at me and his smile is without pity.

I ask without words, How do I get rid of it? and he answers without moving a muscle, Go to Rotorua and find the pool that bears my name. It will come off in the pool.

'That will kill me!'

and he shrugs, still smiling.

The elder snuffles round her cigarette, unruly shreds of tobacco leaking out in a fan. She grates, 'It's all for the best, dear' and grins, an eldritch mahogany unsuitable grin.

There's a pigeon beside her with bright black eyes.

'They often come to me dear,' she says hoarsely, 'though they never admit they're lonely,' and a strong wind from the east came up and spun her and the bird away.

The Tantalising Maze

Is there ever a real answer to anything or a true end to any story?

I hope you realise I tried so hard to stay away from the boiling mud of Rotorua but the strongest of people would be daunted by a fortypound weight clenched forever in one hand.

Yes, I tried cutting my hand off. Whatever the sinker is made of, it is impermeable and has grown all through my arm.

Yes, I tried taking my hand to every doctor and quack under the sun, but they couldn't see anything or feel anything.

It all boils down to this: there are things quite outside humanity and we can't do battle with them. We have to leave it to their own kind to bring them to heel.

Doubtless they will, if they feel we and the world are worth it.

Would you like to know the brightest dream I had of the future? (No, you wouldn't like to know the other ones at all.)

Never Trust a Dreamer Who Can Also Tell Stories

'Give me that bottle. This one's gone dry.

I've been out picking cockles. It's spring tide. They dig themselves down to normal level but the water leaves them exposed early. When you walk over the mudflat, you see them clamping shells, squirting water in bepuzzlement. I have two kit of cockles – I know, that don't mean much to you. All I know is that two kit give you a feed and enough left over to swim in apple vinegar, put in the cool place for tomorrow.

I think sometimes of those squirts. A watercry of help.
Dismay. Horror. When you pour them out of the kit into the pan,
they don't make a noise, not like mussels. They sik and hiss and
squeak sometimes. Cockles just lie there and die in the steam.
Only some don't. Obstinate. You get this feeling when you finally
crack the shells that they hoped their shutness would save them.
It doesn't. Of course. Crack them on that stone.

I like my cockles raw. Smack two shells together, like
cracking walnuts. The weaker always gives. That's sweet, living
meat. Or, just steam them open, the flesh not burnt, just lushly
half-cooked. Add a sauce. Vinegar if you're feeling harsh. Or a
mix of rootginger (did you see the big lilies blooming up on the hill
as you came through the big swamp?) and garlic and soy. We still
get the soy from Dunedin. The people of heaven never quite left
there. Just as well, eh? There'd be none left otherwise. Add
some sherry – now, that cask I have comes from Nelson, they got
a rich crop there. I swap my bulks for that sherry. And the wine of
course. Have some more.

Anyway, you got this sauce, sherry and ginger, garlic and
soy, and you dip the nearly-dead not-cooked meat into it, and eat.

O it's sweet.

I almost wouldn't mind someone eating me, like that, did they
it with appreciation, like that.

My glass?

O, there's one here can mould glass. Blows it. Makes fires
and breath and silica sand to a magic. Containers. Jewellery. A
weapon or two. My glass. That's her over there, squatting next
to the hunter with the copper earrings. Drift we call her.
Lightning we call him. I'm translating, of course.

Anyway, momentarily, and we can eat the cockles I picked.
Friend, you'll understand if I say I'm a little surprised to see you
here bare? I mean nothing coarse. Yes, that's the old worm . . .
you'll know that worm eh! Eh, the times the creature has coursed
the worm. The last season I saw you was Thunderstorms. Seven
cycles ago. Here in the simple seaward hills, we don't take note
of more than a year-name. But you know that of course. It's not
that we pride ourselves on ignorance. No-one but a fool does.
Just, our way is working up more bones, lapping our own fat

cover, growing our own strength. Eating and growing. Us. Basic.

Yes, bare is maybe a wronging word.

I see in your silence your woundedness showing.

Look, when you walk round in your metal skin someone sooner or later is going to think, Ah hah! Flesh *and* cooking pan. That's the way we are round here and you've been on expeditions enough to learn that. We don't think your armour protection or superiority. We skewer.

Taking that metal hide off isn't trust though. Trade for trade is what every thing is. You didn't leave us that worm, for nothing. Your skin's not off, for nothing.

Well, you know better than to misunderstand the savagery and viciousness of us children, heh?

I'm sorry for all the smoke, the cavern is new and unfiltered yet. Nah, it's no special fire, just a joy-thing for this night. Night comes, we must have shelter. Sometimes a fire too. Smile against it, but you wouldn't be out there either, in your suit or out of it. It's wilder than us, night, and too many things tramping around with a taste for soft meat.

Metalmaster, I can ask you bent questions. You come from Cityrace. Can you answer this? Lately I have these night-thoughts. Whatever the Singers tell, I don't think we've changed. Did we ever love each other? Say the Singers. Me, I think we're just the same as we always were, humans, cockles.

A pity you're bare. It's so nice, cracking shells.

Have that bottle, there's wet enough in it, yet.'

I Mean, It Probably Was a Dream

That's all it was. Ten minutes of talk, our kind of language yet not our talk. Sitting in a dark smoky place, with a lot of people around chatting their not-our-language and gnawing things. Sitting in somebody else's head and knowing they were terribly afraid. Sitting in their head and listening to a skinny old man ramble on about how he liked cockles. Wishing his eyes weren't so shiny, weren't so black, and especially wishing I couldn't see what all the other black-eyed people were chewing on.

If it was a dream, the future is going to be way worse than the past.

I don't like thinking that today is the high crest of humanity; tomorrow, we all fall down.

The Jewelled Frame

It's funny, trying to encapsulate your own life. As I said at the beginning, it's only the peculiar bits that make any kind of sense, but I am disappointed in my hope of them also making a pattern.

What I seem to have created for you is an old spiderweb, the kind that is a gallery of past feasts. Here an emerald shard of manuka beetle, there the plundered silken hold of a wolf spider's egg-case; some delicate purple-blue, powdery blue tussock butterfly wings interspersed between the coarse and glassy remnants of blowflies, and in this broken corner, kept as ruby as in their strident heyday by some nasty arcane skill, the little lights of cicada eyes . . .

What is missing, what is needed to make sense of it all, is the spider.

If You Can Raise Up Islands, You Can Push Them Down Again

I know exactly what is going to happen when I drop the sinker in the boiling pool.

There will be a few indescribable seconds of passing between consciousness and nothingness but that doesn't worry me.

The body will drift down, down, and the snooded sinker will slide down further and faster. Some time later, it will reach the place where the crustal plate is tender and touchy and then, like a good little bomb, it will shed its protective skin and be what it is, a seed of antimatter.

And just before the fish shatters into an archipelago, the incandescent cloud will roar helterskelter over Auckland and boil all the northern sea to a frenzy. And all along the line, the volcanoes will gout and the wild tsunamis rear up and speed in huge glassy walls over every innocent island there is. And the canoe will rock and most of it slide under the waves.

Unless my Dad is killing a horse at the time, he will probably be looking at a picture of his vanished daughter and wondering why he can't yet decently take it down and leave the room to the laughing horses.

A Question for the Spider at the Heart of Matter

Who made the fatal mistake?

There was a childhood spent fishing up islands and wasting Granny's fiery nails. Snickering over Tuna's dirty jokes and then massacring Tuna in a dirty-joke way. Putting stutters in the sun's path, battering down a star's pride, because it was a way to make the world happy. But then you wanted to play saviour and there is *no* fury like a saviour scorned.

Your fury was an impotent sputtering for so long; you were reduced to small deadly jokes. Then, I think, you learned to fly from mind to mind and time to time as easily as you formerly flew from man to bird and back again. After that, it was an easy jump into another world altogether where you could play at large again.

There was this troublesome reminder here and now though, a splinter that irked. Maybe you would have been content to let the matter rest, let the Old Lady keep what you had unwisely made available for her to take.

Somebody offended your pride so much that you made a sinker where before you'd made a hook, that you made lucky me over to find it.

Who?

The Windeater

There isn't such a word, eh. There's a lot of us around though.

I came across the term as a gift, if you like, a sort of found gift.

For instance, you break up a perfectly respectable word, happily married in all its component parts: you know it means several things, like a loafer or a braggart. Or a woman who takes part in certain rites. Or it can mean the acquisition of property without any return being made, as well as a spell that is cast to punish somebody behaving in such an unmannerly fashion. That's when it's a whole unbroken word, but if you split it, a power leaks out and becomes a woman trying to make sense of her self and her living and her world.

Which all goes to show the charming naivety of us humans. Sense of a world indeed!

Now, ask me anything you like because
my hand is getting too heavy and
in another second,
I'll be gone.

HEADNOTE TO A MAUI TALE

There are many stories
told:
how, surprising his mother by a month or more
she deemed him unready for life and laid him on seaweed,
covered with meconium and that strange slick foetal fat
and lastly, as a comfort to small disorderly souls,
his parent's long and treasured hair –
parent?
Ah, thereby a tale: tikitiki a Taranga in the North
but tikitiki a Te Raka in the South and he,
in at least one telling, was father to the youngest,
the man who could fly, who borrowed fire every morning for the
     world
from his incendiary grandfather, Mahuika,
who, in turn, flitting from time to time and space to space
spent a long life brooding in abyssal deeps
as mother to islands
– but I hear you snap That was his grandmother! Mahuika!
     Grandmother!

Well, it is a weird family tree: I mean it was definitely his auntie
who rescued him from the sea and nurtured him on sunlight and
     water until
he came full term
(which, for a trickster, is a longer or a shorter time)
but, was she really The Wind? Or just one among many?

And there is speculation, much later on, about the number
of sisters Irawaru had
but none over the fact he turned Irawaru into the first dog
– not the kindest thing to do to your brotherinlaw
even if you can't stand the lazy sod –
but then, no-one ever accused him of kindness –
heroic prowess, ungodly ingenuity, devastating wit? O *yes*
but there is that small difficulty with the not-fully-human
being, well, not fully human . . .

Anyway, it *was* Tuna the father of all eels
(and sometimes half the bush as well)
whom he slew for taking indecent liberties with one
or both, or more
of the aforesaid wives,
and there is no doubt his end:
crushed between the thighs of Hinenuitepo.

(I have not gone into the hasty sun;
the mystic jawbone of that grandother,
or the fishing up of (yawn) o so many islands –
I do admit to a friendship with fantails)

– seriously, there he was slithering and wriggling
    bellydown
stopping the outlet of Death and She
watching beady-eyed already – talk about Tuna's revenge
heh!

Was it just
his mana She killed?
Or the man (or whatever)
himself?

It all depends
on what story
you hear

THOMAS KENEALLY

THE PLAYMAKER

Based on historical fact, THE PLAYMAKER is set in Sydney Cove, the remotest penal colony of the Empire where, in 1789, a group of convicts stage a play after travelling 'eight moons distant from their homes on the other side of the sun'.

As felons, perjurers, whores and thieves, captives and captors unite to reenact a story, their playmaker becomes strangely seduced. For the power of the play is mirrored in the rich and varied life of this primitive land, and, not least, in the convict and actress, Mary Brenham.

'Formidably good . . . strong, subtle, echoing and profound'
Bernard Levin in The Sunday Times

'A magnificent and moving documentary, a tribute to his roots'
David Hughes in the Mail on Sunday

'Keneally's mature fiction goes from strength to strength, finding ever new subjects to press within the vise of its historical imagination. He has now provided a brilliant fictional corollary to Robert Hughes' impressive THE FATAL SHORE The Nobel committee ought to start looking at Keneally now'
Kirkus Reviews

sceptre

THOMAS KENEALLY

A FAMILY MADNESS

His most ambitious novel yet – a searing story about the culmination of a life-long obsession, a clash between the old world and the new, a grand passion that is the prelude to a terrible tragedy.

'It's a brilliant book. More than any other contemporary writer, the author deals in moral concern . . . It's worth betting it'll be ten times better than most novels we're likely to see in the near future'

The Guardian

'Thomas Keneally has always been remarkable for the breadth of his vision . . . This is an impressive performance, ingeniously constructed, extremely telling'

Daily Telegraph

'Mr Keneally seems to me to have pulled off a major Australian work of art . . . a memorable reading experience'

Auberon Waugh in the Daily Mail

'A master in fine fettle . . . a brave, brisk book, loud with the lessons of history. And what a springy style Keneally employs, every phrase alive on the page'

Mail on Sunday

'This is a book to keep you awake at nights. The subject is extraordinary and the book a technical masterpiece'

Punch

THOMAS KENEALLY

SCHINDLER'S ARK

Winner of the 1982 Booker Prize

In the shadow of Auschwitz, a flamboyant German industrialist grew into a living legend to the Jews of Cracow. He was a womanizer, a heavy drinker and a bon viveur, but to them, he was a saviour.

This is the story of Oskar Schindler who risked his life to protect the beleaguered Jews in Nazi-occupied Poland, who continually defied the SS, and who was transformed by the war into a man with a mission, a compassionate angel of mercy.

'An extraordinary achievement'
Graham Greene

'Brilliantly detailed, moving, powerful and gripping'
The Times

'Thomas Keneally has done marvellous justice to a marvellous story'
The Sunday Times

'Keneally is a superb storyteller. With SCHINDLER'S ARK he has given us his best book yet, a magnificent novel which held me from the first page to the last'
Alan Sillitoe

'The best Australian writer alive'
Auberon Waugh

THOMAS KENEALLY

VICTIM OF THE AURORA

In the waning years of the Edwardian era, a group of gentleman
adventurers wait out a raging blizzard in the perpetual darkness of the Antarctic winter, poised for a strike at the South
Pole. As the storm lifts, a new challenge faces Captain Sir
Eugene Stewart – to discover which of his twenty-five carefully chosen men has become a murderer. The quest for
adventure has become a quest for justice.

'I was riveted by this tale of a man fighting the elements and his
fellow explorers'
The Daily Telegraph

'The absolute dark, absolute cold of the Antarctic is skilfully
evoked'
The Sunday Times

'His story is tightly reined: terse, ironic, reflective. His depic-
tion of Edwardian innocence and stuffiness crashing against the
Antarctic void is superb'
Jonathan Yardley in The Washington Post

'The period gives this book its strength and character . . .
altogether an admirable accomplishment'
The New Yorker

'A powerful and subtle writer . . . a remarkable novel'
Spectator

'The best Australian writer alive'
Auberon Waugh

sceptre

MELVYN BRAGG

THE MAID OF BUTTERMERE

'A detailed, eloquent and affecting panorama of truth and lies
. . . His new novel thrusts him into the front rank'
David Hughes in the Mail on Sunday

'This is the story of an impostor and bigamist, a self-styled
Colonel Hope, who travels to the North, where eventually he
marries 'The Maid of Buttermere', a young woman whose
natural beauty inspired the dreams and confirmed the theories
of various early nineteenth century writers . . . It is a fine
story . . . This is historical fiction with a human face'
Peter Ackroyd in The Times

'Very much enjoyed; a fine subject treated with great energy
and imagination, and a gusto that Hazlitt would have admired'
Richard Holmes, author of FOOTSTEPS

'Overpowering all is a tremendous sense of authenticity'
Celia Brayfield in The Literary Review

'Bragg achieves the most difficult of feats, the telling of the
changing perceptions and ideals of a radical age . . . He is also
as powerful as ever in his description of nature'
Andrew Sinclair in The Sunday Times

sceptre

Current and forthcoming titles from Sceptre

THOMAS KENEALLY

THE PLAYMAKER
A FAMILY MADNESS
SCHINDLER'S ARK
VICTIM OF THE AURORA

MELVYN BRAGG

THE MAID OF BUTTERMERE

MAURICE SHADBOLT

SEASON OF THE JEW

CESARE PAVESE

THE MOON AND THE BONFIRE

PATRICE CHAPLIN

THE UNFORGOTTEN

BOOKS OF DISTINCTION